SNOW MAN

SNOW MAN

ROGER BUSBY

A CRIME CLUB BOOK

Doubleday

NEW YORK LONDON TORONTO SYDNEY AUCKLAND

A Crime Club book
Published by Doubleday, a division of
Bantam Doubleday Dell Publishing Group, Inc.
666 Fifth Avenue, New York, New York 10103

Doubleday and the portrayal of a man
with a gun are trademarks of
Doubleday, a division of Bantam Doubleday Dell
Publishing Group, Inc.

Library of Congress Cataloging-in-Publication Data
Busby, Roger.
Snow man / Roger Busby. — 1st ed.
p.   cm.
"A Crime Club book."
I. Title.
PR6052.U76S66 1989
823'.914—dc19   88-19195

ISBN 0-385-24617-X
Copyright © 1987 by Roger Busby
All Rights Reserved
Printed in the United States of America
January 1989

First Edition

OG

In memory of Dick Dougherty, my friend and inspiration

SNOW MAN

1

They sat in the car park of the Happy Eater on the top of Sunrise Hill, overlooking the silver swathe of the estuary, and watched the farmhouse in the valley below. It was October and the countryside was blurred with the gold and brown of autumn. Out on the distant river, sails of dinghies and sailboards added a sharper touch of colour, skittering over the water like the fins of multi-hued sharks.

Through the insect-spattered windscreen of the powder-blue Sierra in which they had travelled down the motorway from London, the American and the red-haired girl took it in turns with the binoculars, keeping watch on the farmhouse nestling in a fold between the rolling hills. Magnified in the bright ring of the lens, the sixteenth-century Devonshire longhouse appeared both neglected and abandoned. Paint peeled from the cob walls and window-frames; threadbare thatch choked with moss. The door of the adjacent cow byre swung drunkenly from broken hinges.

There was no sign of life.

"Make up your mind, kiddo," Jack Monroe needled the redhead. "Only way we're going to get this done is to go down there and have us a look-see. All we're going to do up here is grow old together."

From behind the wheel the girl looked at her companion, sizing him up for the hundredth time. She saw a scrub of cropped sandy hair in contrast to the heavy growth of drooping moustache which gave his face a melancholy air, his expression openly mocking. Frowning, Helen Linden reminded herself that she didn't have to be hustled by this pushy narc. Who did he think he was anyway? Charlie Bronson? Clint Eastwood?

"We don't move a muscle, Monroe," she replied, raising the field glasses to her eyes again and staring at the farmhouse. "Not until you tell me what's supposed to be going on here."

Jack Monroe ignored the question. "I thought your people told you to be nice to me."

"Being nice and being conned are two different things," Helen snapped back. "You're just a passenger here, Monroe, you want to remember that. You've got no jurisdiction, no authority, nothing. In my book you're just another civilian."

Lounging in the passenger seat, Monroe chewed on the ends of his moustache and noted the touch of colour rise on the girl's cheekbones. He was getting to her. "Ah, you Jane Fonda types," he deliberately needled her again, "you're all the same. You want to wear the pants but when it comes to the crunch you don't have the balls to go with them. All you've got is attitude."

That did it. Helen lowered the binoculars and gave him her best frosty stare. "You know what my people said?" she inquired, very calm, very cool. "They said keep the man out of mischief, that's what they said, and that's exactly what I'm going to do."

"Hey, Sarge." Monroe drawled the rank to accentuate the sarcasm. "All I want to do is look the place over. Where's the big deal in that?"

Sarge . . . there it was again. Funny, Helen thought, funny how the rank still sounded strange to her ears. She still had that impulse to turn around, see who was being addressed. Oh boy, she had been a detective-sergeant for exactly six days, the promotion coinciding with her transfer from the familiar ground of the division to the National Drugs Intelligence Unit at New Scotland Yard, where she was still suffering from culture shock and had to admit grudgingly to herself that she was a little lost, a little out of her depth, but trying hard not to show it, particularly not in front of this pushy narcotics agent she'd been saddled with. Babysit the guy until we can find you a niche, that's what they'd told her. Wheel him around, give him the treatment, only hey, Helen, you're a DS now, so you've got to start taking some responsibility, start trusting your own judgement. Cut your teeth on the guy, OK? No sweat. Just keep him on a tight rein, OK? OK . . . only this smart alec was beginning to get her down.

"I don't need your opinion, Monroe." She tried hard not to sound defensive. "I asked you what the hell was going on and until I get a straight answer we don't move a muscle. You know we're not even supposed to be here."

Monroe chewed on the ends of his moustache. No style, the British, he told himself sourly. No get-up-and-go. That was their whole problem. Where was all that kick-ass bull-dog stuff? What did you have to do to get them off their butts? Already he'd wasted best part of a month cooling his heels in London, everything a major debate, while time drifted by and he burned with frustration. Cooperation, they'd promised. Anything you want. Nothing too much trouble for our good friends in the U.S. Department of Justice Drug Enforcement Administration. Now just what can we do for you, Agent Monroe? But when he'd told them they'd smiled politely, told him to relax, see the sights. In short, they'd given him the runaround. Now he was stuck with this prissy broad who was not only hard work but was fast becoming a royal pain.

Monroe changed tack, smiled sweetly. "Helen, listen, why fight? What's the problem? We take a nice drive in the countryside . . ."

"That's another thing," Helen interrupted him. "I'm supposed to keep the office informed of our movements. I should have called in . . ."

". . . and your good old buddy here from the U.S. of A. takes an interest in your quaint old English farms. So I'm a tourist, so humour me. Where's the harm?"

Helen hesitated. "I don't know," she admitted, "I just get the feeling I'm walking into something here."

"Come on," Monroe cajoled her. "You don't have to do anything, so who's to know? Just sit in the car. We go down there, you give me twenty minutes to have a look around and we're home free. Tell you what. We'll find a nice little country inn and I'll buy you a steak, all the trimmings. How's that for a deal?"

Despite her unease, Helen Linden felt her resistance weaken. What the hell, she told herself, so Monroe wanted to play his game close to his chest, well, two could dance to that number. Be pleasant to the man, they had told her, turn on the charm, find out what he's really up to. Well, she could manage that easily enough, the guy was practically transparent. Then why was she still so doubtful?

She raised the binoculars to her eyes and swept the countryside again, seeking some clue to her unease. The old dilapidated farmhouse he had taken such an interest in looked harmless enough, surrounded by green fields, a birch copse on the ridge. A scene of rustic tranquillity. Yet still she was uncertain.

"Come on." Monroe pushed harder. "You don't want me to have to tell your people that you chickened out on me, do you, kiddo?"

The jibe so casually delivered stung deep and Helen felt her cheeks burn. They'd told her to play it by ear, just get the feel for intelligence work, take it nice and easy. Yeah, well they'd reckoned without Jack

Monroe's king-sized ego, Helen thought, and the feminist instinct behind her hazel eyes told her that she wouldn't take a slap in the face
from any man.

In the same instant, movement caught her eye and she twisted
around in time to see a red and white police patrol car with a blue
aerofoil ripple-light across the roof and the crest of the local force on
the door cruise slowly into the car park, its forest of radio aerials swaying.

"Christ, that tears it!" Helen muttered under her breath as the
police car passed by with just a touch of the brakes and the driver's face
turned towards her before it rolled on. "Now they're going to PNC
us!" She knew it for certain. She'd have done the same thing herself.
Pick up the radio and make a quick computer check on the registration,
just routine. "When they find out we're a Met job motor they'll want
to know what we're doing on their turf and that's when the phones are
going to buzz." She bit her thumbnail. They weren't supposed to be
here. Shit! All those smart people with their friendly advice. They'd be
pulling rank and roasting her newly minted DS hide.

Helen's jaw set as she reached forward and started the engine, her
mind made up for her. "All right, we're going down," she told Monroe.
"And just for the record, that was my decision. But you put one foot
wrong, Monroe, and I'll personally throw the book at you."

"Yes, Sergeant, ma'am," Monroe flipped her a salute. "Whatever
you say, just as long as you've got that burr in your breeches at last."

The unmarked police car wound down the Devon lanes towards the
farmhouse, turning finally on to a track which ran between high hedge-
rows. The crumbling tarmac was eaten with moss and spiky with tufts
of grass. Wheels drummed over a rusty cattle grid and almost immediately the track ended and they were confronted by a five-bar gate on
which hung a hand-lettered sign: LOWER COOMBE BARTON. PRIVATE.
KEEP OUT.

Helen stopped the car facing the gate. With her hands resting on
the steering-wheel she surveyed the weed-strewn farmyard and the
farmhouse beyond. Up close, the place looked even more forlorn. She
glanced across at Monroe, noticed the intent expression in his eyes and
asked, "Well? Now are you satisfied? Now are you going to tell me
what's supposed to be going on here?"

The American shrugged. "Just curious," he replied, for he had no intention of sharing the information which had led him to this spot on the map. "Just looks like a dump, huh," he added, wondering at the same time: Is this the place?

"Look, Monroe," Helen told him, "I don't know what you're up to. I don't know how you do these things in your country, but I've got to warn you, you go in there, you're breaking the law."

Monroe chuckled. "The law? You want to give me a lecture on the law?" He reached for the door-handle. "Stay here," he told her, "I'm going to take a look around. Anyone comes along, give me two quick touches on the horn, OK?"

Helen felt a further twinge of apprehension. Despite herself, she laid a hand on his arm, recalling her instructions and said, "Look, Monroe, if you've got something definite we ought to make this official. Get a warrant. Call on the local police, tell 'em what we're up to. They're going to be pretty peeved if they ever find out we're treading on their toes."

Monroe laughed. "Come on! I'm just a tourist, remember?" He patted her hand. "Sit tight, babe. Anything happens here, you don't know a thing about it. Blame it on the crazy Yank."

Before she could protest further, Monroe got out of the car and walked over to the gate, noticing the new padlock and chain which held it secure. Well now, somebody was mighty keen on security. He vaulted the gate more out of bravado than necessity, knowing she was watching him. Forty-six years old, he rebuked himself as he landed heavily on the far side, and still showing off for the ladies. You're an old phoney, Jack Monroe. He walked towards the farmhouse, picking his way through the weeds, still conscious of the girl's eyes on his back, wondering if he could second-guess her. Ice maiden Helen Linden, the original bra burner. He wondered idly if he should make a move on her once this little excursion was over. Just out of masculine pride. He imagined her nails digging into his back as he brought her to ecstasy and just as quickly pushed the fantasy aside. There was work to do.

Monroe followed one rough cob flank of the longhouse, confirming its neglected condition. Some dump! But maybe it was deliberate, maybe it was supposed to look like that. Stepping carefully in the knee-high weeds, Monroe reached the front door and saw that it was ajar an inch or so. In the shadow of the thatched canopy which had all but collapsed, he examined the rotten timber of the door itself, wondering: Now why would someone want to padlock the gate, yet leave the door open, unless . . . As he peered closer, faint chisel gouges on the wooden frame made him freeze instinctively and the hairs on his neck began to rise. Had he glimpsed something through the crack, or had it been a trick of the light?

Chewing thoughtfully on his moustache, a puzzled frown creased the DEA agent's forehead. Some sixth sense was sending danger signals. Leaving the door untouched, he continued his progress along the wall even more cautiously, his senses keyed. Skirting the longhouse itself, he came to the cow byre which abutted on the main building. Again a broken door sagged open invitingly and peering inside he could make out a few pieces of farm machinery standing on the dirt floor. Squinting into the gloom, he could see a partition wall towards the rear of the barn, a wall of concrete blocks, roughly constructed. Again his senses counselled caution and he continued carefully around the outside of the barn, running a hand lightly over the cob wall. At the rear he found an aluminium flue protruding from the cob, patched in with new mortar. The flue cowl was soot-blackened and when he ran a finger around the inside the soot came away easily. The frown deepened.

Monroe went back around the farmhouse, which no longer looked so innocent. Now he was looking for small signs which would give the lie to this carefully created impression of rural neglect. At a ground-floor window he stopped and began a minute examination of the structure. Four panes of dusty glass in a rotting wooden casement, putty crumbling away. He reached into the pocket of his windbreaker, took out a thin-bladed penknife and began to scrape at what was left of the putty.

When he had the glass completely exposed he stepped back and contemplated his handiwork. Something else was wrong. It took him a moment to realize what it was. There were no cobwebs! Everything else had been carefully faked, but the spiders hadn't had time to do their work. Monroe whistled softly between his teeth. Suddenly it was looking very suspicious indeed.

Inserting the tip of the knife blade, he prised the glass free and gingerly removed the pane. A dank musty odour wafted out from the interior and he wrinkled his nose at the cloying smell of decay. Now totally engrossed, Monroe eased his head in through the opening and immediately spotted the wiring tacked out of sight behind the window. He followed it with his eye. At the opening point, near the catch, there was a micro-switch, and twisting his head to follow the wire, he found a matchbox-sized plug of plastic explosive taped above the window where it would do the most damage.

Breathing shallowly, Monroe reached in with his arm and explored the explosive with his fingertips. His light touch revealed a stick detonator which experience told him could easily be withdrawn without triggering the plastic. Gingerly he gripped it between thumb and forefinger, held his breath and plucked it free. Nothing happened and he allowed the now harmless detonator to dangle inside the window as he breathed out his relief. Carefully he reached in again, slipped the catch, raised the casement and heaved himself inside.

A brooding silence filled the farmhouse as he carried out a perfunctory search, the film of dust which lay undisturbed on floors and furniture telling him that the place had been undisturbed for some time. The front door had been booby-trapped in the same crude fashion, but Monroe left the device alone, knowing that the farmhouse itself would stand closer inspection but for the moment he hadn't the time for detail. He had seen enough and his intuition was already pointing him towards the barn.

He retraced his steps and left by the same window, walked around to the byre and, steering clear of the broken door, paced out the distances, working out rough dimensions in his mind. The possibility which had occurred to him seemed entirely credible, and giving the walls his full attention, he circled around until he came upon an air vent set into the wall with the same rough trowel strokes which had fixed the flue. He scraped at it with his knife until the grille came loose and he eased it free an inch or two so that he could run his fingers around the interior, feeling for wires. It seemed clean and when he gave the grille a tug it came away in his hands, exposing an opening just wide enough to squeeze through.

Monroe looked around him. Beyond the buildings the hillside rose to the copse of silver birch. High in the sky a pair of buzzards were wheeling over the tree-line. Jack Monroe sniffed the country air, flexed his muscles one last time and heaved himself up into the opening, wiggling his shoulders through the tight space and slithering headlong into the blockhouse, landing on all fours. Inside, he got to his feet and followed the shaft of light slanting in through the opening.

"Well I'll be dipped in shit!" He voiced his own astonishment, despite his expectations. His information had been right! The shaft of light was falling on the paraphernalia of a precious metal smelter. Gas bottles were still in place, connected to a small furnace with a grooved channel running to the smelting bed where metal clips held the mould in position. Stooping to examine the smelter more closely, Monroe could see that it had been carelessly abandoned, for one of the moulds was still in place and minute droplets clung to the crucible. Brushing them into his handkerchief and rocking back on to his haunches, Monroe massaged his ego, imagining the eulogy in the Law Enforcement Bulletin: *Under the noses of the British police DEA agent Jack Monroe single handedly uncovered a major crime organization which dwarfed the legendary French Connection. For his services to law enforcement, Jack Monroe . . .*

"Jack Monroe!" The girl's shout shattered his daydream. "Monroe! Where the hell are you?" Surprised, he glanced at his watch and realized that he had become so engrossed that he had lost all track of time. Forty-five minutes had elapsed. "Jack Monroe! Can you hear me?"

Helen Linden, her voice anxious, looking for him. Monroe dusted his knees, located the door in the blockwork partition leading back into the barn, checked it quickly, freed the five-lever deadlock and pushed the door open. Light streamed into the barn, flooding around the leaning wreck of a door, slanting across the bare earth floor. Overhead a latticework of rafters sagged under the weight of the rotting thatch.

"Jack! For God's sake, where are you?"

The girl came into sight in the opening, walking towards the barn, turning, looking around her as she crossed the farmyard. A self-satisfied smirk formed on Monroe's face. Her quick, strutting, impatient stride, that jerky swing of her hips in her fawn whipcord jeans; the swell of her breasts under her sweater, halo of flaming auburn curls framing the oval of her face. Feeling pleased with himself, Monroe thought, Yeah, all of a sudden little Miss Prissy looks easy on the eye. A nice intimate steak dinner, bottle of good wine and maybe he would make that play for her after all.

"Jack! Jack Monroe!" She was shading her eyes, peering around anxiously. Monroe's smirk widened into a grin as he leaned casually against the door-jamb and stroked his moustache, recapturing his amorous fantasy.

"Hey kiddo, over here!" he called out teasingly, and she turned, looking at first puzzled and then angry as she began to stride towards the barn, walking quickly. As he watched her approach, the lazy self-satisfied grin still on his face, a trick of the light gave Monroe a glimpse of the tripwire strung across the dirt doorway of the barn. His eyes snapped wide.

"Don't!" But the cry formed only in his mind as his memory flashed back twenty years to the jungles of Vietnam, the badlands on the banks of the Song Tra Bong, deep in Charlie country. They'd set out the claymores in a defensive perimeter when the kid soldier with the thousand-yard stare came down the trail.

"Don't!" Monroe had yelled the same word of warning which had jammed in his mind as the kid walked into the tripwire.

The teenager soldier snagged the wire and detonated the claymore anti-personnel mine.

Helen Linden stepped into the barn, caught her foot in the command wire.

The grunt took the blast in his midriff and was flung backwards, throwing up his arms, his helmet flying.

The nail bomb buried in the earth floor of the barn exploded, hurling the girl detective-sergeant into the air.

The images blurred into one as the cry of warning stuck in Monroe's throat; a rag doll ripped apart by a booby-trap. Split between the two images, Monroe flung himself forward, grabbed the soldier, saw the shocked astonishment in his eyes; scooped up Helen Linden and saw the same expression of panic and disbelief. The eyes merged, dulled, faded as they both died in his arms.

Smothered in the swirl of dust in the entrance to the barn, DEA agent Jack Monroe cradled the dead girl in his arms and like an animal in anguish threw his head back to the sky. Kneeling in the spreading puddle of blood, he produced one long strangled curse: "Fat Man!"

2

On the same late autumn day when the alpine air tasted like chilled champagne and the wooded slopes shimmered in a russet haze, a white Jaguar XJS came around the lorry park jammed with a gaggle of articulated trailers and approached an Austrian border post. A grey-caped guard took a cursory glance at the driver's documents and waved the car through. The low-slung sports saloon eased lazily across the oil-spattered concrete and rolled towards the single-storey buildings spanning the entrance to the Bavarian State of the Federal Republic of West Germany at the Garmisch checkpoint. The signal at the barrier glowed red and as the Jaguar came to a standstill an officer in the dull green uniform of the Grenzpolizei, two stars of a Polizeiobermeister on his lapels, stepped from his armoured glass cubicle and approached the driver's side, throwing an admiring glance at the sleek lines of the Jaguar, also noting the British plates. He leaned towards the open window. Again the driver proffered his documents and the corporal smiled pleasantly, nodded and returned to his glass security box, slid open a frosted window at the rear which gave access to the checkpoint building itself and handed the papers to a colleague seated at a console which was hidden from outside view.

In the Jaguar, Gary Daniels cast an incurious eye over the border post with its activities concealed behind closed Venetian blinds, switched his bored gaze to the knot of truckers gathered around the cab of a giant Volvo Roadmaster, swapping yarns as they waited for the interminable border formalities to be completed. Daniels exuded the complacent manner of a beefy man, once powerfully built, but now grown corpulent in middle age, tyre-folds of paunch overhanging the snakeskin belt of his expensive grey mohair suit. The structure of his face had sagged into fleshy jowls from the same indulgence in easy living and only the carefully groomed mane of glistening dark hair gave an indication of his former youthful vigour. As he waited, he idly tapped his fingers on the cruise control and stifled a yawn.

Inside the border post the Polizeikommissar who had received Daniels's documents extracted the passport, opened the stiff card covers and placed the passport face down on a facsimile screen. The picture was instantly flashed to the Central Criminal Computer at Wiesbaden. Within three seconds the response came up on the VDU at the man's elbow, crisp lines of coded text stuttering across the screen. The supervisor nodded his satisfaction. The computer had confirmed his own suspicions when he had studied the photograph in the passport. He allowed himself a brief smile and then carefully rearranged his expression as he slid the hatch open and handed the papers back to the guard outside with a nod of his head to confirm that all was in order. He left the frosted window open and, as the white Jaguar moved off, lifted the phone at the side of his console, tapped a sequence into the key pad and, when the party came up on the security line, spoke a few brief words into the mouthpiece. Replacing the phone he moved his hand to the keyboard below his VDU and informed the computer of the action he had taken. German efficiency, he congratulated himself. Best in the world.

On the autobahn the Jaguar performed automatically in cruise control, but once he hit the two-lane country road Daniels took over, gave the engine the gun and began to drive recklessly fast. His driving reflected his mood, anticipating the pleasures to come. Smiles wreathed his fleshy face as he reached down and fed a Tina Turner tape into the eight-track stereo, instantly filling the luxurious interior of the Jaguar with the raunchy beat. Cutting through forest, dense stands of timber slipping past, Daniels began to take a keen interest in his surroundings, watching the landmarks. When he spotted the turn up ahead he swung the Jaguar on to a rough all-weather track without decreasing speed and raced uphill through the blur of trees. It was a logging track, long disused, the surface breaking up into ruts which tested the Jaguar's suspension as the car rocketed onwards, topped a rise and swung into a wide clearing, tyres crunching on the loose surface. Through the windscreen Daniels recognized the old work camp where foresters had felled stand after stand of timber, well off the beaten track and so long abandoned that the surrounding forest was once more beginning to reclaim its territory. Three trailer caravans, their aluminium flanks painted dull brown, stood in the clearing with their tow-trucks and, tucked out of sight under a green canvas awning, a Mercedes saloon and a gleaming new Audi Quattro.

Daniels braked heavily and the Jaguar slewed to a halt beside the nearest of the caravans. He got out of the car and stretched, but made no further move until the side door of the caravan opened and a woman appeared at the top of the metal steps. His lip curled in a sly smile of greeting. The woman was fortyish, a fading blonde, but well preserved with a complexion like porcelain and light, washed-out eyes which flitted over the newcomer, the car and past him to check the area beyond.

"You took one hell of a risk coming here." She addressed Daniels in German as he walked towards her.

"Nonsense, Kristi," he replied easily, speaking in English, the smile broadening. "This mountain air is good for me, I've been cooped up in Salzburg for too long wondering if you're ripping me off." He wagged a finger playfully. "Got to protect my investment, eh, Kristi, my business interests, eh? Besides I get hungry for a little relaxation, something juicy, a sample of the service."

Without moving from the steps, the woman measured him with her eyes, calculating the risk. "It's still dangerous," she said, this time in accented English. "That damned helicopter was over here again. Polizei . . . makes me nervous."

"Ah, you worry your pretty head too much, Liebling," Daniels reassured her as he heaved his bulk up the steps and embraced her. "Who's going to bother us up here anyway? Didn't I tell you we've got important people giving us protection? Leave it to me, Kristi, didn't I always take good care of you?" He held her at arm's length. "So how's our trade been?"

"More than I can handle," the woman said, disengaging herself to lead him into the trailer. "I had a big wheel up here, some politician with his retinue, that was some party."

"Good, good." Daniels followed her inside. "Only the best, eh, Kristi, stay exclusive, *crème de la crème.* You got pictures?" In contrast to the austere exterior, the caravan was lavishly furnished, a rich burgundy carpet and soft hide loungers, a cocktail bar taking up one corner. The woman greeted the question with a haughty look. "Naturally," she said. "They look like a nest of big white slugs."

"That's my girl," Daniels said approvingly. She crossed to the bar. "Cognac as usual?"

"Big one to get me in the mood," Daniels purred as he undressed her with his eyes. Heavy sensuous breasts under the white silk blouse, narrow hips encased in fashionable black velvet slacks poised on patent high-heeled sandals. Oh yes, you had to hand it to Kristabel Rosche, he congratulated himself on his choice of business partner, she certainly had style. Knew what a man wanted to see.

Reading his face, Kristi allowed herself to relax and her lips parted in a practised smile as she held up the bottle for his approval.

"Looks good to me," Daniels said, his eyes still feasting on her as she poured his drink. But knowing that this would be just the apéritif, Daniels sank on to a settee, stretched his legs and kicked off his Gucci loafers. He took the drink from her hand and sipped the brandy, letting it warm his belly, deliberately waiting for her to broach the subject he knew must be uppermost in her mind. Kristi realized he was playing this game. Jesus, but she loathed him, his pudgy face, blubbery lips,

soft flabby body . . . oh, how he revolted her. The smile on her face
didn't waver.

She sat beside him, allowed her thigh to rub along his leg. He rested
his head against the back of the couch, closed his eyes and breathed;
"Ah, this is good."

Bastard, she cursed him silently, tormenting bastard. She put her
head down on his shoulder, her lips close to his ear. "Baby, did you
. . . did you bring me a little present, something nice?"

His eyes opened, took on a cunning look. "Would I ever forget your
pleasure, Liebling," he murmured, enjoying the game as he reached
casually into an inside pocket and produced a chamois leather pouch
which he held teasingly out of reach of her outstretched hand. "But
first what do you have to amuse me, eh, Kristi? You know my appetites.
Some new delicacy perhaps?" With his free hand he stroked her face.
"I know you won't disappoint me."

Yes, she had something for him, she told herself sourly, didn't she
always. Didn't she need to ensure his patronage, the powerful protection of his associates which allowed her to continue the livelihood
which was beginning to disgust her.

"You won't be disappointed," she murmured, ravenous for the contents of the pouch. "I have arranged something special, but first, ah,
you know, I need a lift too, then it will be so much better. When did I
ever disappoint you?"

Daniels had to confess that she was right. Never once, since they had
been partners. He watched her face, saw those pearly pink lips part a
little as her breathing quickened. Casually he opened the pouch and,
reaching over, spilled a trail of angel dust across the glass top of a coffee
table.

Her eyes blazed ferociously as she lunged past him, intent only upon
the trickle of dust. From her sleeve, Kristabel Rosche produced a six-
inch ivory tube, sank to her knees and greedily did her lines, sniffing
angel dust into each nostril, gasping her relief. Bastard, she cursed him
still, for whenever she was in the depths of despair she had this urge to
hack off Daniels's genitals with a carving knife and stuff them into his
screaming mouth, and the sweet thought flashed before her now, just
for an instant until the cocaine did its work and she rocked back on her
heels, her face relaxing, notions of revenge evaporating in an aura of
well-being.

Daniels reached out and touched her hair, turning her face towards him so that he could inspect her rapturous expression. It never ceased to fascinate him, the way the snow transformed her like electricity. To him it was nothing more than the product, a trading commodity. He didn't need that kind of buzz himself, his pleasures lay in a different direction.

"Going to be plenty more where that came from." He let it slip casually, resealing the pouch and tossing it on to the table. "This deal I'm working on, we're going to have snow coming down like an avalanche, hit the market and clean up. Going to own a bank in Switzerland . . ." He caught himself speaking his thoughts out loud, cut his voice off with a swift rebuke. His tone softened. "Good hit, lover?"

"Rocket ride." Kristi laughed, still kneeling at his feet, reached over and placed a hand on his thigh, not caring now that she had to pay for her lifeline. "Now my present for you. Let's take a walk." She got up and pulled him to his feet. Daniels finished his drink in one, put on his loafers and followed her to the door. Outside Kristi led him towards the second trailer, its aluminium sides painted in the same drab colour, windows blacked out. "I promise you, you won't be disappointed."

Eyes glittering from the coke-induced high, she led him up the steps and paused at the top, her mouth curving in a smile as she pushed open the door and ushered him inside.

Adjusting to the cloying gloom, heavy with scent, Daniels found himself in a baroque boudoir, felt his pulse race with anticipation. Concealed lights winked off brass fittings; purple drapes swept down from gleaming brass curtain rods, and as his sight adjusted he saw that the floor was strewn with dark animal skins, still possessed of claws and heads, fanged jaws yawning open. He peered deeper into the purple cavern and saw at the far end two young girls with identical yellow hair frizzed into haloes, posing languidly upon a pile of gold-tasseled cushions. Daniels was instantly taken with the girls, their gamine faces, houri eyes returning his greedy stare. Each wore an identical Bavarian jacket of green cord, embroidered with intricate gold designs. Their legs were clad in soft leather riding boots. With a sharp intake of breath Daniels saw that they were quite naked from waist to calf, the whiteness of their thighs accentuated by the spotlights, tantalizingly provocative.

Daniels turned to Kristabel Rosche, who was watching him expectantly, and a thrill of anticipation electrified him. "Schoolgirls?" He hardly managed to breathe the question as he continued to devour the carnal tableau. "Runaways," Kristi said. "Little sisters from Cologne. Come, Liebling, don't keep my little darlings in suspense. Look how eager they are to amuse you!"

Saliva flecked the corners of Gary Daniels's slack mouth as Kristi went into her routine and began to help him undress. Slowly, with the studied deliberation of mechanical dolls, the girls rose from their cushions and began to gyrate towards him.

In the depth of the forest an unmarked Mercedes G Wagen bumped slowly down a firebreak between the trees and halted well short of the clearing, remaining concealed beyond the tree-line. Rainer Wolfe got out of the passenger's side, closely followed by three men in forester's overalls. They pulled holdalls out of the jeep, conferred together for a moment, confirming their bearings, then began to creep through the undergrowth towards the clearing. Wolfe, their leader, was a stocky man with unkempt black hair and several days' growth of blue-black beard. He wore a padded combat jacket and carried a walkie-talkie in his hand. As they progressed stealthily towards the clearing they paused frequently to watch and wait, like hunters on the scent. Near the tree-line they sank down and belly-crawled the last few yards between the stumps of the felled pines. Wolfe studied the clearing, his deep-set piercing eyes taking in every detail. The caravans were arranged as he had seen them on the aerial video filmed from the helicopter and the two cars were still in place under the canvas awning, but now an additional car had appeared, the white Jaguar XJS he had been told about by the border post.

Beside the third caravan in line he could see two men in sports shirts and jeans loafing around a barbecue pit, drinking beer out of cans. Two Doberman guard dogs sniffed around their feet. Wolfe motioned his men around him for a final briefing. Stubby Heckler and Koch submachine-guns appeared from the holdalls and one of the group fixed a telescopic sight on to a Ruger sniper rifle.

Wolfe raised his hand, hesitated for a final check and then swept it down, giving them the signal. He ran forward, a machine-gunner on each flank. The rifleman stayed put, rose into a shooting crouch, brought the stock of the Ruger up to his shoulder, sighted the crosshairs, and with clinical efficiency killed both guard dogs with two rapid shots to the head.

Caught unawares, the men at the barbecue pit swung around and found themselves staring into the muzzle of a submachine-gun behind which a tough-looking character ordered them to spreadeagle beside the dead dogs. They did as they were told.

Leaving his other gunner crouched beside the steps of the next trailer, covering the clearing, Wolfe took the steps at a run and booted in the door. The flimsy door burst inwards and he stood framed in the opening, eyes narrowed.

There, kneeling on the animal skins, naked rolls of flesh quivering from the exertion, Gary Daniels had one girl impaled from behind engulfed in a clumsy bear hug, with her sister astride his sweating back spurring him on with the heels of her boots. Kristabel Rosche, delicately poised in her elegant blouse and slacks, still flying on coke, whipped at the man's straining pink buttocks with a riding crop.

White teeth flashed in the dark stubble as Wolfe opened his jacket to reveal a police issue Walther PPK slung in a shoulder holster. But he didn't reach for the pistol. Instead he held out a plastic ID card emblazoned with the blue and white diamonds of the Bavarian crest and announced himself: "Kriminal Polizei München! On your feet, fat man!"

3

The moon cast a pale light over London's dockland, competing with the residual glow of the sleeping city. Steadily through the night anaemic moonlight transformed the waterfront skyline into a fantasy of shadows, from the newly desirable housing projects across the oil-slicked backwaters of the Thames where supine humps of barges wallowed alongside deserted wharves, to the gibs and gantries of the old Rotherhithe docks, poised like stick-limbed predators over canyons of Victoriana. The scene blended into monochrome shades of grey as moonlight conspired with neon and mercury vapour to bleed the urban landscape of all colour.

As the lopsided moon climbed higher, a wedge of silver light stretched slowly down the cobbles of a loading alley running between the blackened walls of disused grain warehouses. The only movement in the moonlight was the slow progress of a Ford Transit, which turned into the alley from the dock road and rolled to a stop near a rusty corrugated fence which protected an iron fire-escape.

Behind the wheel of the van Detective-Sergeant Tony Rowley, attached to SO11, Scotland Yard's Specialist Operations Criminal Intelligence Branch, glanced at his wristwatch: nearly 3 A.M. He turned off the engine and in the ensuing silence stretched and flexed his shoulder muscles against the cramps of the night. But his eyes, sunk in deep sockets, did not leave the rearview mirror, and the gaunt planes of his face reflected a degree of nervous tension which seldom left him. After a few moments, when he was reasonably certain that he had not been followed, Rowley leaned over to the passenger seat and picked up a powerful eight-cell flashlight then reached under the dashboard and switched on a voice-activated tape-recorder. He climbed stiffly out of the van, locking it behind him, and as he moved, the moonlight revealed a badger streak of white which ran through his hair, the most obvious manifestation of his shredded nerves. His clothes, padded jacket and well-worn jeans, hung loosely on a frame which had lost all excess flesh. A taut, nervous man stepping quickly into the protection of the shadows.

Rowley flicked on the flashlight for a second or two and quickly inspected the corrugated iron, finding a spot where the rust had eaten through and prising the sections apart so that he could slip inside. Beyond the fence, following the beam of the torch, his soft-soled trainers picked their way through a clutter of debris until, reaching up, he grabbed a corroded handrail, swung himself on to the lower level of the fire-escape and began to climb, testing each latticework iron tread as he ascended.

When he reached the flat roof of the warehouse, Rowley moved with extra caution across the crumbling bitumen, shielding the lamp with one hand so that only the minimum light showed as he inspected each area of shadow, working his way across the roof to the parapet on the far side. There he doused the light, rested his hands on the rough brickwork of a waist-high ledge, and gazed up into the night sky.

Disappointment blunted his expectations, for instead of the brilliant star canopy which had remained imprinted on his memory from his days in Cornwall when he had first been introduced to the star fields, here the sky was veiled by the airborne detritus of the metropolis which rose in an inverted cone over the capital. Only the very brightest of the constellations managed to penetrate the murk. He made out the bright

pinpoints of Polaris and Vega with Altair faintly visible down near the
horizon. But the sky was dominated by the pale face of the moon and
in the chill night air Rowley felt himself shiver as the moonlight con-
jured up the apparitions which haunted him.

As he sucked in the salty tang of the nearby tidal reaches, he saw his
old mentor, Dad Garratt leering cunningly into his mind: Dad Garratt,
one of the last swashbuckling squad DIs, and Rowley had been his
skipper. Their last case together had been a five-million-pound-bullion
robbery from a bonded facility at Heathrow Airport, a brutal blagging
for which the cunning old DI had stitched up the Twins, a notorious
pair of vicious gangsters whose come-uppance was well overdue. But
before he could finally work his magic, Dad Garratt had been poleaxed
by a massive heart attack which had snuffed out his life, and Rowley,
the foil for his fancy footwork, had inherited the case and the moment
of glory which went with it.

But when the only prosecution witness worth a damn, a supergrass
Garratt had tucked away in a safe house in Cornwall, suddenly turned
sour, the evidence evaporated, the Twins walked free and Rowley felt
the fiery wrath of his superiors as he was unceremoniously thrown to
the wolves. Overnight he became the scapegoat in a conspiracy to
protect the reputations of the Met's CID hierarchy.

Rowley had blown the case. Kicked back to uniformed sergeant out
in the sticks, fate further twisted the knife as the Twins, bent upon
revenge to restore their hard man reputations began to hunt him down.
He narrowly escaped certain death when his patrol car was blown apart
by a car bomb and, living on his wits, Rowley had bargained the death
threat with SO11 and had become bait on the hook. But the strain of
living with an underworld contract on his life was more than he could
handle with no comfort beyond Dad Garratt's artful sneer at danger
and the final whispered bequest of those blue-tinged lips: "Keep the
faith, Tony—keep the faith."

But even with that valediction ringing in his ears, Rowley knew that
he could never rise to Garratt's genius for self-preservation and now his
shattered nerves were beginning to unravel, for he knew it was only a
matter of time before the Twins caught him off guard and then it
would be all over. So he had to make the only possible move left open
to him, the last option which the old DI had bequeathed to him on his
death-bed. Yet now that it was time, staring up into the murky heavens,
preparing to make that move, Rowley fancied the twisted smile on

Dad's bloodless lips was already mocking him because he didn't have the guts to slug it out.

Rowley breathed deeply of the crisp night air. Yes, that was why he was here, skulking on the roof of this abandoned warehouse at three in the morning. He was here to meet the only man his mentor had left him to turn to; a man who held the power of life and death in hands untrammelled by the conventions of the law. Frank Spinelli, the undertaker, capo of London's organized crime.

Rubbing his face, still beset by doubts, Rowley struggled with his conscience, but before he could reach any decision a figure materialized from the shadows, the slight figure of a man well into his sixties, hunched in a Vicuna topcoat, hook-nosed and Latin-featured, with bright birdlike eyes in a seamed and pock-marked face. He came up to where Rowley was waiting.

"Nice night," Spinelli said.

Rowley recognized him at once. He had seen him many times presiding over the lavish showbiz funerals of underworld luminaries.

"Watching the stars, eh?" Spinelli asked and the detective nodded. A nerve twitched in his cheek.

The birdlike eyes fixed on him. "You've got the look of a stargazer about you, Tony. Stars are for dreamers." Spinelli smiled. "Dad was right, though. He said you'd most probably call me sooner or later. Why try to hack it on your own when you don't have to? You did right, my friend."

Rowley looked away. He didn't want Spinelli to see the doubt on his face. "The thing about the stars," he remarked, "they help put the world into perspective. Cut everything down to size."

"But stars have twins." The head cocked to one side, the smile amused.

Rowley tensed. "We've all got our crosses to bear in this life, Mr. Spinelli, but it comes down to the same thing in the end. In the end we're all just so much dust."

"Very good!" Spinelli congratulated him. "A philosopher too! Only let's cut the formalities, huh, Tony. Call me Frank, we're practically family."

This time Rowley was not quick enough to disguise the expression in his eyes, for Spinelli said, "Look, let me give it to you straight. I'm getting to be an old man, you know? I don't have time for mincing words. I just get straight to it. You've got Dad Garratt's ghost looking after your hide, he told me one day you were going to call, and you called and here I am. We're safe here, we won't be disturbed, I've seen to that. So why don't we have a nice conversation, OK? No commitments on either side."

Rowley watched the capo. Here was the man who had major crime under his thumb; extortion, blackmail, vice, all the rackets woven into an empire which he ran with entrepreneurial flair from behind the most respectable of façades, a funeral business, the Sacred Heart. This was the man who traded in legitimate death while at the same time snuffing out the underworld opposition with ruthless efficiency. Why, Rowley had heard it said that during the gangster wars of the Sixties, when the Krays and the Richardsons had been at each other's throats, any hooligan stupid enough to cross Frank Spinelli soon ended up at his own funeral with all the trimmings. Mad dogs who had ignored the warnings had simply vanished without trace. For years the Serious Crime Squad and more recently the newly formed Mafia Squad had pursued Spinelli but had turned up nothing worthwhile, so well insulated was the capo's empire.

Even this rendezvous with an insignificant detective-sergeant had been arranged on Spinelli's terms with the utmost secrecy, and now that Rowley prepared to trade Dad's legacy he felt a flush of betrayal. On the margins of crime, he was preparing to step over the line. This was the man standing before him.

"Look, my friend," Spinelli said, and smiled, reading Rowley's mind. "All we've got here is the night for company. You can say hello to me, you can say goodbye, it doesn't matter." From under his coat Spinelli produced a bottle of wine and a couple of glasses. He set the bottle of Valpolicella down on the slab of the parapet. "Only first we're going to drink some good Italian wine, you and me, then we're going to see if maybe we can help one another in the spirit of friendship."

The undertaker tilted the bottle and filled the glasses. In the darkness the wine ran like blood. Spinelli touched Rowley's glass with his own. "A toast! To the memory of Dad Garratt!" Spinelli swallowed a deep draught, smacked his lips and then dabbed his mouth with a handkerchief. "You see the stars up there, Tony?" He gestured with his glass. "They're counting your blessings. I say to 'em, look at me, for Chrissake, sixty-eight years old and I'm not having to move my bowels in some plastic bag strapped on my waist and it don't feel like red hot needles whenever I take a leak and I didn't get cancer yet. Each day I like the stars a little more."

Rowley drank some wine.

"Where I come from, you know, we have a saying," Spinelli said. "Live for the day. It works pretty well too, saves you from getting ulcers eating away your insides. Dad understood."

Rowley faced the capo. "Dad always had the next day all mapped out," he said. "The next day, next week, next month."

"Ah, in the head." Spinelli tapped his temple. "Only in the head. Did I say anything about that? I'm talking about the heart, Tony. One day at a time, that's the way the heart goes.

"You know your trouble," Spinelli went on. "You're a romantic. You let your imagination run away with you. Ease up on that department and your problems will solve themselves."

"Not my problems," Rowley said. "My problems are a couple of lunatics who want to kill me. That's my problems."

"Hold it there," Spinelli said. "I've got your story. Dad spelled it out to me and that's the reason I'm here. You think I give a damn that you've got yourself sleepless nights watching shadows on the wall? Forget it. I start worrying about every schmuck gets himself at odds with maniacs like the Twins, I'd be planting myself six feet under instead of enjoying my health."

Spinelli peered into Rowley's face, so close that the detective could smell the garlic on his breath. "But don't go getting me wrong, Tony, you're a responsibility, a debt of honour. I saw Dad in the hospital before his heart gave out and he made me swear if you came to me I'd take care of you like you were of his blood, like you were his son. Only you had to come to me, you had to ask. Well, you've taken your step, Tony. You've got Dad's debt of honour in your hand."

Rowley drank some more wine, acutely conscious of the hidden microphone and the tape-recorder running in his van below. For his own sake he had to draw the capo out yet keep his side of the conversation as neutral as possible.

"Before we get into this," Spinelli said. "You've heard of Omertà?"

"Omerta?"

"No, Omert-a, like that." Spinelli drew the word out into its proper pronunciation.

"Yes, I've heard of it," Rowley said. "The vow of silence."

"So bear with me," Spinelli said. "I'm getting old, like I said. I can dispense with the formalities when I want to. I can break Omertà this once, as a gesture of good faith. If I did this in my own country I'd have my tongue cut out." Spinelli shook his head. "But I've still got responsibilities to my people, my associates. So what am I going to do now that we're getting down to cases, the incriminating stuff? Am I going to pat down Dad Garratt's boy looking for a wire, some gizmo no bigger than a belly-button? No. What I'm going to do is take you on trust, Tony, because Dad told me I can trust you. So I'm going to take that chance." The undertaker spread his hands. "So tell me, what is it you want from me?"

"Some help," Rowley said simply. "Some guarantees. I need to know what can be done to ease my situation, what it's going to take to get the Twins off my back."

Spinelli helped himself to more Valpolicella, cocked his head on one side. "Let me tell you a story," he said. "When I first came to this country soon after the war, I was just another dumb guinea looking for a crust. Then I got acquainted with this policeman who was walking his beat in the neighbourhood, hungry like me, eager to make a name for himself. Pretty soon we had a good deal going for us. I did a little something for him, he did a little favour for me, like a partnership. Soon we were both moving up in the world, looking out for each other. You know what we did, Tony? We took the blood from each other's hands and we mingled the blood and that was the bond, that was the trust. So now that policeman's gone, the penalty of growing old too dangerously. And I've got a little of his unfinished business to take care of. So now you know. So now you can tell me about it."

Rowley nodded. "It's not hard to tell. I'm getting tired of looking over both shoulders at the same time every minute of the day wondering when the Twins are going to nail me. The threats don't bother me, they come with the job. But the car bomb was altogether different because that's when I knew they really meant it, and they're both psychos who can't tell a nightmare from reality." Rowley sighed. "You see, the other thing is, I don't have any confidence any more in my people's ability to keep me in one piece. So here I am, skewered on the hook."

Spinelli said softly, "I can take care of the Twins." He snapped his fingers. "I can take care of the Twins like that! I speak in a certain way to my associates and the Twins won't bother you any more. You live your life again." Spinelli held up a cautioning finger. "All you have to

do is ask. But before you do, what you have to know, Tony, is that
favours work both ways. One time, one day, I'm going to call that
favour in. You're going to have to do something for me. Repayment in
full. And you're going to have to swear to that in the old way, mingle
the blood."

Rowley was about to respond when Spinelli stopped him. "Don't tell
me a thing, not now. Think it over first. You've got to take Dad's vow
or nothing, there's no other way, not with Frank Spinelli." He reached
into an inside pocket and gave Rowley a card, black-edged, with the
symbol of the Sacred Heart. "Call me tomorrow. Give me your answer,
then we can meet again."

Spinelli swallowed the last of the wine. "Ciao, stargazer," he said,
turned on his heel and vanished into the shadows.

Rowley remained where he was for a while, leaning on the parapet,
watching the slow transition of the sky. He put Spinelli's card away still
wondering what he would do. If Dad Garratt hadn't hesitated all those
years ago, then why should he? The undertaker could be a powerful
ally. The little man was so cocksure, so confident. Not just a capo,
Rowley thought to himself, more like the *capo di tutti capi.*

Rowley went back down to the alley and automatically checked the
Transit for concealed devices. Ever since the car bomb had seared the
prospect of his own death into his subconscious, excessive caution had
become a way of life. When he was sure the van was clean he got in
and, sitting behind the wheel, quickly unscrewed the end of his torch
and removed the miniature transmitter. Reaching under the dashboard, he rewound the tape, removed the cassette and slipped it into an
inside pocket. At least the evidence of his conversation with Spinelli
would serve as his guarantee, but all the same, the precaution had the
whiff of betrayal about it, for if ever he should be tempted to turn it
over to his superiors, even to save himself, then the memory of Dad
Garratt would be inexorably blackened. No wonder the capo hadn't
bothered to check him for a wire. It didn't matter. There was no need.

Rowley started the engine, set the Transit in motion but did not turn
on the lights until he emerged from the alley into the dock road, then
picking up speed he recrossed the river and joined the night-prowling
traffic in the city as he skirted north to Hammersmith and parked
outside the block of flats where Cindy Miller lived.

He climbed stiffly out of the van and crossed the slabbed walkway to the lobby door, using the key she had given him in the lock. The four-storey apartment block was in darkness except for low-power courtesy lamps which cast a faint orange glow over the stairs. Outside her door Rowley hesitated, the familiar pangs of guilt gnawing at him. Here I go again, he told himself sourly, the fearless detective running shit-scared, using innocent people as a shield. Cindy's place had been his sanctuary ever since the car-bombing. He had used her the way a frightened animal goes to ground, hardly daring to return to his own flat in case the Twins had prepared another ambush. They were crazy enough for anything. Yeah, just a selfish bastard using the girl, exploiting her emotions to keep himself safe. Jesus, put like that he could hardly believe the depths to which he had sunk. Just the same, he let himself in, moved stealthily through the darkened flat to the bedroom, where he could just make out her shape under the duvet, hear the soft sounds of her breathing. Despising himself more and more, he was reminded of the question in her eyes when they had tried to make love. Was it, she had asked him tremulously as he withered to nothing in her arms, was it because she was black?

Rowley had held her face in his hands and had told her that no girl who hailed from St. Kitts with hot Caribbean blood in her veins should ever entertain such self doubts. Then why did he not make love to her, she had asked, and hiding his hollow shame against her breasts he had told her despairingly that the car bomb had not only shredded his nerves, left a badger streak of white across his hair, but had robbed him of his manhood.

Now as he crossed the bedroom he felt drained, just a husk blowing in the breeze. Without bothering to undress he stretched out on the bed, careful not to disturb the sleeping girl. Tonight he had supped wine with the devil and now he had slunk back to his bolt hole like a yellow cur. Tonight he disgusted even himself.

After a while his breathing became more regular as he drifted into sleep. Beside the nurse in whose arms Dad Garratt had died.

4

"Where the hell've you been?" The duty DI turned on Rowley the minute he walked into the SO11 office at the Yard.

"Me, guv'nor? I just came on," Rowley answered with an innocent shrug.

The dapper detective-inspector in shirtsleeves, waistcoat unbuttoned, swung his legs down from where they had been propped on a half-open desk drawer, threw a copy of the *Sun* down amid the clutter on the desktop and gave Rowley a suspicious scowl.

"Not now, last night," he snapped. "We've been searching the undergrowth all over for you, the old man's been going barmy, even had the woodentops out shaking the trees. Where the hell were you anyway —pulling some bird?"

Rowley stared at the DI, who had now risen to his feet to confront him, hands on hips, scowling, his chest puffed out like a bantam cock. He felt the first twinge of apprehension as he wondered which "old man" the DI was referring to, for the term could be applied to any one of a dozen superiors. On the desks key and lamp phones blinked incessantly but the DI made no attempt to answer them. He concentrated his bile on the detective-sergeant.

"You come waltzing over here, Rowley, swanning around after we pull you in from the plod." He shook his head. "I can see why people might want to cream your nuts, my son. I would've done it myself last night with the greatest of pleasure, the way the old man was carrying on. You would've thought I'd lost you personally." His face set into an unpleasant expression. "I don't know why they didn't just let the Twins blow your ass away and solve all our problems."

"Nice to be wanted, guv'nor." Rowley produced an ironic smile. "Gives me a warm glow inside."

The DI smoothed his slick black hair, which gleamed like patent leather, and studiously continued to ignore the phones frantically winking from among the mountains of paperwork which spilled from box files and buff folders.

"Stuck here on my jack," he grumbled. "Half the squad out on loan and the rest jerkin' off somewhere I can't find 'em when his nibs is doing his crust. Gets more of a shambles every day."

"Er . . . who is it wants me, guv?" Rowley inquired tentatively. From his days on the crime squad and his more recent experience of SO11 he knew that it was remarkable for the brass to take any particular interest in subordinates. After all, DSs were so plentiful that any one of a dozen or so hanging around the various squad offices would have done if there was an errand to run or some hiccup in the system which needed ironing out. Rowley sighed to himself. Like most of the detectives engaged in intelligence gathering, he was seldom required to visit the monolith of New Scotland Yard, the Broadway headquarters of the Metropolitan Police, which was saved from total glass and concrete anonymity only by the brushed silver triangular sign which revolved slowly out in front of the building bearing the famous name of London's police force. Normally SO11 detectives relieved the tedium of observation duties by using the facilities of the local police stations, the "factory" in the area they happened to be working. They were like nomads and visits to the Yard were more or less confined to target briefings, when a whole squad would be pulled together, or like this morning when Rowley, a surveillance team "skipper," was required to make the duty call to have his diary of events endorsed by the duty DI and collect any messages destined for the three DCs who were at that moment manning a stake-out on an elaborate and seemingly endless blackmail investigation. The duty DI's caustic greeting was the first hint of trouble.

"I told you, the old man, Christ, what do I have to do, do I have to spell it out, God himself." The DI jabbed a finger upwards to emphasize the point, savouring his own peevish ill-humour and momentarily dispensing with the convention of rank which would normally have precluded reference to the SO11 Commander in such terms. "And he's spitting blood. The word comes down we're sending you over to NDIU, though I'm buggered if I know what they'd want with a wanker like you. I did hear a whisper they're dreaming up some comedy production down there in Disneyland, got everybody excited, bunch of fairies, only believe you me, pal, I don't want to know anything about any of that. I've got enough on my plate as it is." The DI cast a jaundiced eye around the office and returned to Rowley with displeasure. "All I can say is you must have golden balls, my son, you're so much in demand." He jerked a thumb in the general direction of the door. "Take my advice, you'll get your ass down there pronto . . . that's if you can spare the time from your busy social round." Sarcasm twisted his features into a liverish scowl. "Well, what're you waiting for? A commendation?"

Questions surged into Rowley's mind but he could see that he would get nothing more from this lazy apology for a detective-inspector and so he turned and headed for the door. As he went out of the office, the sense of foreboding growing, Rowley noticed the DI sag back into his chair and snatch up the *Sun* to continue his intellectual workout. All around him the lights on the mute phones blinked frantically.

Rowley squeezed into a lift which was crowded with office workers carrying impressive bundles of paperwork under their arms and trying to touch up the girl clerks who fended off their clumsy advances with bored indifference. The lift went down, emptying as it descended until Rowley was left alone, watching the lights on the indicator. When the lift next jerked to a halt, he got out, crossed the lobby, opened a heavy fire door and began to walk down a featureless corridor, past anonymous doors with slips of card fitted into metal slots to identify the denizens of the warren. The echoes of his footsteps ringing hollowly from the composition floor, Rowley tried to recall everything he had been told about Deputy Assistant Commissioner Raymond Moss and his principal aide-de-camp Commander Larry Drake, boss of the Central Drugs Intelligence Unit. Reputations were made and destroyed on the Yard's highly efficient rumour grapevine, so Rowley had plenty to reflect upon, for both men were of the new breed which was sweeping through the hierarchy of the Met: suave, urbane, more at home in the rarified world of high technology and office politics than the seamy side of nicking villains. Dark-suited, neatly barbered, exuding confidence, they looked more like successful lawyers or businessmen than detectives. Yet behind the smooth, carefully groomed exteriors there lurked a ruthlessness which had swept aside the old guard, that collection of grizzled CID chiefs with more sweat and blood years in the job than they cared to remember, turfed out on their pensions before they could blink their whisky-shot eyes. Before they knew what had hit them, the smiling assassins were in their chairs, hand-lasted Oxfords under their desks and wastebins piled high with the memorabilia of a bygone age, to be replaced on the office walls by rows of smooth faces staring out from the group photographs of the senior command courses at the Staff College.

As he neared his destination Rowley recalled that DAC Raymond Moss was reputed to be a brilliant tactician of the political infighting which riddled the corridors of power and Commander Larry Drake was his protégé. Depending on their whim, they could be either powerful allies or deadly as piranha. Rowley wondered again why such lofty powerbrokers should be concerning themselves with his own mundane involvement in the machinery of criminal intelligence. But before he could come to any conclusion, he reached Disneyland, iconoclastic Met patois for the Special Operations Centre deep in the bowels of the Yard.

At a turn in the corridor Rowley found himself confronted by a security guard, who scrutinized his ID and checked him off his clipboard before allowing him to proceed into the no-go area. Surprise was his next reaction for in all the covert drugs set-ups he had previously experienced, jeans and bikers boots, beards, greasy pigtails and ear-studs had been the most evident attire. But here, the gathering of detectives displayed little of such studied lowlife. Tailored suede and leather were much evident, complementing designer casuals, and hairstyles were still raffish but expensively barbered. Plastic identity cards dangled from snakeskin belts.

At first sight the scene reeked of a pampered cadre basking in the reflected glory of its own elitism, but before he could pursue that idea, there was a general movement towards a briefing amphitheatre where semi-circles of tan hide seats rose in tiers around a spotlit dais which bore the lacquered crest of the Metropolitan Police. As Rowley was carried in on the tide he noticed Moss and Drake were already standing near the dais deep in conversation with a clutch of aides. Groups of detectives drifted in and took seats and Rowley slipped in at the back of the room as a technician set up a screen and began to warm up a projector.

When everyone was seated Deputy Assistant Commissioner Moss bounded to the lectern with an energetic stride, his shock of blond hair ablaze under the lights. The murmur of conversation died away.

"Good morning, gentlemen," Moss greeted them crisply, scanning his audience with enthusiasm, "welcome to the ghost squad. You're all hand-picked specialists so I know I don't have to remind you that this little show of ours is strictly need-to-know, so no pillow talk for the baby alarm to overhear." He paused for effect, then raised a hand to still the chuckles. "OK, OK, so let's get down to it. My friends, what we are about to embark upon here is the most ambitious intelligence-gathering exercise ever conceived by the Metropolitan Police. We call it NEL." A visual aid sprang up on the screen spelling out the acronym, which Moss then emphasized with a theatrical sweep of his hand. "Narcotics Enforcement Liaison." He stabbed a forefinger at each word. "NEL. In essence an all-Europe counter-offensive against the drugs trade, the multi-nationals of organized crime." He treated them to a flashing smile. "Yes, that's NEL's little secret, gentlemen, for the first time in the history of the police service we have the potential, the dynamics for a combined assault, the sharp cutting edge." A map of the continent appeared on the screen crisscrossed with the known drug routes and peppered with a rash of coloured markers. "A familiar picture. At the moment, as you can see, the traffickers are beating us hands down, turning the complexities of international law and the unwieldy nature of cross-border cooperation, the creaking machinery of Interpol, to their own advantage. But no longer! With NEL slicing through the red tape of bureaucracy we can, for the first time, beat them at their own game. A combined task force, gentlemen, the finest talent our countries have to offer, one jump ahead." He paused again, gave his audience another sweep of his eyes, every inch a charismatic leader of men.

"At this point in the proceedings," Moss continued, lowering his voice to a more confidential tone, "it is my very great pleasure, no, my privilege to welcome colleagues from our European partners who have already given NEL their support: from France, the Gendarmerie Mobile; from Germany, the Bundesgrenzschutz; from Italy the Carabinieri." He inclined his head towards the individual groups. "Welcome, my friends! You are here to help us forge a new sword of justice." Moss paused again and a small smile played on his lips. "But you know, the most trusty sword is useless without the muscle and coordination to wield it. We have always had the skill, now at last we have the muscle." He made a fist of his right hand. "Political muscle, and there you have the key which will unlock those doors which have been closed to us for so long. The political muscle, the political clout to make things happen. Have no doubt, the politicians are drooling over drug abuse. It's the latest production on the stage of electoral fortune, the show stopper."

He waved a hand expansively. "The politicians have this nightmare, they see a tidal wave coming and they're screaming for action. All we had to do was pick the moment when moral indignation was at fever pitch and present them with NEL. A little something for everybody."

Moss gave them a confident smile. "So the deal was struck and you, each of you hand-picked for your special skills as narcotics investigators, stand on the brink of an undercover operation the like of which has never been seen before." He held up a hand and slowly made a fist. "We're going to grab 'em by the balls and squeeze until they faint. We're going to deal these fat cats such a blow they'll be reeling and then we'll crush 'em. Oh, make no mistake about it, we're going to forge such a crime-fighting force we're going to write our own chapter in history and make a whole lot of reputations along the way."

Moss paused to let the significance of his rhetoric sink in, tilting his face a little so that the lights caught his best profile, eyes ablaze with sincerity, blond hair flickering with fire. Playing to the gallery, Rowley concluded as he caught himself admiring the performance. An Oscar winner, dripping with charisma. All he needed were the dancing girls.

With immaculate timing the DAC swept a hand towards the partition behind the amphitheatre. "Back there, my friends," he announced, "we are setting up our new muscles, our own dedicated intelligence computers, the very best. Our computers will be talking to their cousins not just here at the Yard but right across Europe, Wiesbaden, Paris, Rome. The high tech of law enforcement at our fingertips."

Moss paused again and a self-effacing smile formed on his face. "Well, that's enough from me for the time being, gentlemen. Time to get down to work. Your team leaders are waiting to brief you and so I'll leave you in their capable hands." Moss turned from the dais, but then as if an afterthought had struck him, swung back, gripping the lectern with both hands like a young lion, the crest gleaming in front of him. "All you need is a sense of purpose, a sense of mission. Let's get this act together and by God we'll show them something."

He stepped down with the same youthful bound and was immediately engulfed by his aides, who hustled him away. Superstar quality, Rowley thought to himself at the back of the room. A succession of tactical briefings followed, covering computer codes and a rundown on technical back-up equipment for every conceivable situation from fibre optic probes, infra-red video and starlight scopes to the latest in eavesdropping equipment. The session was concluded by a logistics specialist, who ran through the duty scheme format and covered the special funds which had been salted away to sweeten informants.

When it was all over, Rowley eased his way through the crowd to where Larry Drake was talking with a couple of his own men. Still in his early thirties, the NDIU boss had struck just the right combination of patronage, ambition and political savvy to become the youngest Commander in the Met, the bloom of youth still lending a boyish appeal to his otherwise bland features. He cut an elegant figure in his chalk stripe double-breasted suit with a polka-dot show handkerchief spilling ostentatiously from the top pocket to complement a pure silk tie. As Rowley approached, Drake turned and under his steady gaze the DS cleared his throat and said politely, "Detective-Sergeant Rowley, sir. Er . . . C11? I was told to report to you."

The nimble brain took less than half a second to make the connection. "Ah yes . . . Rowley. Good, good." Drake reached out and gripped the sergeant's hand in a warm handshake as if they were old friends. "Tony, isn't it?"

"Yes, sir," Rowley stammered, trying hard not to appear too astonished. First-name terms from a Commander was beyond his experience.

"Good, good," Drake repeated, giving Rowley his undivided attention as he casually steered him away from the others. "Were you in for the briefing, Tony?"

"Yes, sir."

"What did you think?"

"Well, sir . . ." Rowley was cautious about offering an opinion. "It sounded pretty high-powered, European forces, that sort of thing. Bit out of my league."

Drake chuckled. "You want to try horse-trading with the Carabinieri, everything a big production, very status-conscious our Italian friends, and the French . . ." He shook his head and glanced at the gold Rolex on his wrist. "Come on." He gripped Rowley's elbow in a proprietary gesture. "Let's get something to eat and I'll fill you in. Brunch is one of the more civilized habits I picked up at the FBI Academy, the others you'd need a polygraph to get out of me!"

He escorted Rowley out of Disneyland, nodding affably to the duty officer who booked them out and they were in the lift speeding upwards before Drake spoke again. "One thing you've got to remember, Tony. The old man puts on one hell of a show. Fire in the loins, but I tell you, he's worked the oracle, we've got open sesame on this deal right up to No. 10. Politics, politics, that's the name of the game. If it doesn't have voter appeal then you might as well forget it. But drugs, hmmm . . . so sexy with the image-makers, it's like a dream come true."

The lift stopped before Rowley could get his bearings and it took him a moment to realize that Drake was leading him into the Commissioners' Mess, that holy of holies reserved for the very highest echelons of the force. Sensing the sergeant's incredulity, Drake patted his shoulder reassuringly as they made their entrance, drawing glances from a couple of Deputy Assistant Commissioners already ensconced at a table near the door.

"That's what I mean, open sesame, Tony," Drake said, laughing, but the DS couldn't help but feel overawed by such flagrant disregard for the time-honoured etiquette of the Met. For a mere sergeant to set foot in the Commissioners' Mess was tantamount to sacrilege. Unperturbed, Drake sauntered over to the buffet laid out on crisp white linen spread over an oak servery resplendent with silver adornments. A far cry from the plastic and formica of the canteens where the tables were graced with sticky sauce bottles.

Hovering over the selection, Drake helped himself to a dish of Roquefort dip and a handful of breadsticks, picked out cornets of smoked salmon and was moving on as Rowley, trailing behind and trying to remain as invisible as possible, grabbed a bowl of Waldorf salad before hurrying after the drugs chief to a corner table which was dominated by an overflowing fruit bowl. It was not until they were seated that Rowley had his first real chance to inspect his surroundings and immediately spotted Deputy Assistant Commissioner Moss, fresh from his performance down in Disneyland, sitting at a table across the room in earnest conversation with a sallow-faced man with lank dark hair flopping across his forehead. Drake followed Rowley's gaze as he plunged a breadstick into the warm creamy cheese. "You recognize the guy with the guv'nor over there?" The question was posed softly, with a secret smirk, and before Rowley could even hazard a guess Drake told him confidentially, "That's Peter Ashworth, or I should say The Right Honourable Peter Ashworth MP, Minister of State at the Home Office and chairman of the Commons Select Committee on drug abuse. Guv'nor's got him eating out of his hand."

Drake tasted a little of the dip, dabbed a trace of the rich cheese from his lips with his napkin and told Rowley, "Was in here just the other day with the Prime Minister. Commissioner's do. You should've seen old Peter, mesmerized like a rabbit. The PM was giving drugs both barrels and old Peter there was practically having an orgasm." Drake dipped the Roquefort. "I kid you not, Tony, the way you've got to treat these politicians, it's like giving sweets to the kids. You tell 'em what it's like on the streets and right away they see a crusade, knights on white chargers, and old Peter over there, boy, he can't get enough of the spurs in his flanks." Drake chuckled to himself and signalled to a waitress, who immediately brought them a bottle of chilled Chablis. Dazzled, Rowley busied himself with his Waldorf.

"So—" Drake finished the dip and pushed the bowl aside, carefully brushing breadcrumbs from the pristine tablecloth. "I imagine you're wondering what the hell you're doing here, Tony . . . am I right?"

"It's crossed my mind, guv'nor."

"Well, what you've got to know first off is, you're sitting at the start of a rainbow." Drake picked up the Chablis and filled their glasses. He suddenly seemed preoccupied.

Rowley sipped a little of the wine. Last night Italian red with the capo, today French white with the brass.

"But I'll tell you this straight." Drake spoke again, a slight frown furrowing his brow. "We've got a little problem, little black cloud out there on the blue horizon."

The wine seemed to thicken in Rowley's gullet as if he had lost the ability to swallow as he told himself, Here it comes.

"I've got to tell you this straight off, strictly *entre nous*," Drake continued. "We lost an officer yesterday."

Rowley flinched. "Lost an officer?" He sounded parrot-stupid.

"Hmmm." Drake pursed his lips. "An undercover. Girl called Helen Linden, newly minted DS off the squad. Nice kid too, but Jesus, isn't that always the way."

Rowley felt a dead weight pressing down on him. "How'd you mean lost, guv'nor?"

"Lost . . . waxed . . . wasted." Drake popped a curl of smoked salmon into his mouth, swallowed before he added, "Killed on duty."

Rowley felt a buzz of alarm. "Killed? I didn't hear anything about that."

"No, and you won't either," Drake said. "Nobody knows. We've got

the lid on this thing for the time being, but that won't last for ever."
He inclined his head, watching Rowley. The cat and the mouse.

"And oh boy, when it hits, we're going to have to dance some fancy
steps, otherwise"—he nodded across the room—"otherwise you won't
see good old Peter over there, or his pals on the committee, for dust."
Drake leaned forward. "Nothing like the old blue granite to scare off
the politicians. They'll be long gone and away and all that brave talk
you heard downstairs will be floating away like so much hot air."

Rowley tried to swallow, found he couldn't. "How'd it happen,
guv'nor?" His voice sounded unreal.

"Oh, how's it ever happen?" Drake sighed, slipped another cornet
into his mouth, washed it down with Chablis. "Stupid, too stupid for
words." He sighed more heavily. "Our good friends across the pond,
DEA, got to hear about NEL on a crosswind and wanted in. The old
man wasn't happy about it and neither was I for that matter. The
Europeans are enough of a handful without DEA prima donnas
showboating all over the place. Only before we could squeeze 'em out
we got guiding light. Be nice to our American cousins."

Drake finished off his smoked salmon with gusto. "So they sent over
an agent, supposedly for liaison, a watching brief, only their guy turned
out to be a firebrand, running around the minute he got here. A real
balls-acher. We tried to keep him pegged down, gave him Helen Linden to show him around, keep him occupied and out of our hair. You
know, a little female company, a little diversion. Only this guy, this
Jack Monroe, must have rocks for balls, because instead of getting into
the girl's knickers, he takes her down to Devon, some farmhouse down
there all wired up and booby-trapped and gets her blown away." Drake
sat back, steepled his fingers and watched the DS keenly. "So there you
have our little black cloud, Tony."

Rowley blinked. "Jesus!" He breathed the word.

Drake reached out to the fruit bowl and helped himself to a big
succulent William pear and a handful of black grapes. He picked up a
knife and began to dissect the pear. "There's a huddle on this right
now, Commissioner, Dep, AC Crime." He carefully scooped out the
pear's core. "The local law didn't even know these two were on their
turf, so there's a few fences to be mended, only as luck would have it
the Chief down there's ex-Met so we've bought a little breathing space.
But I don't have to tell you, Tony, dead policewomen are the worst
kind of bad news, and an undercover at that. When this does get out,

the media's going to have a field day, so unless we can pull something spectacular out of the bag there's going to be problems, big problems. Could wrap up NEL and send everybody home with black marks. That's the pity of it."

Drake sucked a sliver of pear as Rowley tried to grasp the enormity of what he had just been told. In the silence, the question he had tried to keep trapped in his mind suddenly escaped. "So what's all this got to do with me, guv'nor?" It sounded gauche, stupid.

A crafty look crossed the drugs chief's face and just as quickly disappeared. He popped a grape into his mouth and the benign smile returned.

"You heard the boss, Tony, everybody on this little firm's been picked for special skills, special talents. You've got the perfect credentials!" Drake sat back again but his eyes didn't leave Rowley's face. "You've got the Twins after your blood."

"The Twins?" The stupid parrot spoke again.

Drake nodded slowly. "Monroe, this DEA guy has got some angle on the Twins and the Heathrow blagging you were on, only he's playing it close to his chest, very cagey." Drake leaned forward. "But now we've got his balls in the nutcracker. He's the clown got our girl killed, so he's going to have to unlock this thing for us and it'd better be good. But we've not got much time, so we've got to work on him neat and fast, and that's where you come in, Tony. We want you to be his new minder. We want you to stick to him while we put on the squeeze. So that's the size of it. Your chance to shine, Tony, help us blow the cloud away. Think of it like this: putting something back into the service. How long've you been in the job? Fifteen, sixteen years? So you owe it, you owe it to the job. Think about it. Not just a dead policewoman, a dead undercover, her sweet young life snuffed out, no warrant, no correct procedures, no back-up, no jurisdiction, no nothing. Just another king-sized Met cock-up. You want to see those headlines? *News at Ten, Times* leader, *Panorama* special. Clobber the Met, that'll be the name of the game."

Drake sucked pear juice from his fingers. "All we want you to do is see this clown Monroe, talk to him, get close to him, get everything you can out of him as quickly as possible. Soon as we know what he was up to with the girl we can move in, only we can't sweat him officially because whatever else he may be, he's still one of us, one of the family, so we've got to get into his head another way, and if he's on to something, we want it. Nothing like results for shortening the memory, Tony, something spectacular is what we need right now. So what I'm asking you to do is get together with Monroe, be his friend. You'll find him at the Inn on the Park, licking his wounds."

Rowley dropped his eyes and stared at his salad, playing Russian roulette in his mind. The hammer fell on the live round and he asked the question: "Do I have a choice, guv'nor?"

Commander Drake raised his wineglass to his lips. Slowly he shook his head.

5

The hotel room on the eighth floor of the Inn on the Park was in semi-darkness. Curtains drawn across the windows stained yellow by the autumn sun, the rainbow blur of a colour television sending pinwheels of light skittering around walls and ceiling. A video cassette of Francis Ford Coppola's *Apocalypse Now* was playing with the sound turned off. Sprawled on the crumpled bed, Special Agent Jack Monroe of the United States Department of Justice Drug Enforcement Administration watched the ghostly silhouettes of helicopter gunships flit silently across the screen and succumbed to the waves of memory.

He was naked but for a pair of jockey shorts and the old Marine Corps dog-tags nestling in the fuzz of greying hair which covered his chest but could not obscure purple tracks of scar tissue from the collarbone down across the pectoral, indelibly marking the path of the grenade shards which had all but ended his life. Fingering the dog-tags, Monroe gave himself up to the dark mood.

Once Jack Monroe had been a dreamer, an idealist. The small-town kid from Sweetbriar, Virginia, with a single-minded ambition which had taken him through to a criminology degree at New York's John Jay, only to gutter like a dying candle in the emerald jungles which flanked the brown sluggish waters of the Song Tra Bong. Instead of the FBI Academy, by a twist of fate Jack Monroe had first become a cop in the hell-hole of Vietnam.

On the screen he watched the pensive Martin Sheen as his Swift boat sliced down the brown river and a light buzzing of memory began behind his eyes. Through the shimmering images he began to see a reflection of himself. Monroe had gone to Nam as a Marine second lieutenant, a brownbar grunt on the Advocate General's field investigation staff. First he had learned the tricks of survival, wading through waist-deep paddies and swishing elephant grass, senses straining for the staccato crackle of AK fire from the tree-lines, the telltale snick of a Bouncing Betty anti-personnel mine; creeping down jungle trails in heat so sweltering that it could boil your brain inside the steel pot of your helmet. Monroe watched Charlie slaughter the teenage troops in merciless firefights in the last desperate throes of the South-East Asia conflict, crawled into his poncho hooch at night, and through the same jaundiced eyes saw the boy grunts escape the relentless nightmare of conflict by shotgunning angel dust from the flash suppressors of their M16s, chase the dragon across the steel of bayonet blades or simply embrace oblivion in a pipeful of Cambodian Red.

Sprawled on the bed, he watched the fictional war unfold on the TV, the images mingling with the relentless scenes inside his head. Once he had learned how to stay alive in the treacherous boonies, Monroe had been assigned to an SIB unit inside the First Marine Division so raddled with drugs that Command had ordered an undercover investigation. He had been briefed by no less a celebrity than a Westmoreland aide, a florid-faced major with starched jungle utilities and disgust in his eyes.

"We're not losing this war to the little people," the major told Monroe. "We're losing it to this shit." He broke a sachet of cocaine and scattered the white dust across the top of his trestle table in the CP tent. "VC's greasing us with nose candy and Westy's roasting ass." He brushed the snow away with an angry sweep of his hand and jutted his jaw. "Intelligence says there's a potful of junk coming in on the river, so we want you to get out there, Lieutenant, and bring us some hard evidence. Co-ordinates we can zap with a Phantom strike, B52s, all the ordnance you want." He gripped Monroe's shoulder. "As far as the grunts are concerned, you'll be just another brownbar boonierat, only you'll have five-star firepower. That'll be our secret. You, me and Westy."

The raw meat of the major's face melted into the TV screen. Sprawled on the bed, Monroe watched the video war unfold through heavy-lidded eyes, fingering the old dog-tags like a rosary. He had become one of the despised snoopers, tracking an elusive snow trail, finally sinking to the depths of frustration, interrogating suspects with callous indifference, but it was always that last mission which had scarred his mind more deeply than all the others.

Bleakly he relived the bone chill of dawn under the triple canopy of the Vietnam jungle. A relentless drizzle plastered fatigues to his back as the platoon picked its way single file down the trail where the green formed an impenetrable wall along the banks of the Song Tra Bong. They were dog-weary from a week on the march, moving ever deeper into the jungle, two fire teams strung out, so far into the badlands that nerves twanged like piano wires at the slightest sound. All except the kid on point, jaws moving mechanically on a wad of gum, the plastic plug in his ear giving off an insect buzz of the rock-and-roll blasting into his brain. Eyes glazed, jaws working as he humped the heavy M60 machine-gun and led them down the trail through grey veils of drizzle, boots slithering in the sticky red clay. For the hundredth time Monroe paused to squint at the square of map in its waterproof wallet, checking his surroundings for the pencilled cross which marked the spot where he would meet his guide and part company from the patrol.

Suddenly up ahead the kid on point stopped, his mouth fell slack as he dropped to one knee and unleashed a withering fire into the dense foliage ahead. A golden cascade of spent cartridges rained into the red mud. Half a bandolier had been aimlessly expended before Monroe could scamper forward and grab the grunt by his shirt, pulling him down, hissing in his ear, "What in the sweet name of Christ . . ."

"Contact down the trail . . ." The kid gave him a toothy grin, "Charlie on the prowl, uh-huh . . . I just give him a taste of The Gun."

Monroe looked into the grunt's face and recognized the thousand-yard stare. Stoned on angel dust. He felt the heat of his own desperation as his grip tightened on the sodden fatigues making the kid's eyes pop. "Hey, cap!" the kid protested. "Recon by fire, uh-huh, SOP in the boonies. Charlie ain't going to buck the mean machine, no sir." He went to raise the M60 again but Monroe slapped the barrel down and hissed, "You want your ass shot off!"

Behind him the fire team had scrambled nervously into the jungle and were setting up a defensive perimeter. Squirming under Monroe's grasp the grunt began to giggle. "Don't mean nothing, cap, uh-huh." Jaws began working on the gum again.

Up ahead a lone figure emerged from the drifting rain curtain. His face was berry brown under a rag bandanna, tiger fatigues moulded to his wiry frame. He moved silently as an apparition, unperturbed by the hail of gunfire which had shredded the fleshy foliage all around him. The LURP came out of the jungle grinning, a flash of white teeth. "Which one of you girls is the actual?"

Monroe shoved the point man aside and got to his feet. The green man thrust his berry face forward, lips pulled back into a leer. "What's the worst thing you can imagine, slick?" Monroe knew that the Long Range Recon Patrols, LURPs for short, were a special breed infected with jungle madness, so he merely shrugged and the green man slapped the bowie knife dangling from his belt and said, "Luke, when you find him some other bad dude's had his ears."

Monroe's eyes fell to the belt. It was festooned with prunes of wrinkled flesh. The LURP chuckled deep in his throat and something crazy showed in his eyes. He grabbed Monroe by the forearm. "Saddle up, slick," he said, "you and me, we've got a date with the little people."

The buzz inside his head faded and Monroe found himself back in the hotel room staring at the TV, a light sheen of sweat on his face. He wiped the back of his hand across his forehead and tasted the salt on his lips as he chewed at the ends of his moustache. The video played silently on, and with an effort Monroe reached out and switched off the recorder. He had lost his appetite for the movie.

He winced as muscles knotted in his arms and back, and in an effort to relieve the nervous cramps, he swung himself off the bed and with a sigh went into a routine of fifty press-ups in fast time, rolled over and performed twenty knee crunches. Gasping for breath, his heart pumping frantically, the burst of activity eased the tension in his body and he hauled himself to his feet, crossed to the window and jerked open the curtains. Squinting at the sudden rush of sunlight, Monroe raised his eyes from the traffic streaming down Park Lane and surveyed the green oasis of Hyde Park. He was back in the present and he forced himself to review the events which had culminated in the girl's death, cursing his own fallibility.

When he had first arrived in London and had made his number at the Yard, Jack Monroe had found the traditional reserve of the British mildly amusing. But as time went by and his irritation grew, amusement gave way to anger. He was supposed to be working with NDIU, but whenever he put up a plan of action, all he seemed able to generate was polite prevarication. A watching brief, he was mildly rebuked, meant exactly that. Then when they put him under the thumb of the prissy girl sergeant, Helen Linden, with a tight-lipped lecture on jurisdiction, Monroe had fumed inwardly and had grabbed his chance the moment their guard was down, tricking the greenhorn girl detective to take him down to Devon and ending up on his knees in that barn, choking on the dust as he cradled the dying girl in his arms. It was all so stupid . . . so pointless . . . so sloppy.

Monroe turned back into the room, his face darkening under a scowl of self-recrimination. He went over to the bed and pulled on an old sweatshirt and a pair of faded blue jeans. Frustration burned like white-hot embers. Dammit, they hadn't even given him an opportunity to explain when they brought him back from Devon under escort to be lectured by painfully polite men with loathing in their eyes. Instead of listening to him, they had ignominiously relieved him of his passport and had advised him in no uncertain terms to stay put until further notice. In the end Monroe was left with the clear, if unspoken, impression that he was now under what amounted to house arrest, obliged to languish in his hotel room while those perfect gentlemen at the Yard decided how best to nail his hide and ship him back home in disgrace.

Seething at the prospect, Monroe had put in an indignant call to his bureau chief in Washington, but the wires had already been buzzing and all Monroe received was a flea in his ear over the transatlantic line and a frosty admonition to do nothing to further sour relations. Mend fences, he was instructed, cooperate, kiss ass if need be. Monroe slammed the phone down in disgust.

He had slept badly, replaying the sequence of events over and over, straightening it out in his mind. He always came to the same conclusion. He had been right. All those strands of information, those cryptic messages coming out of South America by way of Miami that a gold-greedy drugs syndicate calling itself The Enterprise had laid a brand new pipeline to pump the product into the virgin markets of Europe. All that speculation had meshed together in that moment at that farmhouse, in that barn. Bingo! He had found the smelter and with it the key to the whole cocaine running operation.

But right there and then fate had decreed that triumph should turn to ashes. He had taken a chance and he had succeeded in getting a fellow cop killed. Damned by his own impatience. And the hell of it was that even by his own cavalier standards, such recklessness was unforgivable. Monroe chewed at the ends of his moustache. He had been politely instructed to stay in his hotel until they got around to his problem. Do nothing . . . say nothing . . . keep out of our hair. Shitfire! They'd got him over a barrel.

Squatting on the end of the bed, recalling this admonition, Monroe repeatedly slapped a fist savagely into an open palm in an attempt to vent his boiling emotions. When the house phone buzzed he snatched it up and growled his name into the mouthpiece. But instead of reassuring words from the other side of the Atlantic, another voice, carefully neutral, announced itself from the lobby below and asked if it would be convenient to come up. Monroe almost laughed. Even at times like this when they had his balls securely in their grip, the British were so goddamned polite! Sourly he muttered his agreement and dropped the phone, telling himself that he had no alternative but to go along with their charade.

A few moments later when Monroe opened the door to his visitor, he found himself confronted by a man of about his own height, probably somewhere in his middle thirties, but looking older thanks to the heavy crease lines slanting down from nose and mouth, dragging the expression with them. The light of the hallway accentuated the man's most striking feature, a thick white streak running through his hair. Monroe immediately checked with the eyes. They were the familiar blank wary eyes of a street cop.

"Tony Rowley." The man reintroduced himself with the name he had given on the phone. "I'm the DS from SO11 you had the call about." Monroe's eyes fell automatically to the police identification card offered for his inspection. It confirmed the name and rank.

Monroe moved aside. "You'd better come in then, slick, make yourself at home." There was the merest hint of hesitation as the cautious eyes swept the hotel room. Monroe laughed without humour. "Oh, don't worry, you're safe with me. I'm not killing cops today."

He immediately regretted revealing this inkling of his own black mood, and as Rowley stepped inside, their eyes met and telegraphed some common degree of understanding. The American washed a hand over his face and said, "Ah, what the hell . . . forget I said that. Guess I'm kind of keyed up, that's all."

"You don't have to apologize to me," Rowley said. "I'm just the new minder. Drake sent me over, thought maybe you could use some company." He shrugged. "It's all the same to me."

Monroe went over to the bedside dresser, took a White Owl from an open packet lying there, spent a few seconds stripping off the Cellophane and then clamped his teeth around the plastic mouthpiece, picked up his old Zippo and thumbed a flame. The lighter was engraved with the eagle on the ball and the Marine Corps legend: *Semper Fidelis*.

He turned to Rowley, his face wreathed in blue cigar smoke. "Never kid a kidder, slick," he replied. "Right now it's covering your ass time back at the ranch, damage limitation. Correct?"

Rowley shrugged. "Something like that."

"Brass tap-dancing like all hell?"

Rowley nodded.

"So they send you over here to make sure old Jack Monroe's behaving himself."

"Yeah. I'm just the errand boy."

Monroe sucked on his cigar. "You know, slick, it's always been my experience that there's a whole world of goddamn injustice out there waiting to unload and sooner or later we're all going to end up in the hurt locker."

Rowley smiled. "Maybe what you need is a friend."

Monroe sank down on his haunches beside the bed, rummaged in an airline bag and produced a bottle of Jack Daniels Old Time No. 7 sour mash. He held it up for Rowley to see. "I've already got one," he said. "Maybe what you and me need to get us acquainted is a little taste of the stomp-down Tennessee sippin' whisky just to sort of oil the works."

Rowley looked at the whisky bottle. "If you say so," he said, "I'm not going to argue with that."

He fell into one of the easy chairs, brown tweed on a tubular chrome frame, and watched Monroe prowl around the room picking up the toothbrush glass and a tumbler from the drinks dispenser which stood on top of a miniature fridge. The American exuded the pent-up energy of a caged tiger as he returned to the bed, perched on the end and broke the seal on the bottle. He sloshed whisky into both glasses, handed one to Rowley. "Here you go, slick, drink to the cop-killer."

Rowley raised his glass. "Cheers," he replied.

Monroe took a swig, then put the glass down, puffed at his cigar. "Let's clear the decks," he said after a long moment's silence. "What we'll do is tell each other stories, OK? See how we get along. Like the confessional. And seeing as I'm the host, I'll go first." His expression grew flinty. "Yesterday I screwed up." He stabbed the air with the cigar in an angry gesture. "Yeah, I admit it. Your people jerked me around so much I lost my cool, my sense of perspective. I got careless, I got sloppy and your girl got deep-sixed on my account. And if you think I'm proud of that miserable performance you can walk out of here this minute before I throw you out on your ass." He breathed a heavy sigh. "Oh boy, good old Jack Monroe, so laid back it hurts, coolest god-damned narc in the business, gets his balls busted all because some liberated broad couldn't bear to do as she was told."

He shook his head and Rowley went to speak, but Monroe held up his hand and said, "Your turn in a minute, don't be so hasty." He ground the half-smoked cigar into an ashtray with savage jerky movements. "That place, down there in Devonshire. I knew it was dirty the minute I saw it. Just like the man said, this snitch of mine who turned to Uncle for his salvation when I grabbed his ass running product into Miami just when he thought he'd got that whole bunch of flaky cops down there squared away. The guy was so terrified he'd take a fifty-year fall he was falling over himself to cooperate. What he told me would've made your hair curl, slick. So I turned him loose, put him to work and one fine day he told me The Enterprise was so hot to ship product into Europe they were offering a discount to a bunch of your gangsters. He told me there was a farmhouse way down in the countryside where the deal had been struck. Just came out with it, like he knew his days were numbered. And he was not wrong. I tell you this in the past tense because the next day my man went over the side of his speedboat wrapped in anchor chains."

Monroe leaned back and took a pull at the Jack Daniels. "When we heard about NEL, my people wanted in. It was too good an opportunity to pass up. Perfect cover for what I had in mind." He hunched his shoulders, working the muscles. "Only when I got here, your people dickered around so much I could hardly take a leak without a chaperone, and when I did slip the leash I had your little lady in tow, and that's when Lady Luck dealt me out. Oh, that place . . . Jesus, that place was set up for the sucker punch, come-on signs flashing like neon and enough C4 to take the lid off the world."

Monroe proffered the bottle. "You want some more anaesthetic?"

Rowley shook his head and the American grimaced. "For what it's worth, I told the kid, stay put, stay in the car, but she didn't. I was in back of the barn when she came waltzing in right on to the command wire."

Monroe gnawed at his moustache. "Nail bomb buried in the ground
. . . took her apart." He shook his head as though endeavouring to
dislodge the memory. "Oh yeah, one whole big fat world of injustice.
Now your people have got me in the pickle jar. Ballsbuster Jack
Monroe, the original cop-killer."

Dispensing with his glass, the American took a deep swig from the
bottle and wiped the back of his hand across his mouth. His eyes
watered from the jolt of raw whisky. "You want to take a turn now,
slick," he said to Rowley. "Tell me a story that's going to beat that."

Rowley paused for a moment, sensing that the DEA agent would
close up on him as the brittle glint of indifference settled behind his
eyes. He needed some quick inspiration. Slowly he rocked forward until
he was leaning his forearms on his knees, rolling the glass between his
hands, watching the whisky swirl.

"Mr. Smooth tells me you've got an interest in our Heathrow job,
the bullion blag." He paused for effect. "Well, you've got the right
man, right here, that's the one I screwed up. Could be we've got more
in common than you think."

"Drake's smarter than I thought," Monroe replied, suddenly attentive. "You were on that caper?"

Rowley nodded slowly. As he stared into the whisky he could see
Dad Garratt's face reflected there, smiling the secret smile. "Why
don't I give that story a whirl, see what you think?"

Monroe watched him, chewed at his moustache, said, "Try me."

He reached out with the bottle in his hand and sloshed more Jack
Daniels into Rowley's glass, drowning the image of Dad Garratt.

"We never did work out who plotted the job up," Rowley began,
falling into the vernacular of the Met. "Never got so much as a sniff on
that. But a local firm blagged the gold away. A tasty tickle all right, five
million in bullion bars tucked away at the airport en route to Nigeria.
They had it away sweet as a nut. All the squads were after it, Sweeney,
serious crime, central robbery, C13, all the glory boys looking for a
chance to make a name for themselves. I was a skipper on the RCS at
the time and my guv'nor got the first whisper. He was the old breed, a
snout on every firm, nothing moved in the Met he didn't know about
sooner or later." Rowley smiled at the memory. "A real chancer he was,
they broke the mould when they made Dad Garratt, he was one in a
million." He shrugged. "Well anyway, we jumped in first, lifted one of
the tearaways who'd been on the job. They'd gone in tooled up and

mob-handed, buggered the security cameras and given the guards a petrol bath, scared 'em shitless when they torched one just to show they meant business. Bad bastards. Anyway we dropped on the happy-bag-man while the dew was still on him, just Dad and me. Stuck him up a deal he could hardly refuse. Supergrass the firm and we'd set him up with a nice long holiday in Spain, immunity from prosecution, new life, the whole package in return for his testimony in court. Guy was staring twelve right in the face so he jumped at it."

Rowley took a sip of whisky. "Well, Dad slipped him away to a safe house down in Cornwall and we pulled a pair of first-division robbers on the strength, the Pollard Twins, kind of lunatics would cut your heart out as soon as look at you. Got 'em in their fancy Knightsbridge drinking club, hit 'em at three in the morning and hauled 'em down to the local factory while the rest of the squads gnashed their teeth in frustration. That was Dad's style. Thing he liked best, next to nicking villains, was rubbing the wallies' noses in it." Rowley stared into his glass. "And that was when it all went off the rails. We'd got the Twins banged up on remand, even got those back-it-both-ways legal eagles down at the DPP singing our tune when Dad's ticker gave out and the swedey down in Cornwall trumped our ace in the hole."

Rowley fleshed out the story as briefly as he could. How when the heart attack poleaxed Dad Garratt he'd been ensnared by temporary promotion to acting DI, set up for the sucker punch and then thrown to the wolves as a face-saving expedient of the CID hierarchy. He recapped his desperate dash to Cornwall to salvage the supergrass, only to discover that the blagger had been shafted for a double murder on a Cornish clifftop from which he could not be extricated. A perfect fit-up. How once the evidence evaporated, the Twins had walked free with a vow to purge the stain from their underworld egos with Rowley's blood. Finally he sketched in his own ignominious demotion and ban-ishment to the uniformed ranks out in the sticks where the Twins finally caught up with him and he escaped death by seconds when a car bomb ripped apart his patrol car; how SO11 had rescued him from the blue serge and he had become a stalking horse, a moving target waiting for the Twins to try again.

Although he had the American's undivided attention Rowley stopped short of describing his own mental torment, the slow fraying of the nerves which had streaked his hair white and set him jumping at shadows. He drank some of the whisky, allowing it to linger in his mouth before he swallowed.

Monroe watched him, an infectious grin forming under the ox-bow curve of his moustache. "So what happened to the gold?" he asked finally.

Rowley shrugged. "All we ever got was circumstantial. We didn't even get so much as a sniff of the gold."

Monroe got up, walked over to the window and stood with his back to the room, looking out towards Hyde Park. "You want to know what happened to your gold, slick?" he asked softly. "It went over to Europe on the magic carpet where it ended up financing the biggest cocaine scam you ever dreamed of. My inside man on the cigarette boats, running the product into Miami, he knew that before he was fed to the fishes. It was all part of the grand slam." Monroe frowned thoughtfully, watching the joggers in the park. "You see, there's this freewheeling bunch of entrepreneurs expanding the South American coca industry. Big, big bucks. The government down there's weak as water and turns a blind eye, most of their flaky economy's propped up on angel dust anyway. These guys are really cute, hooked into some of the middle-ranking *mafiosi* down there in Florida, running the product across the water right under the noses of the Dade Metro dummies. Swift as a starship, that's why they call 'emselves The Enterprise."

Monroe paused, getting it straightened out in his mind. Then he said, "Before he was deep-sixed m'man got word to me that The Enterprise was set up to move the product into Europe like a blizzard white-out. And they weren't talking no plastic either, the deal was strictly market negotiables on the barrel head, and that meant gold."

Thinking aloud, Rowley said, "Nigerian bullion?"

Monroe turned from the window. "You got it, slick. Five million in yellow bars buys you product aplenty. You get yourself twenty mill pounds sterling as she comes off the boat, step on it once, you've got forty mill, step on it twice, you've got eighty, pushing a hundred million and you're still hustling supergrade four-star freebase Colombian dust. Big, big bucks."

Rowley sucked in a breath. "You mean the Twins . . ."

"Hell, no." Monroe laughed the idea aside. "They'd just be the mechanics. Oh, I don't doubt they pulled the heist, but they would never have seen the big picture. The Enterprise is goddamn shrewd and even more goddamn cautious. Contract labour, everything negotiated through middlemen and shyster lawyers with corporate offices. A maze of deals leading nowhere. Everything neatly laundered before it moves the next step. A hierarchy with no upward lines, just a bunch of numbered accounts in the Cayman. Sweet, sweet set-up."

Rowley hunched forward. "But you said you knew about this farmhouse down there in Devon?"

Monroe looked pained. "Yeah, that was the chink in their armour, it turned out. The jump-off point." He clenched a fist and held it in front of Rowley's face. "And I got it right there before my main man went over the side."

"How do you know that?" Rowley asked. "For certain."

Monroe's face went blank as he appeared to debate the question, then he shrugged as though making up his mind, and recrossed the room to the bedside table where he took a polythene bag from a drawer. Carefully he spilled the contents out into the palm of one hand. Tiny yellow droplets. He held the hand out for Rowley's inspection. "Gold, slick," he said. "Gold. You see, I found the smelter in that barn, tucked away down there, that was where they burned down that gold of yours, turned it into something else, something even the most gung-ho Customs man wouldn't suspect, then they just spirited it away. That was the magic carpet. Only there's one problem with contract labour. Sometimes the help gets a little hasty or a little careless. What do they care?" He let the droplets fall back into the bag and grinned without pleasure at his own powers of deduction. "So I got to the gold and what's more I've got the name of the courier who handled this end, the magic carpet driver."

"Yeah?" Rowley said. "And who might that be?" He didn't really expect an answer.

Monroe tapped his temple. "That stays here, slick. Because that's the key that opens up the whole can of worms. Now I've got to have something to barter with when your Mister Smartass Drake and the rest of those dudes down there at good old Scotland Yard decide they're going to ship me back States-side in disgrace."

He considered Rowley, a cynical smile on his face. "But I tell you what I will do, slick, seeing as you and me are practically buddies. You get Drake to cut me loose and I'll give you the name." He was watching Rowley but his thoughts were on the fat man. "Because in case you've forgotten my friend, there's the matter of your little lady on my tab and that don't exactly make me an attractive proposition, if you get my drift. So I've just naturally got to keep a little something up my sleeve so that when the day comes as it surely will that your Mr. Drake decides the time is right to shaft old Jack Monroe, then I've got to have something he wants more than my hide. Call it self-preservation."

"Yeah, well, maybe I can convince him," Rowley said without much conviction.

"You'd better," Monroe said. "Get me a guarantee and you get the name, simple as that."

"You don't trust me?" Rowley asked.

"Would you in my place? Far from home and deep in the shit?"

Rowley saw the logic in that. "I know the feeling. I've been there myself."

"All the more reason we give it a shot," Monroe said, reaching for the sour mash. "I've got a feeling maybe you and me can do some business on this deal." He raised the bottle, squinting at its contents. "Only right now me and my old friend Jack Daniels here have got a heavy date. Got to drown that little lady of yours right out of my mind before I can get the all-singing, all-dancing act together again. You're welcome to join us, slick?"

Rowley hauled himself to his feet and declined the offer with a shake of his head. "No, thanks all the same, I'd just be in the way. Besides, I've got some nonsense of my own to take care of." He crossed to the door. "I'll talk to Commander Drake. I'll see you later. You're going to stay by the phone?"

"Sure." Monroe didn't look up as he dispensed with the glass and drank straight from the bottle. "Me and my friend here, we ain't going anywhere."

6

Detective-Sergeant Tony Rowley debated whether he should wear a wire for his second meeting with the capo. In the end he decided that he should, for he had no doubt that his superiors in the shadowy world of SO11 were devious enough to have him tailed and at least this way he would have some scope for convincing them that his encounter with Spinelli was a legitimate offshoot of his surveillance work, even though there was no notation to that effect in his diary. On the other hand, if the capo found a listening device then his life would be in even greater jeopardy.

While he turned the possibilities over in his mind Rowley selected a hoop device concealed in an alligator belt which had a miniature transmitter built into the chrome buckle and an aerial concealed behind the suede lining. Of the various coverts available from technical support this seemed to him the most likely to evade detection should Spinelli or one of his henchmen suddenly take it into their head to pat him down. Trouble was, this particular system could only function for a short time over a very limited range. Another drawback was the bulky radio receiver/recorder which could be fitted into a number of disguises ranging from a briefcase, handbag or plastic lunch-box but could not be easily concealed. As he made up his mind, Rowley drew the belt around the waist of his dark grey slacks, left the button of his sports jacket undone so that the buckle mike was not obscured and then wrapped the receiver in a ball of old newspaper which he stuffed into a black plastic sack, tying the neck with the wire aerial. When he was satisfied with his handiwork Rowley took the underground over to Rotherhithe and walked the last couple of streets to the funeral parlour. The Sacred Heart was a converted town mansion, heavy with black wrought-iron and polished brass, set back from the roadway by a tarmac run-up and bathed in floodlights. A stretched Granada hearse was parked on the forecourt.

As he approached the place, Rowley casually studied his surroundings and his eyes finally alighted on a council skip dumped at the kerbside in front of a similar Victorian mansion across the street which was undergoing renovation. Without further consideration he walked briskly past the skip and dropped the plastic bag into the brimming rubbish, stepping away without breaking his stride and hoping that some scavenging vagrant wouldn't help himself to this seemingly innocuous piece of refuse. It was a calculated risk that he would just have to take.

Rowley's inclination towards caution was reinforced when Spinelli greeted him with exaggerated bonhomie, seizing him by the shoulders and slapping him on the back, fingers lightly exploring the usual places in which a miniature tape-recorder might be concealed. Rowley did not resist.

"You've got a nice attitude, Tony," Spinelli remarked affably as he ran a hand over Rowley's shoulder. "Not pushy like these young guys in your line of work these days. Gimme this, gimme that. Nice attitude. I can see how Dad would've taken a shine to you."

"You don't get very far in this game by throwing your weight around, Mr. Spinelli," Rowley agreed, but the undertaker held up a hand and said, "For Christ's sake it's Frank, Tony. We're friends, no? So why so formal? Good manners I can take, but didn't I tell you before, call me Frank."

The capo steered him down a gilt-mirrored hallway and into the chapel itself. "Humour an old man, OK?"

The chapel was ornate gothic, hung with crystal chandeliers and cherub wall lights. Underfoot a heavy dark-fringed carpet lay inside a border of polished dark oak floorboards. Rows of seats finished in burgundy plush were arranged before a trestle, the sawhorses supporting a plain wooden coffin in front of a gilded triptych. Spinelli guided Rowley towards the coffin. "Just humour me, OK, Tony?"

Rowley said, "I'm afraid I ran short on humour a while back. Try looking over both shoulders at once. All you get is a pain in the neck."

Spinelli exploded with laughter, which echoed hollowly around the high plaster cornice from which more cherubs looked down on them. "You're like Dad was all those years ago, Tony, the spitting image. Nice attitude, nice and polite, like I told you already. Only you've got to have the balls as well, Tony. Oh yeah, let me tell you something, in this world, you've got to have the balls one hundred per cent."

Rowley said, "Well, some of Dad's quaint old-fashioned ways must've rubbed off, Frank, otherwise I wouldn't be here. As for the balls, well, you'd better take that up with the Twins."

An artful look crossed the birdlike face. "Ah yes, the Twins. Look, loosen up, stargazer, relax, show a little goodwill, eh? It's not every night I get a visitor drop by I can exchange the time of day with. That's the whole trouble with stiffs." He waved a hand around the chapel. "You don't get no conversation."

Rowley pictured Dad laid out in this house of death, entertained the morbid thought for a second but did not allow it to linger.

Spinelli went over to the coffin, indicating that Rowley should follow. He tapped the lid with his finger. "Yeah, that's the trouble with the world today, Tony. No time. Everything hurry, hurry. You'd think conversation was a dirty word. I tell you, take my business here, there was a time the mortician was an artist, did you know that? Took his time, no detail too much trouble. Nowadays? Jesus Christ, it's like a production line down at Ford, stamping 'em out. No craftsmanship any more. Another dirty word." As he talked, Spinelli raised the lid of the coffin and Rowley saw the waxen face of its occupant flushed a healthy pink from the embalming formaldehyde. "You know, they're planting 'em in plywood boxes, chipboard. Slap on some Fablon instead of veneer even. What a way to take the final bow, huh. Cheapskates!" Spinelli spat his distaste. "But not Frank Spinelli, oh no. I've got a reputation to keep up. Nothing but the best, Tony." He ran a hand around the coffin. "Look at that, matured oak. See 'em out right, even if they're going into the municipal furnace." Looking inside the lid of the coffin, Rowley noticed a carved emblem in the shape of an angel with outstretched wings and when Spinelli noticed the detective's curiosity he explained, "Angel's wings. Signature of my cousin Umberto. Best damned coffin-maker around. Angel wings to carry the departed straight to heaven." He lowered the lid and the blank eyes of the corpse disappeared as the coffin was closed.

"We laid Dad out here, Tony, with flowers, lots of flowers. Had 'em flown in especially. Only the best of the best is good enough for the special friends of Frank Spinelli. Me and Dad, we were like that." Spinelli crossed his fingers. "Like brothers."

"I was at the funeral," Rowley reminded the capo.

"Yeah, yeah, I know you were. You've got respect, Tony. I admire that."

Rowley nodded towards the coffin. "Who's in the box today?"

"That's Mr. Joseph T. Prizzario, Old Joey Prizz, the olive oil king in person. A good old-fashioned Catholic, made his pile swindling everybody in the import-export racket but never missed a Hail Mary. Ladies man all his life, old Joey, seventy-three years old and he could still get it up like a young stallion. Blew his bulb on the job with a cocktail waitress in the goddamn Dorchester. Bitch nearly screamed the place down when Joey expired on her. We got him out the service entrance and told his old lady he'd choked on a piece of steak having dinner. Still, he went out doing what he liked best, bitch said he erupted just like a volcano before he pegged out." Spinelli chuckled in his throat. "Nice embalming job too, Tony. Looks better'n he did alive. I took care of him myself, with these hands, knowing the way he'd want to go. Going to fly to heaven on Umberto's angel wings and meet his maker with a king-size hard-on." Spinelli chuckled again, then grew more serious. "I wanted you to come here, Tony, because this is the place Dad and me did our business. Ended it here too, when I laid him out, so it's fitting we should start here, Tony, you and me. Dad would've approved."

"I can see that," Rowley said. The macabre setting would have certainly appealed to his old DI's sense of humour.

"So I have to ask you the question now, Tony," Spinelli said, growing even more solemn. "You want to do this thing? Take over where Dad left off?"

"Like joining the Masons?"

"Like taking out life insurance," Spinelli corrected him. "Only first we honour the traditions. Give me your hand."

Rowley extended his hand and the capo took a pearl-handled penknife from his pocket, snapped open the blade and drew it across his own forefinger, raising a bead of blood.

"The mingling of blood was always a ritual of trust," he remarked. "The custom of the old country, before AIDS got everybody nervous."

Rowley hesitated.

"You want to do this?" Spinelli's eyes were bright.

"Dad did it?"

"Sure."

Rowley gave the capo his hand and felt the sting as the knife drew blood. Immediately Spinelli gripped the finger with his own and as the blood mingled a single droplet fell to the carpet at their feet. Spinelli released his grip, dabbed the cut with a handkerchief and then passed it to Rowley.

The detective said, "That's it?"

"That's it," replied the capo.

"What about the Twins?"

"Already taken care of," Spinelli said. "I never doubted you, Tony. The word's already on the street, you and me are of the blood." He shrugged. "Cut you and I bleed. Cut me and you bleed. You can forget the Twins. They got a message tonight, personal delivery. They touch you, Frank Spinelli's going to bury them with their dicks in their mouths and send the pictures to the papers."

"What if I'd said no? What if I hadn't turned up?" Rowley was curious to know.

Spinelli smiled a sad smile. "You forget I'm a man of honour first.

I'd've had to take care of you myself. It would've given me no pleasure."

"So what is it you want from me, Frank, what's the price?"

"Same deal I had with Dad," Spinelli said. "Every once in a while a file takes a walk and never comes back. Some tapes get wiped, video gets spoiled. Just little accidents, no big deal."

Rowley nodded slowly, anxious to avoid any show of emotion.

"Hey, not so serious." Spinelli laughed. "You just saved your own life. We've got to celebrate that." He clapped Rowley on the shoulder. "Come on, I've got some champagne upstairs. We'll drink a glass together. Your worries are all over."

Much later when he left the Sacred Heart, Rowley crossed the street to the skip and casually retrieved the black plastic sack.

It was gone midnight when the detective-sergeant returned to his flat in the deep Victorian reaches of Rotherhithe, now becoming fashionable with the avant-garde as the crumbling old warehouses of the once-bustling dockland were reclaimed piecemeal and transformed into warrens of trendy apartments. Rowley had had a flat on the third floor of just such a warehouse building since long before the boom, when the three rooms were all he could run to after his marriage broke up. The gloomy former grain warehouse loomed over Russell Street, and when he let himself in, the flat smelled musty, for he had neglected the place since the car bombing had driven him into hiding, hopping around the single men's quarters or camping at Cindy's place whenever the monastic existence of the section houses became too depressing.

Without turning on any lights, Rowley walked through the flat, wrinkling his nose at the stale odour. When he reached the lounge window overlooking the central courtyard he paused and looked down at the occasional rectangles of light cast from similar windows into the dark well of the yard. Curtains were drawn against the night but as Rowley's eyes travelled down they stopped as though by prearranged signal at one window where the shades were not drawn. Looking down into the living-room as he absentmindedly sucked his cut forefinger, Rowley could see a dark-haired girl disco-dancing alone across an off-white Indian carpet, the scene bathed in soft light from table lamps. He could almost catch the strains of the beat as the girl gyrated sinuously to the music, stepping it out in gold high heels, the skirt of her scarlet dance dress swirling around the outline of her hips and thighs.

As Rowley watched, the taste of his own blood on his lips, the girl paused, crossed to the window and looked up, smiling. There was no way she could have known he was there, hidden in the darkness, watching unseen, but the guilty thrill of the voyeur electrified him as, with her eyes fastened on his window, she slowly reached behind her neck and unzipped the flimsy dress, which fell like a feather. She was naked underneath. Face upturned towards him, she parted her crimson lips in their secret knowing smile before she turned with a toss of her black mane and picked up the frenetic beat again, her olive tan catching the light as she danced for him.

The detective turned from the window and slumped into an easy chair. Suddenly he felt drained, exhausted. The still darkness of the flat closed around him, conjuring the ghosts. Confirmation that his mentor, Dad Garratt, had willingly entered into a blood contract with a major figure in organized crime had come as no real shock, but that he himself had agreed to follow suit in fear for his own skin now seemed like a betrayal. He had no stomach to play the Spinelli tapes, for he knew that in his present mood they would offend his ears. He could always turn them over to SO11 and clear his conscience, but there again he had no faith in the ability or even willingness of the hierarchy to protect him. Ever since the car bomb, despite their soft-voiced assurances to the contrary, he knew full well that he had become the stalking horse of their ambition to ensnare the Twins. At least with the capo there was something tangible.

Sprawled drowsily in his chair, he began to review the events of the day, carried along like a piece of flotsam caught in a powerful current. He came upon Jack Monroe with the realization that he and the American agent were the victims of similar quirks of fate. Perhaps he could work on that. Rowley allowed the idea to mature but before he could reach any satisfactory conclusion he slid into a shallow sleep with Dad's spectre whispering to him through the web of his dreams. As always, the words were just too indistinct for his straining senses to catch their meaning.

7

"I've got your number, Monroe." Larry Drake leaned across his desk shooting five inches of crisp white cuff and, without raising his voice, displayed the first hint of anger.

"I got your card marked by Burghoff down at the Embassy, we go back to Harvard. He told me you're a Vietnam veteran, I should have guessed. Gung-ho Marine, blood and glory. Well, you're not John Wayne in *The Green Beret* any more, you're playing this game by my rules."

The NDIU chief eased back into his chair, smoothed the lapels of his suit and the moment passed. When he spoke again, Drake had regained his poise. "What we're supposed to be engaged in, in case it has somehow escaped your notice, is intelligence gathering, deep background. We don't go around booting in doors and getting our ass blown off. Not our style at all. Shadows in the night, my friend, shadows in the night." He gave Monroe a searching stare. "Nice and subtle. You know how long it took me to set up NEL? Eighteen months toil and sweat massaging political egos. Then you come waltzing in and run us right on to the rocks. Lacks a certain delicate touch. You got an officer killed in circumstances which don't bear close examination, and hey presto! suddenly we're on the rack. When this goes public, and believe me it most certainly will, a lot of people are going to be backpedalling like fury. Lots of pressure to close us down, reputations going up in smoke." Drake gave the DEA agent his ballbearing stare.

Jack Monroe, insolently casual in sports jacket, polo neck and Levis, slouched in his chair and waited for the drugs chief to finish the lecture. He had to keep reminding himself of his boss's admonition to play ball, which meant ignoring Drake's jibes about Nam. He consoled himself with the view that the effete popinjay who was chewing him out wouldn't have lasted ten minutes on the line.

"Oh, and in case you're still not getting the big picture," Drake continued, perfectly at ease again, "just between ourselves, I don't propose to lose a single brownie point over this fiasco. That's why I've got the hold button down on you, Monroe. That's why when the hounds of the media start baying for blood, looking for someone to nail, you're going to be our star turn. They can tear your worthless carcass to shreds."

Sitting to one side in the drugs chief's office on the CID floor at the Yard, Tony Rowley wondered how the DEA agent would handle Drake. He had suffered himself from the Pontius Pilate manoeuvrings of the CID hierarchy when it came down to self-preservation and despite Helen Linden's death he felt a twinge of sympathy for Jack Monroe.

There was a long silence in the office, then Monroe stirred himself and said lazily, "You can jerk my chain all you want, don't mean nothing to me, I've been jerked around by experts. You and your buddy Burghoff can do what the hell you like, only it won't get you out of the hole."

Drake raised an eyebrow. "You've got a better suggestion?" he asked with undisguised sarcasm.

Monroe waited again, leaving the question hanging in the air. Then he said, "I tell you what, my friend, I'll give you a deal, not that it matters a good goddamn to me. I'll give you the biggest dope bust you ever wet-dreamed about. Twenty million in uncut angel dust. That'd get you off the hook clean."

Drake produced a humourless laugh. "You're priceless, Monroe, you know that? Here I am, I've got you by the short hairs and you're trying to horse-trade me. What d'you do for an encore, whistle *Dixie?*"

"It's just a question of attitude," Monroe said, unperturbed by Drake's sarcasm. "Positive attitude. Screw me and in the long run you'll be screwing yourself. Cut me some slack and I'll give you The Enterprise." Now it was Monroe's turn to lean forward. "Hang me out to dry and I'll make a few phone calls, talk to some people I know who spend their time in nice air-conditioned offices over in Washington and maybe have breakfast a couple of mornings a week with a few influential Senators up on the Hill, and before you can blink, my friend, strings will be pulled and you'll be waving me goodbye from the gate at Terminal Three and then all you'll have for a patsy is fresh air." He waved a hand in a dismissive gesture. "OK, so maybe I get my ass roasted for letting your girl get herself zapped, then again maybe I don't. The way my people are going to see it, I was just the tourist, remember, she was the cop."

Monroe stared into Drake's eyes giving nothing. "Who takes the rap then, eh buddy? I don't see too many volunteers. If I read it right the brass is going to be looking to the squad commander for some answers. Same guy who sold 'em a dummy with NEL, I wouldn't be surprised, who all of a sudden is beginning to look like a three-time loser going down for the last time. They'd probably figure he burned out the judgement circuits, maybe give him the runaround, a nice tidy shoe-fly job, then put him out to grass. Brilliant career down the tubes." Monroe smiled. "How'm I doing so far?"

Drake's face settled into a mask and Rowley, watching from the sidelines, had the distinct impression that Monroe had scored a direct hit. He almost savoured Drake's discomfort as the possibilities sank in. True, Monroe was probably just shooting a salty line of breeze but the scenario seemed so plausible that Drake began to look rattled.

"What kind of deal did you have in mind?" the drugs chief asked after permutating the possibilities in his mind and ending up with a more than fifty-fifty chance that the DEA narc had the edge on him.

Monroe chewed on the ends of his drooping moustache. "I know who the bagman was, the courier, the one who wired the farmhouse."

"Is that so?" Drake remained studiously unimpressed. "Well, what makes you think we need you? I've got my own team down there, they'll get that for themselves. It's just a matter of time."

Monroe shook his head. "Time you don't have," he said. "The Enterprise is tight, took me five years to get in on an inside track. Starting up from cold, you think you can hang in that long?"

Drake's eyes conceded the point. "So tell me something I want to hear and we'll take it from there," he said.

"Wait a minute. Before I get into that," Monroe said, "I'm going to need some guarantees."

"Such as?"

"Such as I get first shot."

"What kind of deal is that! You could take off."

"He'll be with me." Monroe jerked a thumb at Rowley. "Looking after your interests. He can hold on to my passport, we'll be like Siamese twins."

Drake looked sharply at Rowley as though aware of the detective-sergeant's presence for the first time. "You in on this con job, Tony?"

Rowley said, "Not me, guv'nor. I'm just the minder, remember."

"But you've got an opinion?" Drake's eyes were speculating.

"I don't see how we can lose." Rowley chose his words with care.

Drake turned back to Monroe. "Just the two of you?"

Monroe said, "Just the two of us."

Drake pursed his lips, running the prospect through his mind. He had never been averse to a little creative manipulation and his instinct told him that if he was going to go along with this, then he should play it very close to the chest. No one else need know what was in the wind. It was the prospect of the multi-million-pound bust which Monroe had left dangling in front of him which was really tempting, made him want to believe Monroe's promise of a sweet deal. Now if he could pull something like that out of the bag, he conjectured, channel the glad tidings through the political network, consolidate his position with the Select Committee, curry some favour with the Home Office mandarins, maybe, just maybe, he could outflank Moss and set up the DAC for a bloodless coup. With Moss out of the frame, he'd be a natural to move up to DAC, broker some more political power, leapfrog to Assistant Commissioner and then . . . Drake took a grip on himself before his imagination reached escape velocity.

Across the room Rowley thought: Clever. Monroe had probed Drake's weakness, the blind pursuit of power and was playing it low key, spoonfeeding the man. Clever move.

"If I do buy any of this horseshit"—Drake gave some ground—"this deal of yours, Monroe, what's in it for me?"

"You get the courier, the main man this end," Monroe said. He counted off on his fingers. "You get the man for one, you get conspiracy to smuggle controlled drugs, you get conspiracy to cause an explosion and you get conspiracy to commit murder. That's the package."

"And what do you get, an Oscar?"

Monroe said, "What I get is a lever on the U.S. end. The Enterprise is a big operation, there's plenty in this for all of us. Oh, and I almost forgot, I get a clean bill of health from you."

"Any other little favours I can do for you?" Drake said sarcastically.

"Yeah, one other thing," Monroe said, his eyes half closed as though none of this mattered. "I'll need the NEL database, run some computer checks. If your system's as good as it's cracked up to be, it'll take no time at all."

"You've got to be joking." Drake tensed, unease dancing behind his eyes. "D'you have any idea the level of security we had to guarantee just to get that system accepted? Triple clearance, approved by all participating agencies. The Italians and the French are still bitching about it. That database has got an awful lot of raw intelligence in there, stuff straight out of the field. We've got data protection around our necks and you're telling me you want to tap into that dynamite?" Drake shook his head. "It's out of the question."

Monroe eased himself deeper into the chair and gave the drugs chief an eloquent lift of his shoulders as if to say: Take it or leave it, I couldn't care less.

Drake turned to the window and gazed out over the London skyline. Now that Monroe had tempted him with the prospect of a big bust, he was becoming consumed with the idea. In fact his grand design depended upon it. But could he risk giving this treacherous DEA narc access to the NEL intelligence databank, hooked up to the unrefined snooping of a dozen nations? If it backfired, Moss would destroy him. On the other hand, if he slammed the door now . . .

He swung back into the room. "All right," he told Monroe. "Tell you what I'll do. Convince me you're not just peddling a fairy story and I'll take a chance and get you some time on the computer. Only it'd better be good."

Monroe levered himself upright as though arousing himself from a nap. He gave Drake the story much as he had told Rowley, touching the highspots and including only enough detail to string the sequence of events together. When he finished, Drake gave it a further moment's thought and then said, "Something else Burghoff told me about you, Monroe. He said you were a fantasy merchant. A dreamer. Well, just for the record, if all this turns out to be so much hogwash I'm personally going to see to it that you don't pull any more stunts ever again. You'll be so *persona non grata* that you won't even get a job as a dog warden." Drake drew his lips back, exposing his teeth. "But if this works out the way you say it will, we'll all be wearing laurel leaves. You know what they say, my friend; nothing succeeds like success."

Drake got to his feet and came around the desk. "I'm calling your hand, Monroe," he told the DEA agent. "Let's go and talk to NEL."

Inside the special operations centre, the computer suite was like a vault, protected by layers of security. Their ID badges took them through the checkpoints into Disneyland, but it was only Drake's personal authority which permitted them to proceed beyond the red-lettered sign which stated: NO UNAUTHORIZED PERSON BEYOND THIS POINT. Cocooned from the outside world, the computer room was softly illuminated by uplighters and contained two banks of terminals, twenty-four VDUs in all, hooked into a McDonnell Douglas mini with uprated power to interrogate the big crime intelligence computers across the continent of Europe. The system, Drake told them, as though conducting a guided tour, had been expanded on the principle of HOLMES, the Home Office (Large) Major Enquiries System, developed in the wake of the Yorkshire Ripper fiasco to provide an interlocking exchange of crime information between police forces. NEL had elevated the Holmes system of comparable intelligence to an even more rarefied plane and checks and balances had been built into the system so that no one operator could ever see the full impact of the information which was being processed into target profiles.

Drake moved over to the command console and watched the staccato lines stutter across the grey screen of the VDU as the shift supervisor, an SO11 DI, monitored progress from a thick concertina of print-out data.

The DI looked up and recognized the drugs chief.

"What've you got on there, Sid?" Drake asked with casual informality.

The DI pulled a face. "Carabinieri rubbish, guv'nor. Most of it don't make any sense at all."

"Par for the course, eh?" Drake shared the grumble. "Listen, you want to take a coffee break while I run a test check on your terminal?"

The DI looked surprised. "I'm not supposed to leave here while the system's running, guv'nor," he replied warily, wondering if Drake's unheralded arrival was a security spot check designed to catch him out. "It's against the rules."

"You know who made those rules, Sid?" Drake asked lightly, resting a paternal hand on the man's shoulder.

"Why er . . . you did, guv'nor," the DI replied uneasily, still expecting a trap.

"Then I'm the only one can break 'em, right?"

The DI looked relieved. "Well, I could use a breather," he conceded. "This Italian gibberish is driving me bonkers. Beats me how they ever nick anybody on the strength of this lot."

He moved out of his seat and Drake said, "I'll give you a shout when I've finished. Everything else OK?"

"Sweet as a nut," the DI said. "Humming like a bird." He reached for his jacket and when he'd gone Drake slipped into the seat and glanced over his shoulder at Monroe. The DEA agent was intent upon the screen. Rowley was standing back watching the show.

Despite his rank, Drake felt a childish pride in his own creation as he turned his attention to the screen. He concentrated for a moment. The NEL database was protected by a complexity of codes, the operator's individual *logon* signature, the operational access sequence and the code of the day, which was changed every twenty-four hours. Security was obsessive and the slightest keyboard error would abort all the command and control circuits.

Drake flexed his fingers in the manner of a pianist preparing for a recital and began to tap the keys from memory, hardly needing to check the affirmative responses appearing on the screen as he went through the start-up sequence. When the terminal was set up he eased out of the chair and with a flourish offered it to Monroe. "Now show me something I don't know already," he challenged.

Monroe sat down, his casual manner unruffled. With slow deliberation he tapped out the name which obediently appeared on the screen: GARY DANIELS AKA GRAHAM DOUGLAS GERRY DELANEY DOB 060938. He pressed the key to start the name search, took his hands off the keyboard and waited. There was a three-second pause as the computer explored the possibilities, the cursor blinking like a heartbeat. Then, triggered by a distant pulse of compatibility, lines of green text began to stream across the screen.

"That him?" Drake asked, peering over Monroe's shoulder.

Monroe nodded without taking his eyes from the VDU. The NEL computer was talking to the West German crime computer at Wiesbaden, the brisk electronic chatter revealing that Gary Daniels was currently in police custody at Munich on vice charges and border violations, all within the jurisdiction of the Bavarian Minister of the Interior, who had ordered his detention without formal charge. Daniels was being held for interrogation.

"That him?" Drake asked again.

Monroe nodded. "That's him," he confirmed.

"Well, what d'you know. Looks like the Polizei got him in the bag," Drake said.

"Looks that way," Monroe said, still watching the screen.

Drake reached over Monroe's shoulder and quickly keyed the sequence to cancel the data search before anyone else could pick it up. The screen went blank.

"You sure that's him?" he questioned Monroe.

"Oh, I'm sure," Monroe confirmed. "No doubt about it."

Drake straightened, barely able to conceal his excitement. He rubbed his hands together and said, "Well, well, looks like our German friends don't know what they've got. I want him laundered and out of there before the State Ministry get any bright ideas of their own." He thought about it for a moment and then said, "We'll get him out on the old pals act, no problem." He tapped Monroe's arm and then gestured to Rowley. "My office. We've got more talking to do."

"For a minute there I thought you were going to push his nibs over the edge, Jack," Rowley said with a grin on his face as they came out of the lift and crossed the wide foyer of New Scotland Yard, pushed out through the revolving glass door and began to walk down Broadway.

"Ah, you've got to play a con artist like Drake," Monroe said. "All you've got to do is roll high. Offer 'em something so tempting you've got 'em hooked right off the bat. After that you could kick 'em in the nuts and it wouldn't wipe the smirk off their face. That's the knack."

The two detectives stood on the pavement waiting for a break in the traffic streaming down Victoria Street. They had slipped out for a bite to eat while the drugs chief cleared the diplomatic lines between the Yard and the Bavarian Ministry of the Interior.

"Are you really on first-name terms with senators or was that eyewash too?" Rowley asked.

"Oh no, I've got 'em, slick," Monroe said, slapping his back pocket. "Right here. Mostly slippery Sams though, sell you down the river soon as look at you. That's politics."

"So where's your pull?" Rowley asked. Ever since the encounter with Drake he had felt more and more comfortable in the American's company.

"My good old Uncle Sam," Monroe said. "Best buddy a man ever had. Taught me how to kill people, sent me to Nam."

They crossed in a haze of diesel fumes behind a red bus and Rowley led the way into Strutton Ground, still subconsciously scanning faces, nervously watching his back as they walked into the narrow street with its ragged collection of stalls, typical of a London street market. Since striking his bargain with the capo, Rowley had forced himself to relax a little, but he had not dropped his guard altogether. There was still the possibility that a couple of renegades like the Twins might not succumb easily to Spinelli's blandishments. A double-cross was always on the cards. The same applied to Drake, who had drawn Rowley to one side in the ante-room to his office and had sought to clinch his personal loyalty with a little sweetener, the promise of promotion. "Tony, you do something for me, I don't forget it. I'm going to look after your interests OK, see if I can't return the favour." The Commander checked that Monroe was out of earshot, making a phone call. "You're going to Deutschland with the cowboy and you're going to bring home the bacon. I want a result on this, I don't care what it takes. So here's a little something on account. Come through this with your colours flying and I'll put you up for DI. You've got my word on that."

Rowley almost laughed out loud at such transparent insincerity, but only Dad Garratt would have appreciated the irony.

Now with Monroe beside him he elbowed his way through the sea of rubberneckers crowded around the stalls where the spielers vied with each other in the colourful language of the market trade, and together they ducked into a snack bar. At the formica counter they perched on bar stools and ate chilli con carne with plastic forks. Squinting around the brashly cheerful luncheonette, Monroe remarked that it reminded him of home. Now that they were on their way, the DEA agent exuded rare good humour.

"You want to tell me about this Daniels character?" Rowley asked, ordering coffee which came in plastic beakers adorned with the slogan HAVE A NICE DAY.

"Guy was a bullion dealer," Monroe replied without hesitation. "Legit. An original jet-set swinger. Used to shuttle between New York and the Middle East, only his home base was always right here in good old London town. We first got wind of him in Beirut, where he was into some fast action laying yellow metal on the Druze, only we couldn't work out his angle so we lost interest in him. We figured what the hell, guy's into some bullion scam with the militias, one fine day he's going to wind up dead in an alley with a snootful of AK rounds, so we passed him on to the CIA. Only before the spooks could get their act together he'd dropped out of sight."

Monroe sipped his coffee. "Big guy," he said. "Fat as a tub of lard. Lives high on the hog and likes to keep moving. If we'd known he was connected with The Enterprise we'd have kept a hook on him." Monroe shrugged. "Some you win, some you lose."

"What's he like?" Rowley wanted to know.

"Smoothie," Monroe said. "Big with the ladies. Always finds time to charm the pants off some broad even when he's hustling." Monroe put his coffee down and gave the girl with a pink Mohican hairdo behind the counter a friendly smile. "You married, slick?" he asked Rowley casually.

"Divorced," Rowley replied. "We didn't see eye to eye, so we called it quits. How about you, Jack?"

Monroe was watching the girl as she moved away down the counter so Rowley couldn't see his face. "I was," he said. "She was killed in a car crash while I was out in Vietnam. Funny how it worked out . . . they sent me a wire from The World." He hunched his shoulders, picked up his cup and drained the last of his coffee. "Crazy. Zapgrams were supposed to travel the other way."

"I'm sorry . . ." Rowley began but Monroe cut him off with a flip of his hand. "Don't be, slick, you get one life, you've got to grab hold of it while it's around. We had good times."

To cover his discomfort Rowley consulted his watch and then said, "We'd better get back to the factory or Drake'll be spitting blood. D'you have any contacts in Munich, Jack?"

Monroe pushed himself off the stool. "Only Uncle," he said, "only Uncle."

When they returned to the Yard Commander, Larry Drake was waiting for them. The euphoria had evaporated and he was looking grim.

"The vultures have got a whisper on that Helen Linden business," he announced. "Was bound to happen, this place leaks like a colander. Our bullshit boys have got her loved ones downstairs learning their lines for the telly for when the lid blows off. The clock's running on this one, so you two had better look lively. It's all going to hit the fan any time now."

8

A pale green Mercedes 280 SE staff car from the Staatsministerium des Innern came through the gate in the chainlink security fence around the low blockhouse police station adjacent to the terminal buildings at Munich Riem airport, made a slow turn on to the parking apron and picked up speed to catch the Volkswagen "follow-me" van. In the front passenger seat, Kriminalpolizei Hauptkommissar Rainer Wolfe stared moodily across the expanse of runways fading purple in the dwindling light. Wolfe hated the airport with a deep and unreasonable passion. For it was here as a young uniformed officer, a polizeiwachtmeister, back on that fateful night in 1972, that he had stood by incredulously as the Puma helicopters of the Bundesgrenzschutz exploded in balls of orange fire as Black September played out the final bloody act of the Olympic massacre.

The impotent rage he had felt that night, watching a handful of Arab terrorists humiliate the cream of the German police, had stayed with him down the years. And he had vowed to himself as the coils of oily black smoke billowed skywards from the crippled helicopters that come what may he, Rainer Wolfe, would never hang his head in shame again.

"I hate this fucking place." Wolfe inadvertently voiced his thoughts with such venom that the driver, Dieter Muller, a pudgy-faced staff officer from the Ministry of the Interior, shot him an amused glance and said, "The airport? What's wrong with the airport?"

"You'd been here, you'd know," Wolfe replied cryptically. He had already dismissed the flabby aide as of no real consequence. Although he wore the uniform with the gold star of a Polizei Oberat on his epaulettes and clearly outranked the detective, Wolfe knew that he was nothing more than a deskbound lawyer who had entered the force as a ranking administrator and had little conception of the practicalities of police work outside the comfortable offices of the Ministry.

"Some stewardess stand you up, eh, Wolfe?" Muller asked with a chuckle. "I didn't know you detectives wore your heart on your sleeve."

Wolfe merely grunted. He didn't try to explain.

They passed under the tailfin of a parked Tri-Star and the black and yellow striped tailgate of the "follow-me" van swung to the right around the expanse of plate glass of the terminal. Muller eased the wheel over, tucking in close behind.

"Who are these characters anyway?" Wolfe wanted to know, scowling through the windscreen. He was clean-shaven, but already a shadow of blue-black stubble darkened his jawline and added a sinister touch to his narrow features which were dominated by piercing eyes set deep in their sockets. A black cotton polo-neck under a leather jacket added a further hint of menace.

"Visiting firemen," Muller replied. "The boss says we're to be nice to 'em, Rainer, hundred per cent cooperation, so how about wiping that scowl off your face and stop looking like you're totally pissed off with the whole thing."

Wolfe said, "All of a sudden you Ministry people yank my prisoner and start giving the bastard the kid glove treatment and you're asking me to be nice! In case you've forgotten, it's my case you're fooling around with."

"Just be nice, Wolfe," Muller repeated the instruction, this time with an edge of authority in his voice. "If it's what the old man wants, then we do as we're told, accommodate our allies, hands across the ocean, you know the procedure as well as I do."

"I still say it stinks," Wolfe protested. "The fat bastard's my prisoner."

"I told you," Muller said. "Nobody's about to steal your thunder. We just borrowed the guy, that's all. State business. You'll get the credit for cracking the case."

"So why've you got him under wraps?"

"We want him sweet."

"You want him sweet." Wolfe prodded his chest to emphasize his next point. "I want him in prison, doing time, that's what I want."

Muller chuckled. "You know your trouble, Rainer. You've got no idea how to make friends and influence people. You're just a kick-the-door-down cop."

"We're talking about an animal who gets his kicks screwing underage schoolgirls. Even if they consent, that's rape in this State."

"Ease up, Rainer," Muller advised. "Where's the problem? So we put your man on ice for a couple of days to accommodate our friends, what's the harm? You get a nice spell of special duty and you'll still have the vice thing when this is all over."

"You can't see it, can you?" Wolfe said plaintively. "Strings are being pulled. We're being taken for a ride."

"Look." Exasperation crept into Muller's voice. "We're all sucking on the Government tit, we do what we're told to do. So the old man gets a call from Scotland Yard, a request for cooperation, Interpol priority. The world's a small place, Rainer, and getting smaller all the time. Maybe one day the boot's going to be on the other foot and we're going to be in London."

"I still don't have to like it," Wolfe grumbled as Muller braked in behind the black and yellow striped VW. In the gathering dusk the runway lights came on and a British Airways 737 came in from the glide path, wing flaps flared, and touched down with a squeal of rubber, the engines screaming as the pilot slammed on reverse thrust.

"Well, you'd better get used to it," Muller shouted above the din. "Here they come."

Polizei Oberat Dieter Muller watched the Boeing come in, sitting in the Mercedes tapping a finger on top of the steering wheel. He had been briefed by a special assistant to the Minister, a lawyer he happened to admire, and that had coloured his thinking. Over apple brandy and thimble cups of coffee in an ornate ante-room off the Minister's own suite of offices, he had been told what was expected of them. What the old man wanted to happen. It had all been very civilized. He had passed on to Wolfe only as much as he deemed the detective needed to know because he had taken the precaution of casting an eye over Wolfe's service docket and had seen that the detective could be unpredictable, a dynamo who could easily spark off trouble if he wasn't carefully handled. Ideally he could have done without Wolfe, picked somebody who would have been more amenable, but the fat man was the Hauptkommissar's prisoner and to have cut him out would only have created waves inside the force. Muller had picked up enough police sensitivity to appreciate that hassle with the street cops was something to be avoided. So he was saddled with the mercurial detective. Well, he thought to himself as he watched the jet finish its braking run and turn towards the terminal, he supposed he could live with that.

The Boeing approached, a dry whistle sounding from the idling jets and soon the airliner was looming over them, breasting up to the disembarkation gate. In the wash of light from the terminal the covered passenger tunnel was positioned at the main doors, but the policemen in the Mercedes were watching the crew steps which had been rolled up to the forward exit. The engines cut abruptly and the hatch swung back. A stewardess appeared in the opening and locked the rail, a fixed smile on her face as she ushered the two passengers earmarked for VIP treatment out of the aircraft ahead of the herd. All formalities waived, courtesy of the Bavarian state police.

Muller had his door open and was already easing himself out of the car, putting on his cap with the gold strap and starred crest over the peak, straightening his green uniform jacket. Wolfe hesitated, his hand on the door-handle, watching the new arrivals start down the steps. He wanted to form first impressions his own way, aloof from Muller's official reception. He wanted to make his own judgement. Through the windscreen of the Mercedes he looked for the faces. The first man coming down was casually dressed in sports coat and blue jeans, a nylon travel bag slung from his shoulder. He had a cropped scrub of brown hair and a drooping moustache which gave his face a mournful appearance. That would be the DEA agent, Wolfe guessed. Behind him came the second man, in a blue suit, lugging a BA holdall. His hair was shot through with a heavy white streak, his expression drawn. Detective-sergeant from Scotland Yard, Wolfe made the bet with himself as he followed Muller out of the car. An unlikely pair, he decided, watching the careful movements of their eyes as they came down the steps, taking it all in. Wolfe came around the car, still hanging back, avoiding Muller's effusive greeting. The world-weary look in those eyes reassured him. At least they were street cops like himself.

The detectives met at the foot of the steps, exchanged handshakes as Muller kept up the trivial chatter, asking how the flight was; had they been to Germany before; telling them that the Minister was taking a personal interest in their request, all official lines cleared, green light all the way. While Muller prattled on, the street cops measured each other.

Eventually Muller ushered them into the Mercedes, got back behind the wheel and gunned the engine, still talking over his shoulder. Privilege of running the airport, he told them, passports, baggage, all taken care of, don't give them another thought.

They wheeled around the terminal building, parked the car at a side entrance and went up to one of the VIP lounges.

"While you're here you must make time to look around Munich," Muller was saying in flawless English. "Marienplatz is worth a visit, and the old town. You must see some of our countryside too, very beautiful in the autumn, perhaps we could get you up into the Alps. We've got our own ski-lodge up at Sudelfeld. What d'you think, Rainer?"

Wolfe shrugged without offering an opinion and Monroe said, "You know, chief, the thing of it is, we're going to be running pretty much against the clock."

"Ah yes." Muller smiled. "Nose to the grindstone, as they say. But you mustn't miss out on our traditional Bavarian hospitality, that would never do. It'll soon be Oktoberfest time, we could drink ourselves some fine beer."

Monroe gnawed his moustache, got right to the point. "Look, I don't want to seem pushy or anything, chief, but can we do some business on Daniels? Or do we have to see the man?"

Muller waved them to low seats around a glass-topped coffee table on which had been set out refreshments, wine, ginger pastries, a Thermos jug of coffee.

"Why so hasty?" he said. "Sit, relax a little, have a drink, eat. We should get to know each other."

"You didn't answer my question," Monroe said, sitting down.

Rowley said, "Excuse my friend, he's a little anxious, that's all. We presume you know what this is all about."

"We've seen the Interpol traffic naturally," Muller said.

"We believe Daniels to be implicated in the murder of a police officer back in England," Rowley said, seeing no point in prevarication.

The Germans exchanged glances.

"We weren't told anything about that," Wolfe said.

"It was a booby-trap bomb in a house," Rowley said. "A farmhouse. We think Daniels set it up."

"We haven't seen anything on that," Muller said, surprised.

"My people are keeping the lid on it," Rowley explained. "That's why we're in such a tearing hurry to see your man."

"We were given to understand drugs," Muller said.

Monroe said, "Yeah, there's that too. We've got this guy Daniels pegged for an angel dust hustler. Waxing the officer was just an extra to normal service."

"Seems like quite a boy, our fat man," Wolfe said to Muller.

"So what's the score here?" Monroe went back to his original question. "Can we deal with you guys or do we have to go through the palaver again, higher up?"

Muller turned to him and said, "My instructions are to give you our full cooperation, gentlemen. Instructions of the Minister himself. We can make any arrangement you want . . . within reason."

"Where's Daniels now?" Monroe asked. "Here in Munich?"

Wolfe said, "Dachau."

"Dachau?" Monroe raised an eyebrow. "I thought that was a concentration camp."

"It's a museum now," Muller explained blandly. "We Germans, we can never let go of the past." He waved a hand across the table. "Please, eat something, drink some wine, coffee at least."

"We've got him in the Inspektion, the police station at Dachau," Wolfe explained. He shot Muller a barbed glance. "Or I should say our good friends at the Ministry have tucked him away out there. Only the very best for our colleagues from the famous Scotland Yard."

Muller smiled, unperturbed. "Wolfe here is BCI, Bureau of Criminal Investigation. Very jealous of their reputation, the BCI. We at the Ministry like to take the broader view. Dachau is a pleasant little town, nicely out of the limelight for our mutual purposes. We asked for Daniels to be moved into custody there and naturally the BCI were only too pleased to oblige."

Wolfe's face darkened and Rowley said, "Look, can we clear the air here? We're just here to do a job, we don't want to tread on any toes, create any local problems. Whatever you can do for us, we'd be obliged."

He said to Wolfe, "It would be helpful if you could fill us in on the background of how you came to pick up Daniels."

Wolfe hunched forward, dug into the pocket of his jacket and produced a small round tin from which he tapped a little snuff into the valley formed between thumb and forefinger. He took a sniff.

"There was some trouble with the girls working the autobahn, the prostitutes," Wolfe said. "They started a new stunt, flagging down motorists, pestering drivers in the rest areas. Flag 'em down and then take the clients into the woods for a little *al fresco* fun. It grew into quite a business once the girls got organized, like shelling peas. Oh, the traffic patrols ran 'em off from time to time but nobody got too excited about it. Live and let live."

Wolfe took another sniff.

"Only one day," he continued, "a State judge with a high moral reputation out for a picnic with his family got propositioned. Well, the judge took one look at the high jinks in the woods and started screaming for a clean-up."

Wolfe brushed his nose with a handkerchief.

"By that time the girls had got themselves nicely fixed up, caravans and motorhomes in the lay-bys. One set up a group of trailers in the woods down by the Austrian border. My group was assigned to keep this particular knocking shop under observation, on direct orders of the judge."

Wolfe dusted snuff from his fingers.

"We sat in the trees like the boy scouts and watched what was going on. When we'd seen enough, got some video film, we went to the judge, swore out the warrants and hit 'em."

He gave the visitors a smile. "Caught the fat man sampling the wares, couple of schoolgirls, runaways. Got his lady-friend too, Kristabel Rosche, a bagful of money and some drugs."

Wolfe put his snuff away. "You never know how your luck's going to run in this job."

Monroe said, "That's for sure. So how long've you been holding Daniels?"

"Two days," Wolfe said. "We needed a little time to get all the evidence together and we were going to charge him when we received instructions to hold off."

"What about his lady-friend?" Rowley asked.

Wolfe said, "She's hooked on coke, drug-dependent. We've put her into a treatment centre, a secure facility, for the time being. She's amenable to our requirements, so she'll probably end up a material witness, depending on how the prosecutor views the case."

Muller interrupted, saying, "Naturally we've suspended all legal procedures while you've got an interest. Tell me, what do you want to do first?"

"Take a look at Daniels," Monroe said. "Can we do that right away?"

Muller smiled. "Certainly. Whatever you want." He glanced at his watch, pursed his lips and then announced, "Gentlemen, I've got to run along. Wolfe here will take care of you. Whatever you want, just ask."

He slid the car keys across the table and said to Wolfe, "Take the car, Rainer. Anything else these officers need, just let me know."

Muller got to his feet, straightened his uniform jacket. "I hope this will be a productive visit, my friends. I can assure you that we are anxious to be helpful. There are certain influences at work, how shall I say, at the political level. Need I say more?"

When Muller had taken his leave Wolfe said, "He means strings are being pulled in the State government. In BCI we don't give up the reins that easily, not even for visiting firemen. You must have friends in high places."

Rowley sensed the chill of the German's displeasure and hastened to thaw their relationship. They would need the BCI detective's active cooperation.

"We know how you must feel," he told Wolfe. "It's pretty galling when some joker pulls rank and won't tell you the reason. But believe me we don't have anything to do with that. We're just the errand boys and it's going to be a lot easier all the way round if we can trust each other."

"He's right," Monroe said. "We just want to do what we have to do and get out of your hair. Look, why don't we take a run out to Dachau? We'll fill you in on the way."

Wolfe rasped a finger along the line of his jaw, contemplating the options, easing up a little, his professional curiosity taking over.

"Well, no offence," he cautioned them finally, "but you're on my territory so the first thing you do which you haven't cleared with me, the first indication I get that things are happening which I don't like, then I'm going to pull the plug on you, Muller or no Muller." He allowed his teeth to show in a smile. "Nothing personal, you understand."

Rowley nodded his agreement and Monroe said, "Sure. Understood."

Wolfe's smile relaxed. He reached for the wine and poured a good measure into their glasses. "It'd be a shame to waste the chief's hospitality, why don't we drink to that?"

9

Travelling fast despite the heavy traffic, the Mercedes entered the city from the east, crossed the Isar at Maximilian Bridge, skirted central Munich on the ring road and, maintaining speed, took an exit heading north-west on to Dachauerstrasse. Wolfe drove aggressively, straight-arming the wheel and exerting the authority of the powerful car over less adventurous drivers. A night mist was settling, combining with the early darkness in blurring the features of the city into swirls of light and contrasting shapes. They made good time through the suburbs and escaped from the sprawl of the Bavarian capital. Only the flare of opposing headlights punctuated the ride to the town of Dachau, and when the Mercedes swung into the driveway of the police station, set back from the main street, Rowley, riding in the back seat, ducked his head and took his first look at the functional square building with the green and white striped blinds over the windows. In the yard where Wolfe stopped, Audi and VW patrol cars in the same two-tone livery with black numerals painted on their roofs were lined up in the parking spaces. The Dachau Inspektion had all the familiar signs of an operational police station anywhere in the world.

They got out of the Mercedes and Wolfe led the way inside, waving a hand to the uniformed man behind the hatch to let them through. As the automatic catch whirred he pushed open the security door and they went through into the station. The three detectives had covered much of the subject during the journey and now confined their conversation to logistics as they prepared to take the fat man by surprise.

In the station office Wolfe rapped out instructions in brisk German and then took them down to the basement cell block where the gaoler had already installed Daniels in a featureless interview room. Basic tubular metal furniture was bolted down to the composition floor and matt beige walls absorbed the worst of the harsh light shining down from mesh-protected ceiling fixtures.

Gary Daniels, his fleshy features waxen, sat hunched at the table, jacketless, his shirt open at the neck. His tie and belt had been removed as a routine precaution. The uniformed gaoler who met them at the door exchanged a few words with Wolfe and then left, closing the door behind him.

Daniels watched them, nervous surprise registering in his eyes. "Who are these two?" he addressed Wolfe, the only one of the trio he recognized.

"We're the sunshine boys," Monroe said before the BCI detective could answer. "Come to save your worthless ass."

"Americans?" Daniels's eyebrows shot up as he queried the accent.

"He's smart," Monroe said to Rowley. "Didn't I tell you he was smart?"

"You shitting me?" Daniels said.

"I wouldn't shit you, buddy," Monroe said, leaning back against the wall. "You're my favourite turd."

"Hey, come on. What is this?" Daniels went to rise but Wolfe crossed the room and pushed him back into the chair. "What's going on here?"

"What's he look like to you?" Monroe asked Rowley.

Rowley said, "Fat."

"Yeah," Monroe said, "the original fat man." And then to Daniels, "So how's it going, fat man?"

The prisoner searched their faces looking for a sign. "Who the hell are you?"

"We're your new friends," Monroe told him. "We're going to be pals. You're going to be one of the gang."

Daniels's heavy jowls trembled and a sheen of sweat formed on his forehead. "Hey, look," he said. "I don't know what any of this is about. I've never met either of you before. You've got the wrong man."

He turned to Wolfe, a pleading note creeping into his voice. "When are you going to get me a lawyer so that I can get out of here? I know my rights."

"Maybe he's not so smart after all," Monroe observed, frowning and chewing at his gunfighter moustache. "What d'you think, slick?"

Rowley shook his head. "He can't be that stupid. Perhaps he just can't believe his luck, getting two new friends right out of the blue like this."

"You're English?" Daniels exclaimed, swivelling his attention to the Yard DS.

Ignoring him, Monroe said, "Yeah, that must be it. Nobody in their right mind would want to be dead."

The word stung the prisoner like a slap in the face. For a moment Daniels tried to brazen it out, holding their stares, which bored into him, anticipating a response. Then his shoulders sagged and he said to nobody in particular, "Have you got a cigarette? I need a smoke."

Monroe took a packet of menthol More out of his pocket, pushed himself off the wall and dropped the packet on the table. Daniels took one with shaking fingers and Monroe thumbed a flame from his Zippo and lit it for him. The fat man drew in smoke, burning down half an inch in one deep drag, exhaling with a long sigh.

Monroe watched him calm his nerves and then said to Rowley, "You think he could've forgotten the farmhouse—where was it?"

"Devon." Rowley supplied the location.

"Where he smelted down all that gold," Monroe said.

Rowley said, "Be hard to forget, five million in bullion bars."

"Well, if he could forget a thing like that," Monroe said, "maybe he doesn't remember The Enterprise either, or how he's going to convert the gold into angel dust."

Rowley shrugged. "Doesn't seem likely."

"Or how The Enterprise is going to blow him away when they find out he's been doing a deal with the guardians of the law, just because they're careful people who never take a chance."

"I can't believe he'd forget something like that," Rowley said.

Monroe returned his attention to the prisoner, a bored expression on his face. "Could be his memory blanked out. Amnesia, something like that, it can happen."

Rowley said to Wolfe, "Did he take a knock on the head or anything?"

The BCI detective shook his head, his face solemn, and Monroe said to Daniels, "Doesn't look like amnesia's going to do the trick then, does it?"

There was a silence while Daniels sucked greedily on his cigarette, his shoulders slumped.

"OK, let's stop playing games," he sighed wearily. "What d'you want?"

The DEA agent said, "We want to be friends, that's all. So why don't we put this down to a courtesy call. We'll do some horse-trading in the morning. So long, buddy."

Abruptly Monroe turned on his heel and left the interview room. Rowley and Wolfe followed and in the corridor the BCI detective signalled the gaoler to return Daniels to his cell. Then he said to Monroe, "What the hell was that all about?"

"Just giving him something to think about while he gets his beauty sleep," Monroe replied easily. "We can nail this jackass any time we choose, but what's the point when with just a little extra effort we can put him in the frame of mind to lead us to the jackpot. For now we'll play the fish on a long line."

Wolfe took them back up to the working area of the station and then to the second floor where there was a rest-room finished in Portafleck, brown on beige with cheerful yellow formica tables and chairs. Wolfe went over to the coffee machine and poured three cups. He put them down on the table in front of his guests.

"What's your bag, Wolfe?" Monroe asked, weariness drawing lines down his face. "You on vice or what?"

Wolfe was feeling more comfortable with the pair now. He liked the no-nonsense way Monroe had handled this first encounter with Daniels. String the man up and then leave him dangling. Very smooth.

"Anti-terrorist," he answered Monroe's question, stirring his coffee. "Grenzschutz group. We work on Baader-Meinhof, Red Brigades." He spent a moment or two explaining his role in diffident tones, but he stopped short of the Olympics massacre. That was a private grudge which he kept to himself.

"So how come the vice thing with Daniels?" Rowley asked out of curiosity. "A bit off your usual beat, wasn't it?"

Wolfe drank some coffee before he explained. "You have to remember we have political masters and from time to time we get drafted into other areas of activity where our, how shall I say, our special skills are required. Usually a request from one Polizei Direktor or another." He lifted his shoulders and let them drop.

"Did you ever work drugs?" Monroe asked.

"Occasionally," Wolfe said. "Same sort of arrangement."

"You know the man you've got down there is into drugs in a big way?"

Wolfe nodded.

"Plus the little matter of the death of a policewoman," Rowley added.

Wolfe drank his coffee.

"That's a very bad man you've got down there. That's why we appreciate your help," Monroe said.

"Anything you want," Wolfe replied. "It's all laid on."

"Well, I've been thinking," Monroe said, working around to the point. "Just mulling over ideas. I'd like to set up a little outing for our fat man. This mountain lodge the chief mentioned, any chance we could take him there?"

"Sudelfeld?" Wolfe looked surprised. "Certainly, if you want to."

"Can we use a chopper?"

"Helicopter?"

Monroe nodded. "Be quicker if we can. You know how it is, we don't have a lot of time to play footsie with this joker."

Wolfe considered the request for a moment and then said, "I'll call Muller. He can probably arrange an Edelweiss from the Grenzpolizei."

"Edelweiss?" Rowley queried the word. "Isn't that an alpine flower, like in *The Sound of Music?*"

"It's also the call sign for our helicopter flight," Wolfe explained, and then turned to Monroe, unable to contain his curiosity. "First you're very eager to talk to this man, yet you don't ask him any questions, and now you want to take him riding in a helicopter to the mountains. What've you got in mind?"

The DEA agent smiled. "We call it rat hunting," he said. He didn't offer any further explanation.

Wolfe finished his coffee and got up. "I'll phone Muller right away. See what we can fix up for you. In the meantime I've arranged for you to stay here on the station. We've got guest quarters upstairs. It's not the Hilton, but it's adequate. I've had your bags taken up." The German looked from one to the other. "Is there anything else you need tonight?"

Monroe said, "Do you think you could rustle up a TV and a recorder, something plays VHS? Oh, and the camera kit too, for in the morning. We'll be making a home movie."

Without batting an eyelid Wolfe said, "No problem."

Their rooms on the third floor were well away from the activity of the Dachau Inspektion and while Wolfe was away on his errand Monroe dumped his jacket on the cot, unzipped his airline bag, picked up a bottle of duty-free Scotch and took it into Rowley's room. He gave the Yard DS a conspiratorial wink and poured nightcaps into the toothbrush glasses.

"Why do I get the feeling that rat hunting isn't in the manual of good police practice?" Rowley said.

"Because you're a detective. And because we don't have time to play this game according to the book. We've got to convince our friend down there that it's in his best interests to cooperate with us. A quick sharp shock is all he needs."

"He looks like a tub of lard to me," Rowley said. "Are you sure he can deliver the goods, Jack?"

"This firm doesn't give guarantees."

"That's what I was afraid of. Because in that case we ought to be thinking about shipping the fat man out of here. Pretty soon Commander Drake is going to be screaming for results and that's going to mean a body on the sheet. If we can't produce, Jack, he's going to cancel our open sesame, which is the only reason we're getting the red carpet treatment over here."

"You worry too much," Monroe said easily. "Let's try it my way first. If we strike out, we can still cut our losses and run with the ball."

"There's no way we can go for legal extradition." Rowley voiced his doubts out loud. "That would take forever. It'd have to be an under-the-counter arrangement. Buy the man a ticket and put him on the plane. That's going to need an awful lot of friendly cooperation, Jack."

"Hey, just hang loose, slick," Monroe said. "This is too good to hurry. We've got the chance of pay dirt if we handle it right, snow worth a hundred mill on the street. That's a jackpot worth shooting for."

"I hope you're right," Rowley said, draining his glass and stretching out on the bed. "Because if you're not, I'm the mug who's going to have to blow the whistle."

He thought about that possibility for a moment and then said, "So I'd be obliged if you don't get into the Helen Linden thing with our fat man. If we do ship him out, then my people will want that little episode to come as a big surprise."

Monroe raised a forefinger to his eye and drew down a lower lid. "D'you see any green in there?" He lifted his glass, squinted thoughtfully at the last drop of whisky and then tipped it back. "Besides, in my book that was just a sideshow. Don't let's start getting pessimistic, this joker'll come through for us, you'll see. He's a businessman, he'll be looking for the best deal he can get. The way I'm going to sell it to him, he won't have any option."

Rowley said, "What about our friend Wolfe? He's not going to play along forever. I get the distinct impression he's not too keen on us anyway, probably thinks we're going to steal his thunder."

"Wolfe'll be all right," Monroe reassured him. "You have to understand these State police organizations. Whatever they might think privately, they obey the orders from the top. He may not like it, but he'll do what's required all the same."

"Until somebody pulls the plug."

"That's when our problems start," Monroe said. "But by then Wolfe is going to see a great big drugs bust right in front of his eyes. Lots of glory. If we give Wolfe an angle, he'll be lapping it up, you'll see."

Back in his own room Monroe found that a portable colour TV with an Hitachi tape-player had been set up in the corner. Beside the set was a carry-case containing a Sony Betacam portable video camera. The DEA agent took a video cassette from his luggage, slotted it into the machine and turned out the lights. The central heating had created a soporific warmth in the room and Monroe stripped off his shirt and in the darkness slumped on to the bunk as he watched the picture appear on the screen. Another sequence from *Apocalypse Now*, this time Robert Duval in the white cavalry Stetson leading a flight of helicopter gunships into the attack. The psy-ops bird was blaring out "The Ride of the Valkyries" from speakers slung under its belly. The formation dipped and began to strafe a village, buzz-saw rasp of mini-guns, streams of red tracer and rocket trails, black-edged balls of orange flame erupting from the hooches, figures clad in black pyjamas and conical hats scurrying for cover. Mayhem. A dust-off dropped into the village square, an ornamental garden, to pick up wounded crewmen while the flight laid down a carpet of suppressing fire. A girl ran to the medivac bird pleading with outstretched arms as the rotors slapped air, spooling up for take-off. A corpsman stretched out to her and at the last minute she reached inside the folds of her tunic and tossed a stick grenade into the helicopter, which was torn apart by the explosion.

Monroe felt the sweat jump from his pores as he fondled the dog-tags hanging from his neck and massaged the jagged scar running across his chest. His mind was back in Vietnam.

They were five days moving through the jungle, just the two of them, the green man leading like a Natty Bumppo of the woods. They followed the meandering course of the Song Tra Bong, stopping only to sleep, curled in their ponchos in the exposed roots of giant trees. The drizzle was continuous. They dined on cold C-Rats, defecated in cat-holes and when they came to the ville on the river bank they climbed high into one of the massive trees, perched themselves in a creeper-matted fork seventy feet up, hidden in the leathery dark green foliage of the canopy, and watched the sullen brown river. Below, a bamboo jetty, precariously supported on rotting wooden piles, jutted out into the river. A well-trodden trail led back to the collection of ramshackle huts which formed the village proper. Wisps of smoke rose from cooking fires.

This was the trading post, the green man explained, lounging comfortably in a hammock of creepers, to which shipments of drugs came by the river. Anything your heart desired, Cambodian Red, Laotian Green, grass by the bale, smack or coke in big clay pots, all of it shipped in to satisfy the demand. The little people adapting to free market forces. The green man grinned, his eyes bright. He took a dog-eared paperback, Conrad's *Heart of Darkness* from inside his tiger fatigues and began to read, withdrawing into himself. He told Monroe to watch the river.

After a while a motorized sampan came down, heavily laden, and nosed into the jetty. There was a flurry of activity as eager hands removed wooden slats from the decking and unloaded the boat, humping the cargo up the trail to the ville. The green man put aside his book and looked down on the scene. A shipment had arrived, he explained. Charlie's goodies. He went back to reading his book.

At night, from his perch in the great tree Monroe watched the ville through a starlight scope. A curious smell drifted up to his nostrils. He asked his companion if he knew what it could be. Face hidden in the darkness the green man said, "Sure, burning flesh."

In the darkened guest-room on the top floor of the police Inspektion in the German town of Dachau, DEA agent Jack Monroe shuddered and dragged himself back to the bright square of the TV screen. They were down on the beach, the Air Cav Colonel in the immaculate Stetson, oblivious to the lunacy of the firefight swirling around him as he watched the kid riding a fibreglass board while AK rounds spattered into the surf. The kid finally falling . . .

Monroe used the remote control to switch off the video and the scene dissolved. With the back of his hand he wiped the clammy sheen from his forehead and sagged back on to the bunk. It took him some time to fall asleep.

10

They breakfasted on sugar-dusted sweet buns, strips of smoked ham, strawberry preserve and thick cold black-currant juice brought up by a uniformed man from the desk below.

"So what's rat hunting?" Rowley asked as they further fortified themselves with coffee in the cheerful rest room at the Dachau Inspektion.

"You'll see, slick," Monroe replied cryptically.

Wolfe came in loaded with padded clothing. He gave each of them a quilted anorak and an alpine trooper's cap. "Getting colder in the mountains," he explained.

"What about Daniels?" Rowley asked.

"I'll take care of Daniels," said Monroe, tipping back in his chair. "The fresh air'll do him good." He turned to Wolfe. "When's the chopper going to be here?"

The BCI detective consulted his watch. "Half an hour."

"OK," Monroe said, clasping his hands behind his head. "Here's what we're going to do. We don't have time to take this schmuck to the show, so we've got to do a quick number on him, scare the shit out of him, mess up his mind, then sell him the round-trip ticket."

"Just how are you planning to achieve that?" Wolfe asked with professional interest.

"Easy. First we take him up there to the snow line, up there in the mountains with the wolves and the bears, and then we throw him out of the helicopter."

He watched their faces with amusement as he proceeded to outline his plan to crack any further resistance from the fat man, painting a picture of the soft city slicker flung into the harsh environment of the wilderness. Trauma shock. Then he said, "Look, we don't have time for the niceties of interrogation. So we're going to violate some cherished human rights, that's the name of the game, amigos, nothing's sacred in this dirty end of the business. We're going to have to cut some corners. Now are you two going to stop looking at me as if I'd just trod in something? It's time the fat man had his wake-up."

They went down to the cell block where Wolfe had Daniels brought out to the interview room. In the corridor outside, Monroe said to Rowley, "I'll do the heavy and you do the nice guy. You're going to be his friend. Just take your cue from me, slick."

They went inside and Monroe did his cool casual routine, stroking his moustache with thumb and forefinger as though none of this mattered. Daniels was seated behind the table. He looked strained but there was defiance in his eyes.

"How're you doing?" Monroe asked genially.

Daniels said, "Are you going to tell me who the hell you are?"

"Sure." Monroe took his wallet out of his pocket and opened it so that his ID was displayed. "United States Department of Justice Drug Enforcement Administration. Federal Agent Monroe."

He gestured to Rowley, who made a similar show of producing his warrant card. "Detective-Sergeant Rowley, Crime Intelligence, New Scotland Yard."

The fat man's eyes popped.

Monroe indicated the German detective. "With the chief here from the BCI you're looking at the cream of the balls-busters."

Daniels said, "Hey, what is this, what's going on, what'd I do?"

"You know what you did," Monroe said. "We also know what you did. The question is, what are you going to do now, that's what we've got to find out."

"Hey, look," Daniels protested, "I don't have the faintest idea what's going on here. I'm not doing anything, I'm not saying anything, until I see a lawyer. I'm a reputable businessman, I don't have to take any of this shit."

Monroe said, "Seeing as you're such a hotshot businessman, we're going to take you somewhere nice and quiet for a nice friendly business meeting. We're going to give you our sales pitch."

"What!" Daniels looked baffled. "You can't touch me, I'm not going anywhere." A sickly smile formed on his face. "Look, fellows, I'm a businessman, I've got contacts. If we've got a little problem here, we can work it out, you know what I mean? You're men of the world, no sense in getting things out of proportion. Am I making sense?"

Without warning Monroe lunged across the table, his hand flashed out and grabbed Daniels by the mouth, seizing the fleshy upper lip. The fat man yelped in surprise and excruciating pain.

Rowley laid a restraining hand on Monroe's arm. "Pack it in, Jack. You don't have to do it this way. Give the guy a chance."

"I ought to tear his face off," Monroe growled.

"For Chrissake no," Rowley said. "Leave it out."

Monroe released his grip and Rowley pulled his arm away. "Just take it easy," the Yard DS counselled. "Let me talk to him, maybe we can work something out."

"Yeah?" Monroe sneered. "You think so? I tell you what's going on in this catknacker's mind right this minute. He's working out how to string us along and slip the hook. Practically burning out the circuits working that one out. You want to know about your friend there, your good old buddy, well, I'll tell you. He's not just a fat man with a penchant for little girls. He's one bad fat man full of shit and up to his ass in angel dust. Isn't that right, fat man?"

Daniels nursed his swollen lip in silence, tried to keep his frantic panic in check. Hang on, stay calm, find out what they want.

He looked up at Rowley with the appeal of a fellow countryman on his face. "You know I don't have to stand for this," he muttered thickly. "I've got my rights, I want to see a lawyer."

Across the table Monroe gnawed at the ends of his moustache. From the recess of his memory an image bubbled up and burst with great clarity. He saw himself cradling Helen Linden in his arms. The blood and the astonished look on her face bored into him. His eyes glazed into frozen intensity and the hand resting on the table clenched into a fist, his expression twisting into a snarl.

Daniels was visibly shaken by the sight and flinched back in his chair.

Rowley said calmly, "Jack, for Chrissake, it doesn't have to be this way."

Monroe blinked, broke the spell; felt a cold flush of sweat along his ribs. With an effort he relaxed, then jerked a thumb over his shoulder. "It don't, eh? Well, we'll see . . . saddle up!"

Out of the grey-blue blur of the morning sky a Messerschmitt-Bolkow-Blohm BO 105 of the Bavarian Border Police circled overhead and then fluttered in to land on the heli-pad at the rear of Dachau police station. The Grenzpolizei pilot in crisp khakis and white bone dome, eyes concealed behind aviator shades, kept the power from the twin Allisons running as four figures emerged from the building and hurried towards the green and white helicopter.

Daniels, now dressed in jacket and tie, was flanked by Monroe and Rowley. Wolfe walked a little apart, filming the others with the Beta-cam perched on his shoulder, panning from the white Jaguar XJS parked in the yard. The detectives hustled the fat man into the helicopter, the wash from the spinning rotors snatching at their clothing. Wolfe reached up to stow the camera and then climbed in beside the pilot.

They exchanged nods of greeting and the BCI detective raised a thumb, at which the pilot set his instruments for the mountains, reached a white gloved hand up to the throttle levers, brought the Bolkow up into the hover, spooled up and then pitched the machine forward into flight.

They climbed steadily, the town of Dachau dropping away behind them, the urban landscaping changing into a green and brown patch-work of farmland dotted with the red-roofed houses of rural Bavaria. After a while the monotony of the terrain began to break up into wooded slopes cushioning jagged ridges as they crossed the foothills and flew on into the Bavarian Alps. Hostile peaks wreathed in mist slipped by and saw-toothed mountain ranges streaming ragged white cloud came into view, rock on snow, purple on white. From a thousand feet the pilot picked up the winding thread of a mountain pass and began to descend towards the pine-dotted slopes, following the road which led to the mountain lodge of Sudelfeld, easily identified by its steeply pitched roof surmounted by an alpine campanile. The Bolkow dropped down to land on the gravelled roadside outside the lodge and the pilot cut the whine of the engines.

Without waiting for the rotors to stop turning they hustled the prisoner inside by way of the heavy wooden doors and took him to a room which had been earmarked in advance. Massive dark beams contrasted with whitewashed walls and ceiling and the room was plainly furnished with heavy wooden furniture. The scent of pine was sweet on the alpine air. A video player had been set up at one end of a heavy refectory table and as Daniels was invited to take a seat he became aware of a growing intensity about the detectives which made his flesh crawl. Hang on, he told himself. Work something out. But his resolve was already beginning to crack.

"I'm going to tell you this right off the bat," Monroe started the session. "We've got you by the balls, fat man, you'd better believe it. Every time we give you a tweak you're going to squeal. Every time you try to get smart we're going to squeeze your nuts. You understand?"

Daniels said nothing, tried to return their hard-boiled stares without letting his eyes waver. It was getting more and more difficult.

"So here's our proposition," Monroe went on. "We get your active cooperation on a little deal we have in mind and you get the chance to walk away from the deep shit in one piece. Believe me, that is a very, very good deal."

Daniels gathered the remnants of his resolve, not knowing what to expect but still believing that if this was just a bullshit session, then he could still brazen it out. He shot Rowley an anxious look, wondering if the man from the Yard might become an ally. He forced a weak smile. "Look, fellows, you've got me all wrong. OK, so I've got a little problem with the local law, but it's nothing I can't work out. Apart from that I don't know why you're taking such an interest in me, and that's God's honest truth." He looked around him. "I mean . . . I don't know . . . look, why have you brought me here?"

"Tell you what, fat man," Monroe replied patiently, "we'll give you a sample of our executive service, seeing as you're such a big noise. We'll give you a sneak preview. We're going into the movie business, make ourselves a pop video. And here's the best bit, buddy; you get the star billing."

Monroe reached out, slotted a tape into the deck and pushed the play button. A picture came up on the screen, Daniels talking to the detectives at Dachau police station, shots of the fat man hurrying to the waiting helicopter, his own white XJS clearly visible in the background.

"Looks like a guy who's pretty thick with the fuzz, wouldn't you say?" Monroe said. "Getting the VIP treatment."

Watching the screen, Daniels tried to moisten his lips but could only run a furred tongue around his dry mouth.

"All we need is a few more intimate sequences," Monroe said. "Dub on the jingle, edit the package and then send it special delivery to your pals in The Enterprise. How's that grab you?"

The colour drained from Daniels's face; his jowls began to quiver.

"Be like signing your death warrant," Monroe predicted with a lazy grin.

A greasy sheen formed on Daniels's brow.

"Still not convinced?" Monroe said. "Well, let's see if we can do something about that." He looked at the others. "Why don't we take a breath of air?"

They prodded Daniels to his feet, donned their cold weather gear and took the man outside into the crisp autumn morning. Gravel crunched under their feet.

Bunched around the prisoner, they herded him towards the parked Bolkow and Monroe spoke the thought as though it had just occurred to him: "Why walk when we can fly?"

The helicopter pilot, who was checking the machine, stopped and watched them approach. Monroe said to Wolfe, "What about a little joyride for our strong silent friend?"

Deep-set eyes intrigued, Wolfe said, "You really want to do this?"

"Sure," Monroe said. "Let's do it."

Daniels said, "Hey, do what?"

And for the fat man's benefit Rowley feigned concern and said to Monroe, "Jack, wait a minute, this is crazy."

Daniels searched their faces with growing alarm and tried to hold back, but Monroe shoved him on, and as he stumbled forward the DEA agent grabbed his wrists and snapped on a pair of ratchet handcuffs.

"Hey!" Daniels yelped in alarm.

"Shut up," Monroe ordered, prodding him along.

Rowley grabbed Monroe's shoulder, said, "We don't have to do this."

But the DEA agent shook him off and told Wolfe to instruct the pilot to crank up.

The BCI detective shrugged and gave the order and the pilot got into his seat, strapped in and began flipping switches on the console in front of him. He had flown for the Kriminalpolizei often enough to be accustomed to taking orders without question, and even when Wolfe got in beside him and explained what was required, he raised no objection. If they wanted fancy flying, then he would give it to them. The rest was none of his business.

Monroe shoved Daniels, still protesting, into the back, leaving the sliding door locked open, and Rowley stepped on to the skid and followed them into the cabin. Red and yellow lights winked as the pilot continued to activate the systems, pausing only to turn his head and give Daniels a curious glance through the dark lenses of his sunglasses.

The starter whined and the jets fired, rising to a scream, the swish of the four rotor blades melting into one continuous roar of sound. The Bolkow quivered and parted from the ground as the pilot pulled up on the collective and eased the cyclic over, throwing the machine into a sideways slide, skimming across the mountainside and heading for the snowline.

Scuds of snow whipped up and Monroe grabbed Daniels and thrust him into the open doorway, snagging his manacled wrists on to the abseil safety line. Below, the ground flashed by in a dizzy blur and Daniels began to gasp, his eyes bulging as the slipstream stung his face. Desperately Daniels tried to wrench himself back into the safety of the cabin, but the line held him fast in the open doorway as the helicopter jinked between the fir trees, weaving from side to side, throwing Daniels's belly hard against the safety line, his feet scrabbling for a grip. Monroe braced himself and signalled to Rowley to strap in. No word was spoken.

Snow, denser now, an all-white blur. Skimming the snowfield at fifty feet, white spirals lashed up by the rotors, Wolfe gave the pilot a prearranged signal and the machine canted over, began to describe a tight circle, chasing its tail. Lips pulled back in a grimace, Monroe picked the moment and prodded Daniels out onto the skid. Unable to save himself, the fat man slipped and a Gucci loafer spun away. He began screaming in terror, his eyes rolling in his head. Only the abseil line and centrifugal force prevented his headlong fall.

The pilot tightened the orbit, the blurred arc of the rotors almost touching the snowbanks. Blood draining from his brain, Daniels felt his knees sag as he screamed himself hoarse. Round and round they went, winding in until just at the moment of total disorientation the pilot gave a deft flick on the controls, righted the Bolkow and juddered into a nose-up hover. Monroe, braced in the doorway, brought his knee up into the small of Daniels's back, punched the quick release on the abseil line and catapulted the fat man out of the machine. The fat man fell the few remaining feet and sprawled headlong into a powdery drift which broke his fall.

Relieved of the weight, the Bolkow bobbed up as Monroe signalled to Rowley, who unbuckled, stepped out on to the skid and, as the machine settled, dropped lightly into the ankle-deep snow. The helicopter pulled up and circled away.

Daniels was burrowing in the deep powder of the snowbank, scrambling on his knees. Stark terror had reduced the fat man to a gibbering wreck. His fleshy lips quivered uncontrollably, saliva bubbled with incoherent pleadings and then he began to retch, heaving and shuddering as Rowley plodded over to him.

When the convulsions subsided, Daniels pawed at his moist mouth and looked up frantically at the Yard DS standing over him. There was outright panic in his eyes.

"There's one thing you ought to know about that man up there," Rowley said, shading his eyes to watch the progress of the circling helicopter. "Now he's got you, he won't let up, and there's plenty more tricks like that one up his sleeve."

Daniels heaved himself on to his haunches, sitting in the snow, blinking in the snowdazzle.

"Oh yes, he's pretty crazy all right," Rowley said. "Jesus, you know what? I feel sorry for you, Gary."

Daniels coughed, spat mucus, tried to control his quaking bowels. He stank of the heavy musk of fear. Disorientated and in trauma, the fat man cast around him and experienced the desperate agoraphobic horror of the wilderness.

Hunched in his parka, Rowley said, "I tell you something else. A man could die of exposure out here, easy as that. Could easily look as though he was trying to escape and got lost on the mountain. Yes, that could happen."

As he spoke the Bolkow wheeled and came roaring overhead, buzzing them, the DEA agent leaning out of the open door.

Daniels flinched at the sight of his tormentor. He grabbed Rowley's leg and pleaded, "For pity's sake." The words were accompanied by a gasping sob.

Rowley watched the helicopter. "Yeah, I'd say if he decided to leave you out here that'd pretty well be it. He's crazy enough to do it too."

"Keep him off me," Daniels croaked. "Can't you keep him off me?" The plea bubbled from the fat man's soft pink mouth. "What do I have to do? Just tell me what he wants from me!"

Rowley got a hand under Daniels's arm and hoisted him to his feet. "What can I do?" he said. "You want me to help you, then you've got to give something in return. Otherwise—" He shrugged, leaving the doubt hanging on the air. Then he said, "Look, you know what he wants. It's time you cleared up a few debts, made some atonement."

Daniels's heavy bulk sagged and Rowley tightened his grip on the swaying man. "Hey," he said, "looks like you need a friend."

Daniels's acquiescence was hardly more than a sigh. "I'll do whatever you want. Just so long as you keep him away from me."

They began to trudge through the deep snow.

"But you've got to deliver," Rowley said.

"I'll deliver! Oh Jesus, I'll deliver."

"The problem is," Rowley said doubtfully, "I've got to work with the man, go along with what he wants. OK, so maybe I don't agree with his methods, but what can I do, the man's a Federal agent, he's the boss on this one. I have to go along with him unless of course you can do something to help me."

"What do you want?"

"Well, that's got to come from you. I can tell him you're willing to cooperate, only you've got to prove it. You see, what this is all about is the man up there wants to check you out, see if you've got the guts to help us. Now if he decides you haven't, or you try to get smart, then he'll probably take you up in the helicopter again and keep throwing you out until you don't get up any more. Then he's going to fly away and leave you for the wolves."

"Oh Jesus!" Daniels gasped. The prospect terrified him. "Just tell me what to do and I'll do it . . . anything you want. I can't take any more of this." The fat man clung to Rowley pleading. "Please, for pity's sake help me!"

Rowley said, "Look, I don't like to see you going through the mill. I'll do what I can, see if I can persuade him, only first you've got to give me something, something to work on. Prove you're serious about this."

Daniels's voice was tired and empty. "You think I don't know that."

Rowley patted him on the shoulder. "That's better," he said. "Now you're getting the message. You know how it is, Gary, everything in this life's a trade-off."

Two tiny figures on the white expanse of the snowscape and one of them raised an arm and signalled the circling helicopter to return.

11

"You've got to appreciate my predicament," Gary Daniels pleaded with the detectives, an edge of desperation in his voice. "One false move and I'm dead."

Cleaned up after his ordeal in the snow, the fat man sat at the same heavy wooden table in the stark black and white room at the Sudelfeld mountain lodge trying to make the best of his precarious situation.

"Tell your bosom pal there," Monroe said to Rowley, "if he so much as thinks of reneging we're going to do the sky jump again, only this time from five hundred feet, and we won't be hanging around to pick up the pieces."

"Oh no." Daniels flinched at the threat, a nervous tic twitching his cheek. "I'm not reneging. I didn't say that. All I'm saying is these people, these people we're talking about, they don't mess around. There's no benefit of the doubt. They find out, they'll kill me, that's the bottom line."

"Well, that's going to be your choice," Monroe said flatly. "You're right between the rocks and a hard place."

"Hang on a minute," Rowley intervened, playing his role as conciliator. "There's got to be a way, let's give Gary a chance here. He's going to try for us, aren't you, Gary?"

"Yeah, sure," Daniels agreed swiftly, grateful for the support, "I'm going to try. Jesus, am I going to try. All I'm saying, I mean I've got to think, think ahead, what's going to happen. Take it into consideration, otherwise . . ." His voice trailed off.

"Look, why don't you spit it out, tell us what's on your mind, Gary," Rowley suggested. "Then we'll know better if we can do something for you. Give and take, you know."

Daniels took a deep breath, searching around for the right combination of words. Then he said, "What it is, what I mean is, if I'm going to do something for you, then I'm going to have to have some guarantees up front."

Monroe jerked forward, his face angry. "Fat man," he said, "here's your bottom line as far as I'm concerned. Work it out or the movie's in the mail."

Daniels shot Rowley a pleading look. The Yard DS was still his best hope of escaping from the noose which he could feel tightening around his neck.

On cue Rowley said, "Tell you what, Gary, why don't you just put something on the table, something to demonstrate your good faith, then we'll have a better idea if we can do something for you. For instance, why don't you tell us about the gold."

Daniels breathed a heavy sigh, reached a trembling hand out to the packet of cigarettes Monroe had left in front of him, lit one from a book of matches and sucked heavily on the menthol tobacco like the gasp of a drowning man. As he exhaled he said, "The gold was a contract job. All they had to do was lift a consignment of bullion from the bonded warehouse at Heathrow. The Enterprise plotted it up for them, gave them all the instructions by numbers, they were just the mechanics."

"Let's be clear who we're talking about," Rowley said. "You're talking about the Twins, am I right?"

Daniels nodded. "A couple of nutters. Yes, their firm did the job."

"And delivered the gold to you?"

"At the farmhouse down in Devon. I gather you know about that." Daniels glanced at Monroe and then at Wolfe. He returned to Rowley and said, "They brought the gold to me there right after the robbery and I smelted it down. Gold's my business, but I had no part in the robbery, that's the God's honest truth." Again he glanced hopefully at Rowley, his eyes asking, "How am I doing?"

Monroe gnawed at his moustache, looking mean. "Come on, slick," he told Rowley impatiently, "when's this prick going to tell us something we don't know already? I think we should give his chain another jerk."

Rowley frowned, said to Daniels, "How about it, Gary? If you're looking for our protection, it's going to take more than that."

The fat man squirmed in his chair. "Look, I smelted the gold, OK? You've got me admitting things now, criminal acts. What do you want me to say?"

Monroe took up the questioning. "How'd you get the gold out of the country?"

"Smelted it into tractor parts," Daniels replied. "It was shipped in a container as agricultural equipment, bills of lading, all the paperwork in order, everything above board. Customs didn't bat an eye."

"So where's the gold now?" This time Rowley was the questioner.

"Switzerland," Daniels said. "Reconstituted into bullion and deposited in the vault of the Crédit Suisse bank."

"Was that the first move on the laundry run?" Monroe asked.

Daniels nodded. "The Enterprise set up a complicated series of business transactions, moved the money around until it was washed clean."

Rowley patted Daniels on the shoulder. "See, that wasn't too hard, Gary, now was it?"

Daniels looked from one to the other of his inquisitors. "Will I go to prison for this?"

"Oh boy." Monroe laughed. "You still don't get it, do you, fat man? We wanted to nail your ass, we wouldn't be doing any of this. Your ass'd be nailed so tight you couldn't take a crap." He stared speculatively at Daniels for a long moment. "What we want from you is, we want you to perform, fat man, like a circus trick."

"We don't want to do anything to you, Gary," Rowley explained more kindly, "unless we don't have a choice. Think of this as like a fishing trip."

"And you're the fat juicy bait," Monroe interjected.

"You see," Rowley said, "what Jack means is if you help us set up The Enterprise then we'll see if we can't get you right out of it, drop right out of sight." He made a vanishing motion with one hand. "Think of it like slipping through a window into a new life."

"Have to be a mighty big window to get that fat carcass through," Monroe said to Rowley. "And he's going to have to satisfy our friend Wolfe along the way because right now he's standing out a prisoner." He turned to Daniels. "You're going to have to be one hell of a busy fellow to keep us all happy."

Daniels shot an anxious glance at Wolfe, but the BCI detective seemed preoccupied with his thoughts and offered no comment.

"You mean . . . do I understand . . . I mean, I wouldn't be involved?" Daniels groped around the question uppermost in his mind.

Monroe shrugged. "Depends. Depends on you, doesn't it, this all hinges on how well you can do your stuff. Walk the high wire and you slip either way and that's it, finito." He drew a finger across his throat.

Daniels blanched at the threat.

"Look, why don't we get back to the gold." Rowley resumed the questioning, playing his part in the cat and mouse game, prodding the prisoner into further admissions. "You say the gold was used to finance these business deals. How did that work?"

Daniels lit another cigarette, a greasy sheen gleaming on his forehead. "They set up a string of companies, mostly just on paper," he explained, frowning as he tried to recall the details. "Fricker Freight was the main one, shipped the tractor parts, collected on the gold and then moved the money around through a maze of transactions, handled mainly by a brokerage called Euro Credit and Trust, buying into bonds, negotiables, easy commodities. Worked up a portfolio which was changing all the time, like a conjuring trick. Anybody tried to follow the money they got lost in the maze. Then there were other companies, Snell Engineering, Pecker Trading, Capstan Air-Sea Holdings. In the end the money filtered through to the account of Condor Enterprises, First National Bank, Bella Vista Boulevard, Miami, Florida."

"Quite a paper chase," Monroe observed. "Very neat."

Daniels said, "My involvement was Fricker Freight. I registered the company in Munich and Salzburg and then once I'd run the gold I was supposed to sit tight and wait for the return trip. That was when I made my first mistake and, well, you know the rest."

"Yeah, carnal knowledge of schoolgirls," Monroe said.

"So the money reaches Miami." Rowley resumed the line of questioning. "What then?"

"It pays for the shipment."

"Cocaine?"

"What else? That's the name of the game, prime the UK with top-grade cocaine." Daniels blinked. "That's what it's all about."

"We've got the picture," Monroe said. "You're going to market angel dust in handy packs off the supermarket shelves. The U.S. is played out and The Enterprise is looking for a new sales territory and you got a slice of the franchise. Make you feel good, fat man?"

Daniels said, "Hey, I'm only the middleman."

"Oh, you can do better than that, my friend," Monroe said. "You're the magic carpet driver. You're the man in the know. So what's the next move?"

"Condor ships the product," Daniels explained. "It's coming in through Turkey." He shot another glance at Wolfe. "Five million buys the pump primer, sets it all in motion."

"So when's the shipment due?" Rowley asked.

"It's on its way now," Daniels replied. "Moving in stages, each stage with a cut-off. The consignment gets here"—he looked at his watch, checking the date—"in two days' time, but only if I make contact in a certain way, follow the procedures. Otherwise"—he shrugged—"another cut-off."

Daniels slumped forward, resting his arms on the table, the material of his jacket pulled tight across the bulk of his shoulders. "The only way it'll work is if I'm back in Salzburg. That's the way it's set up. I have to clear my end, then come over the border and wire up the next stage."

He glanced at their faces, biting his lower lip. "You see, what I mean to say is, we're talking about some very careful, suspicious people here. They get the first inkling that something is not running according to the plan, they pull the switch and they're gone, out of sight."

His shoulders sagged further. "This whole operation is so fail-safe, so riddled with cut-offs, there's no way you could get into it unless you're already on the inside."

The fat man sighed. "So you see, the thing is, you want me to work for you, I'm ready to do that, only the really important thing is, unless I'm back in circulation pretty soon, doing all the things I'm supposed to be doing, pushing all the right buttons at the right time, then the product's going to be long gone and you won't see The Enterprise for dust. And that's not all. After that's done, if I don't make all the right connections here in Bavaria, touch all the bases in the right sequence, then it still evaporates. So what I'm saying is, you want me to do this thing for you, and I know I'm going to have to do it, then it's going to have to be done my way, otherwise it's already too late."

Completing his little speech, Daniels heaved his bulk back in his chair, his confidence returning. He watched the detectives trying to anticipate their reaction.

"Who's your contact?" Monroe asked.

"It's like the rest of the operation," Daniels replied. "There's a guy comes and goes according to the timetable. I only contact him when I have to, when I'm ready to hand over."

"Has this contact man got a name?"

"Calls himself Ryker."

Wolfe appeared to rouse himself and spoke for the first time. "Ryker? He's German?"

Daniels switched to the BCI detective, eyebrows raised in surprise. "No," he replied, "not at all. I think he's American."

And there it was. The name Monroe had waited so long to hear, finally confirmed. Ryker! The DEA agent kept his face deadpan, carefully avoiding any outward display of the thrill of discovery which electrified him. Ryker!

"Ryker comes in from Florida," Daniels explained, still addressing Wolfe. "He's like the trouble-shooter, on the move all the time, oiling the works between the stages. Nothing moves without his say-so."

"The honcho," Monroe mused. "We're going to need a look at this guy."

Daniels shook his head. "You don't understand," he protested. "Unless I get back out there and do certain things, you won't see Ryker or anybody else, because none of this will happen. It'll be a cut-off."

"I was thinking the same thing," Monroe agreed, chewing his moustache.

He turned to Wolfe. "Well, that about concludes our business for the morning. Can we get something to eat here, then back to civilization? Time we broke in our new undercover."

Heading east on the autobahn towards the Austrian border, four cars constantly changed position around a white Jaguar XJS cruising at eighty-five. Two Mercedes and an Audi kept station on the Jaguar while a bronze BMW 351i sat in the hang-back position.

The unmarked crime cars were crewed by detectives of Wolfe's anti-terrorist group, who talked to each other in laconic asides over the car-to-car. Beside the driver in the BMW Wolfe issued occasional orders into the radio and monitored the progress of the surveillance block. Monroe and Rowley rode in the back of the BMW and watched the countryside roll by in the hazy sunshine.

Behind the wheel of the Jaguar, Gary Daniels tried to quell the churning of his bowels. His hands were sweaty and phlegm welled up in his throat and threatened to choke him. Daniels's nerves were shot and from the way his insides burned he feared he was starting an ulcer. The prospect dismayed him. The previous afternoon, following their return from Sudelfeld the detectives had briefed him at the Dachau Inspektion. His head throbbed as they coached him in the techniques of his undercover role; simple codes were devised and each detail was drummed into him over and over until they were satisfied he understood exactly what was required of him.

At one point Monroe gave him a "tracker," a miniature electronic locator and advised him unsmilingly that the safest way to carry it without risk of detection was to swallow it and not defecate until the operation was over. Daniels had shuddered at the idea. Eventually, when they had exhausted the subject, the fat man was permitted the luxury of sleep.

But now in the harsh reality of the following day, travelling down the autobahn, aware that his every move was being shadowed, Daniels found himself lapsing into a mood of dull hopeless panic. As he considered his predicament he entertained the fantasy of giving the detectives the slip, warning Ryker and throwing himself upon the mercy of The Enterprise. But logic swiftly dictated that such a course of action would be tantamount to suicide. No, whichever way he looked at the situation, it was clear that he had no choice but to throw in his hand with the American drugs agent in the hope that if he delivered then Monroe would keep his part of the bargain and save his hide. The enormity of such duplicity condensed into acid which dripped steadily, burning holes in his gut as he clutched the steering-wheel, oblivious of the opulent comfort of the sports saloon effortlessly eating up the miles.

In the back of the pursuit car Jack Monroe was equally occupied with his thoughts. The warmth of the morning sun and the meaningless monotony of the radio exchanges finally induced a heavy-lidded drowsiness to which the DEA agent succumbed. Without the benefit of the video player, Monroe let the movie play inside his head.

The Swift boat was coming down the sluggish brown river through a ravine in the dense green jungle; around a curve in the river the tailfin of a downed B52 angled upwards, dripping electronic entrails from gaping holes to mingle with the matted creepers entwining around the wreck. The patrol boat ploughed on, dwarfed by the primeval jungle which reached out as if to strangle the river itself. Dusk was falling when up ahead appeared the incongruous sight of an isolated firebase ablaze with fairy lights.

The scene shifted.

Out of the darkness a flight of helicopters, navigation lights blazing, was coming in to the landing-pad. Hordes of soldiers in a sea of sweat-soaked green fatigues were being held back by a line of white-helmeted MPs. A troop of go-go dancers tripped from the Hueys and began to gyrate on white stilettos, swirling their pink mini skirts. The slavering moaning green hordes swayed forward, overwhelming the snowdrops, and the girls scrambled back into the slicks as the pilots pulled up, abruptly ending the show. The movie faded and Jack Monroe was back in the company of the green man perched in the giant tree above the torpid waters of the Song Tra Bong. The green man said they would have to watch the ville for a while, see what transpired, and so they settled down to wait. It was surprisingly comfortable, lounging in the matt of creepers, each strand thick as a man's arm, shaded under the triple green canopy from the relentless sun which had finally burned away the misty drizzle. Like a hunting animal at rest, the green man was at ease in his hammock, browsing in his dog-eared paperback. He turned a page and asked Monroe if he had ever read *Heart of Darkness*. Monroe admitted he hadn't and the green man smiled and turned another page.

After two days in the tree the green man stirred himself and announced that the time was right. He would reconnoitre the ville and if everything was as expected he would take Monroe in to obtain positive evidence of Charlie's drugs pipeline. Then Monroe could return to the waiting patrol and call in the Air Cav. Monroe felt the green man's eyes mocking him.

When he left on his scouting trip, Monroe, alone now in the hide-away, felt the first twinge of caution. Foremost in his mind was the realization that he did not know who had sent the green man to guide him, and should something go wrong, he had no doubt that the LURP would melt back into the jungle and he would be left without a witness.

He thought of My Lai and the witchhunt which had followed the scandal. He decided to be prudent and protect himself.

Methodically Monroe began to search the treetop hideout and discovered a deep hole in the trunk. Reaching inside, he came upon an assortment of combat gear, several weapons, including a Kalashnikov AK 47 assault rifle and ammunition, grenades, boxes of C4 explosive, some tins of C-rats and a short-wave military radio.

Careful not to disturb anything, Monroe searched through the clothing which was also hidden in the hole for some clue to the green man's identity. When he felt behind the laces of a pair of boots his fingers located a set of dog-tags and on impulse exchanged them for his own.

Time passed and then the green man returned to announce that the coast was clear. They could move down into the ville with impunity and he would show Monroe things which would make his brownbar boonierat eyes pop out of his head. The green man chuckled deep in his throat. Monroe blinked . . .

Monroe blinked and the figure of the green man became a grey-caped Austrian border guard beckoning them towards the checkpoint with his traffic wand. As the BMW came abreast of the guard Wolfe rolled down his window, displayed his ID and said, "Kriminalpolizei, München."

"*Wunderbar,*" replied the guard, waving them through. In the back of the car Monroe massaged his face, reviving himself as they picked up speed again, heading for Salzburg.

While the rest of the surveillance group kept a discreet watch over their target, Wolfe had his driver take them to the police headquarters, an ancient ochre fortress with open archways through which they passed into a crumbling courtyard littered with police vehicles. Soot-blackened windows and decrepit rusting drainpipes added to the generally dismal yard and when the driver had manoeuvred the BMW into a parking slot Wolfe went inside to make his number with the Austrians. Monroe and Rowley got out of the car to stretch their legs.

"I'm going to have to call the Yard soon," Rowley said. "Drake's going to be tearing his hair if he doesn't hear from me."

"Tell him everything's hunky-dory," Monroe replied. "Tell him we're up and running."

"Maybe I'll telex something short and sweet," Rowley said.

They sauntered out of earshot of the Polizei driver, who was lounging behind the wheel smoking a cigarette.

"What about Wolfe?" Rowley said. "D'you trust him?"

Monroe said, "I learned a long time ago never to trust anybody. Our friend Wolfe will be OK just as long as he's getting orders from above to cooperate. If the orders change, then we've got problems."

"What if he gets enough to shaft us?" Rowley asked. "He's not stupid."

"Well, we'll just have to stay one jump ahead," Monroe said. "Keep him guessing."

They turned and walked back across the cracked, oil-stained flag-stones as the BCI detective came out of the building. Wolfe said, "It's all OK. My friends here will turn a blind eye for the time being and my group will babysit the fat man." He smiled. "So it looks as if we've got some time to kill, my friends. Why don't we get some lunch and see the sights."

"This guy Monroe, this DEA agent you foisted on to me. I'm going to tell you something now. That's a very dangerous man we're dealing with," Kriminalpolizei Hauptkommissar Rainer Wolfe told his boss, Polizei Oberat Dieter Muller in the privacy of the latter's office at the Ministry of the Interior that evening.

In the booklined room where a couple of computer screens competed for prominence with several yards of leather-bound legal tomes, Muller sank back in an easy chair, rested an ankle on the corner of his desk and treated the detective to an amused smile.

"Too rich for your taste, eh, Wolfe?"

"You know what he did?" Wolfe continued, leaning forward and resting his hands on his knees. "Only took our prisoner up to Sudelfeld in the Edelweiss you laid on for him and then proceeded to throw him out of the chopper."

Muller jerked upright. "He did what?"

"I just told you," Wolfe said.

"Tell me again," Muller demanded.

Wolfe described in detail the somewhat unorthodox methods Monroe had employed to soften up Daniels, enjoying the change of expression on the lawyer's face. By the time he had finished, Muller was no longer smiling. "That adds up to attempted murder according to our penal code and you let him do it!" Muller exclaimed. "Who the hell authorized a stunt like that?"

"You did," Wolfe reminded him. "Visiting firemen, *carte blanche*, whatever they want. Remember?"

Muller shook his head slowly. "Jesus, if any of this gets out, the old man'd throw the book at us."

"At you," Wolfe corrected. "As they used to say, I was just following orders."

A frown creased Muller's forehead. "Well, at least Daniels is not likely to complain, that's the one saving grace, and besides we could discredit him if we had to. What are our friends up to now?"

"They've got Daniels on a long leash." Wolfe told the story. "Took him over to Salzburg so that he could set his business in motion again. Oh, it's OK, I looked in on Gruber over there and cleared the lines, nothing that's going to cause us any embarrassment. The way this Daniels tells it, this Enterprise is going to bring in snow like an avalanche. They're going to bring it in the back door through Spain and Turkey and we're the jumping-off point for the United Kingdom. I'd say that's something we ought to be thinking about, visiting firemen or no visiting firemen."

Muller digested the information, steepled his fingers. Then he said, "I'm just thinking out loud, Rainer, but could we do anything ourselves, I mean independently?"

"What happened to the guiding light? The orders to cooperate?"

"Oh, I'm only talking hypothetically, you understand; exploring possibilities."

Wolfe said, "Well, that's good, because as of right now I'd have to say, not a chance. The problem is, there's no way we can make the link between Daniels and his next contact, we'd need that at least, because the way they've set this up, there only has to be one slip and everything evaporates into thin air. From what I can gather, this Enterprise is a very cautious organization. They've built in cut-offs for every eventuality and if we tried to move in at this stage we'd be clutching at air. I'd say if you want my assessment, we just don't have enough."

Muller swung his leg back on to the desk, relaxing again. "See, the way I look at it, Rainer," he mused, "is that if we let a big shipment of drugs, cocaine in this case, slip through our fingers, whatever else we've been doing in the name of European cooperation, we're not exactly going to be hailed as conquering heroes here in our own backyard. Am I right?"

Wolfe said, "Is this still hypothetical?"

Muller said, "Just thinking out loud again."

"I thought you said the old man expects us to do the donkey work and hand this one on. I got a very clear impression on that," Wolfe said.

"Well, that's one way of looking at it," Muller replied, "but that's an area which could get a little blurred. I mean, the Minister's a political animal, at the end of the day he's thinking votes and that's all he's thinking. OK, so someone up the line is nudging him right now, maybe calling in past favours, let's say. So on the face of it he's got to appear to be doing what's required. But there are all sorts of nuances, Rainer my friend, all sorts of shifts of emphasis. Now you can't expect an old political war horse like the old man to come right out and tell you what he wants, not in so many words. You have to look for the signs. That's what we're here for, to protect his back, make sure all our best interests are served. You see what I mean?"

Wolfe shrugged. "I'm just a simple detective," he replied with heavy irony. "I don't go in for all this wheeling and dealing. I just get on with the job, and that's getting more difficult by the day."

Muller said, "Your practical experience then. In a perfect world what would be the best way for this thing to work out for us which would also get our revered leader the maximum leverage?"

"We bust the drugs, obviously," Wolfe replied.

"Exactly." Muller unbuttoned his tunic and eased himself into a more comfortable position. "Several million DM in cocaine would be a sizeable feather in our cap. How do you imagine we could achieve that?"

Wolfe said, "That depends on just how subtle you want to be. The visiting firemen have got Daniels where they want him and he's doing his stuff for them. Down there in Salzburg he was hammering digits into an IBM like there was no tomorrow. When he comes back and meets his contact they'll have it sewn up. Now we could jump in and cut them out, only I imagine that would bring some squeals of anguish from our cousins at Scotland Yard, and the old man, having given his word, wouldn't be exactly impressed."

"So we're on the horns of a dilemma," Muller said. "Let's try a more subtle approach. We let them keep Daniels; after all, that's what we agreed to do; and we let them think everything's going their way only when the time comes we step in as a matter of overriding priority. I'm only speculating, of course, but could we arrange something like that?"

Wolfe thought about it for a moment. Then he said, "We'd need another source of information, someone other than Daniels, otherwise it would be too transparent. We'd need somebody who knows the score but would be working exclusively for us, so that if it came to it we could demonstrate our good faith."

"My sentiments precisely," Muller said stroking his chin. "Now who do you think that person could be?"

"The woman," Wolfe replied immediately. "Daniels's girlfriend. There had to be pillow talk with a slob like Daniels, so she's in the picture, no doubt about it."

Muller clasped his hands behind his head, a roguish smile playing on his boyish features. "Kristabel Rosche. Could we persuade her to join us?"

"We might," Wolfe speculated. "We'd have to offer her something worthwhile. It'd be a risk, of course, but we could give it a try."

"Everything in this life's a risk," Muller observed. "What sort of time-scale are we talking about?"

"Hard to tell," Wolfe said. "Monroe's going at it hammer and tongs as they say, and Daniels is nervous as a kitten. Couple of days, three at the most. That'd be my best guess."

"Then we'd better get to work on Kristabel. We could offer her immunity from prosecution, drop the vice charge, guarantee no future harassment provided she plays ball. I could maybe get the old man to square that judge. We could tell her she either sticks with Daniels and goes to prison or she throws in with us and gets a licence to operate her skin game. What do you think?"

"Up to you," Wolfe said. "You're the ladies' man. Why don't you have a cosy little chat with her? I'm sure you'd be good at that. I'd do it myself only she might not be too impressed with my bedside manner and besides I'm going to have my hands full keeping tabs on the firemen." A slow grin spread across his face. "You know where this meet with Ryker is set up?"

"The way you're looking like the cat who got the cream I'm sure you're going to enlighten me," Muller said.

"Would you believe Berchtesgaden?"

"The Eagle's Nest?" Muller raised an eyebrow.

"The very same. And I get the impression this Ryker character is going to prove to be a really sharp operator. He's got all the angles covered. I've got a feeling our visiting firemen are going to have their work cut out with this one."

"Well, that suits our purpose," Muller replied. "Let's maintain full cooperation, meanwhile I'll see what I can do with the lady and start cooling down the old man. I get the feeling in my bones that this could swing our way."

They concluded the meeting and Wolfe picked up his jacket and took his leave. He went down the deserted corridors of the Ministry, his footsteps ringing on the parquet floor, and stepped outside through the security gate in the fortified entrance to the building. Wolfe paused for a moment under the floodlights, breathing the night air and watching the traffic stream by on the M-Strasse. The old Ministry building was set back from the road behind a wide plaza crisscrossed with low walls and walkways which had all the appearance of a landscaped pedestrian precinct but in reality served a much more practical purpose, for it had been designed to protect the Ministry from the car bombers who had marked it down as a prime target during the heyday of Baader-Meinhof.

Even now two Bereitschaftspolizei, turned out in their green leather greatcoats, fingers hooked in the trigger guards of Heckler and Koch submachine-guns, stood guard beside the entrance.

Wolfe hesitated for a moment as he re-ran the conversation with Muller through his mind, wondering at the devious nature of the power games they played at the Ministry. Suddenly out on the M-Strasse there was a squeal of tyres as a VW Mini-bus swerved across the traffic. Just another drunken driver, Wolfe thought, rationalizing the tension which fluttered across his midriff. In the same split second the guards were equally startled and Wolfe saw himself in the same uniform, back at the airport watching the Pumas burn as Black September massacred their hostages and fought a gun duel with the Bundesgrenzschutz. He felt the old flash of impotent rage and spent a few seconds calming himself before buttoning his coat against the sudden chill of the night. He flipped a salute to the sentries, whose young fresh faces had also relaxed. Wolfe walked past them thinking to himself that they had never seen the asphalt running with blood. But he had and the sight had forever stained his memory.

12

Five kilometres into the Bavarian Alps from the town of Berchtesga-den, the Kehlsteinstrasse began its steep, dizzying, hairpin ascent of the mountain from which it took its name. Carved out of the rock in a triumph of German engineering, the Kehlstein Road had but one desti-nation: the Eagle's Nest.

Only purpose-built Mercedes coaches were permitted on the road, weaving through the tunnels and around the twists and turns of the sheer bends poised between the pale rock and oblivion, climbing the four miles from 3,300 feet to the summit at 5,630. On the mountain the powerful Kehlsteinhaus coaches ruled supreme. All other forms of transport had to be left at the Hintereck car park at the foot of the peak.

At mid-morning a frozen food truck manoeuvred into the car park and positioned itself unobtrusively among the rows of air-conditioned tourist buses. In the cab, an overalled driver took out a copy of *Der Spiegel*, ostensibly taking his regulation break on a transalpine journey. Behind the cab of the tractor unit a generator hummed softly, to all intents and purposes supplying power to the refrigerated trailer embla-zoned with a fast food decal. The appearance of the truck effectively disguised its true purpose. Big Boy Burgers concealed a Surveillance Mode and Retrieval Technology, electronic surveillance unit of the Bavarian Bureau of Criminal Investigation. Concealed behind the fi-breglass spoiler above the cab was a communications dish linked by coils of cable to a self-contained compartment within the trailer which housed an array of computerized eavesdropping equipment. Inside the soundproofed compartment two detectives perched on pull-down seats and concentrated on a bank of video monitors.

"Pity this was such a rush job, Sergeant," Kriminal Hauptkommissar Rainer Wolfe apologized to Tony Rowley, "or I could have shown you some fancy tricks with our SMART equipment."

As he spoke, Wolfe tapped instructions into the on-board microcom-puter's keypad and lines began to run across the screens, building up an electronic mosaic which promised to materialize into a picture. "Any

minute now we're going to get pictures clear as *Dallas* on the TV,"
Wolfe said, his fingers moving swiftly over the keys, following the com-
mands on the status line. Rowley watched the computer painstakingly
search for the picture. "That's pretty impressive," he complimented
Wolfe. "Beats the old stake-out routine hands down."

"The advantage is you don't have to be there," Wolfe said. "Cuts
down all the old risks of blowing a cover." Wolfe was still concentrating
on the status line. He had taken considerable pride in explaining the
system to the Scotland Yard DS, for ever since Daniels had revealed the
location of the meeting place, six of his best men had been surrepti-
tiously working around the clock concealing SMART optics in and
around Hitler's old mountaintop eyrie. A low-power laser was used to
beam the signal to the opposite ridge where Charlemagne's slumber
was scarcely disturbed by a hikers' camp concealing more BCI techni-
cians, who were now concentrating on lining up their antennae with
the parked surveillance truck. Steadily the computer enhanced the picture line by line across the monitor screens.

"We don't believe in taking unnecessary risks, not when we have the
technology to do the job for us," Wolfe said, raising his eyes from the
screens.

He gave Rowley a curious look, nudging towards the subject which
was uppermost in both their minds: Jack Monroe's stubborn insistence
that he should go alone to the Eagle's Nest; that he had personally to
witness the meeting between Daniels and the next link with The Enterprise, the man called Ryker. With SMART making such legwork
unnecessary, Wolfe had at first felt professionally slighted, imagining
the DEA agent was not impressed with the latest German technology.
Now he wasn't so sure. His instincts pointed to another motive.

"Nobody wants to take risks when they don't have to, not in this
business," Rowley agreed.

Wolfe turned to face him, a question in his eyes. "Your friend
Monroe, you've worked with him for some time?"

"Why'd you ask?" Rowley dodged the question.

"Oh, I was just curious. Just wondering what made him tick. You'd
think, the way he goes at it, you'd think this business with the fat man
was some sort of personal crusade. But if he keeps on like he's been
doing, I've got to tell you, chances are he'll take one risk too many and
blow it for all of us."

"He's probably just anxious, that's all," Rowley said. "This officer he was working with back home, policewoman who got killed. Monroe blames himself."

"Was it his fault?"

Rowley shrugged. "Who knows? More likely it was just one of those things that happen. Jack pushed his luck, but he wasn't really to blame."

"Are you a friend of his?"

"I only just met him," Rowley admitted. "Tell you the truth, I took the place of the girl that got killed. Sort of a minder."

"Is that why he's so damned pig-headed?"

Rowley glanced away. It was a good question and he let it hang on the air for a moment, recalling his one-sided telephone conversation with Commander Drake the previous night on what he assumed to be a none too secure telephone line. Too much time was ticking by, Drake had complained, the Helen Linden thing was going to blow in the news any time, and something spectacular was needed to deflect the flak. Get the spurs into Monroe, Drake had demanded, get some results. But with Monroe determined to run the Gary Daniels operation his own sweet way, Rowley was beginning to have misgivings of his own.

"Jack plays it pretty close to the chest," he told Wolfe without much conviction. "You know how it is, a thing like that happens, you're apt to become a little paranoid."

"So what if he frightens Daniels off?" Wolfe said. "He goes up there, shows out and everything falls to pieces. These drugs dealers cut out and we all end up with egg on our faces."

"Whatever happens, it's still Monroe's party," Rowley said, feeling obliged to defend his absent colleague.

"Pretty stupid, though, wouldn't you say? Risking the whole thing like this."

"You know how it is." Rowley shrugged. "Something like that happens, everything can get out of proportion. Maybe he just wants to feel right there in the saddle, thinks that way nothing else can go wrong."

"But in his shoes, would you go up there? If you didn't have to?"

"I don't know," Rowley said. "I don't like to take risks, that's for sure, not if there's another way."

"But Monroe doesn't give a damn, does he?" Wolfe pressed the point.

"It looks that way, on the face of it."

"Which means he's either foolish, which I doubt, or there's more to this than he's admitting."

"Like what?"

It was Wolfe's turn to shrug. "Who knows? All I'm saying is, if his judgement is suspect and he runs Daniels on to the rocks, then it's not just him. You and me, we could both go down with him."

Rowley made no reply and after a while Wolfe produced a wry smile. "You know, in Regensburg, where I come from, we have this dry wind, blows all summer long. In the end it drives you crazy. We call it the Föhn. The Föhn and our friend Monroe have got a lot in common."

Was Monroe crazy? Rowley wondered. A chancer, certainly, but crazy? Who could say.

Considering the possibility, Rowley was reminded of Dad Garratt. This was just the kind of ego trip Dad would have pulled without a second thought for the consequences. Relying on instinct rather than logic. No, not crazy, just blinded by delusions of infallibility.

Rowley shook his head but before he could speak the images suddenly crystallized on the screens in front of them and they were looking into the Eagle's Nest.

"What'd I tell you!" Wolfe's attention returned to the computer system. "Just like we were right up there."

Rowley glanced at his watch, saw that it was almost time for the rendezvous and looked over at the TV monitor covering the car park. The camera was built into the ventilator rotating on the roof above their heads and with each revolution the lens scanned the lines of vehicles for the target programmed into its memory. As Rowley watched, the rolling motion stopped and the camera locked on to a car which had just pulled into the Hintereck. The camera automatically zoomed in on a white Jaguar XJS.

"We're in business," Wolfe said, reaching out to tune the fine focus as the Jaguar backed into a parking space.

They watched Daniels appear from the car and glance casually around him. A woman got out of the passenger's side, her hair tied with a yellow scarf.

"Right on the button," Rowley remarked, watching the screen. "And the fat man's got company. Who's the lady?"

"Watch this." Wolfe tapped a key and brought the picture down on to the screen in front of him. He took the shot tight in on the woman's face, gave the computer a search command and sat back. The screen split, freezing the picture on one half and then producing a mirror image beside it, a Polizei mug shot. The cursor blinked, spelled out a name, Kristabel Rosche, and then listed a string of vice convictions.

"I'm impressed," Rowley said. "That's a neat trick. Teach this thing to think and we'll all be out of a job."

Wolfe adjusted the camera, and tracked the couple as they strolled towards the departure point. "Now all we need is a good look at Ryker and we've got the set," the BCI detective murmured to himself.

"Where's Monroe?" Rowley asked as the picture closed in on the waiting Kehlsteinhaus coach. Daniels and Kristabel Rosche stepped aboard.

Wolfe concentrated as he scanned the windows of the coach. "There . . . there he is," he said. "He's already on the bus."

On the Kehlsteinstrasse the yellow coach began its steep climb, engine growling in low ratio. As usual, every seat was taken with a full complement of passengers rubbernecking at the breathtaking view while the driver swung on the power steering, hugging the cliff face with the agility of a mountain goat to the accompaniment of a pre-recorded tape extolling how in just two years an army of three thousand workers had hacked the road out of the mountainside.

The Mercedes rounded a sharp bend, wheels inches from the sheer drop, and as if on command the passengers were treated to the view of eagles soaring in the abyss below. The driver smiled inwardly at the gasps of amazement behind him: the Kehlsteinstrasse never failed to delight. Automatically he glanced in his mirror to make sure they were all enjoying his show. At the back of the coach DEA agent Jack Monroe was playing tourist. He wore a quilted body-warmer over a woollen sports shirt and had a motorized Nikon with zoom lens slung around his neck. Just another tourist. But under a Velcro flap inside the jerkin was concealed a tiny two-way radio tuned to the surveillance net. This safeguard had been his only concession to the exasperated Wolfe when they had planned the strategy for the undercover operation. In truth Monroe had hoped not to alienate the German detective, but in the end he had insisted on playing the operation his way. He was determined to witness for himself the meeting between his new recruit and the next contact, not on some fancy TV rig, and that was all there was to it. In his time Monroe had seen some of the best gadgetry in the world break down at the crucial moment. Well, however Wolfe bitched and moaned, that wasn't going to happen this time, no sirree, there was too much at stake.

Monroe shifted his position, raised the Nikon and pretended to sight the camera out of the window. From the corner of his eye he kept watch on the fat man and his girlfriend up near the front of the bus. He was confident that Daniels hadn't spotted him and he intended to keep it that way. Ryker! Monroe frowned, projecting his thoughts ahead, trying to second-guess this new adversary as if playing a game of three-dimensional chess. The man was probably up there already, at least that would be the way he would play it in his position, the safe way, check out the location ahead of time. After all, that must have been the reason for choosing this mountaintop eyrie in the first place. Easy to reconnoitre, no surprises. Oh yes, a stealthy customer, this Ryker. Monroe chewed on his moustache. Be very careful, he told himself, show out now and it's all over.

Hauling up the last incline, the coach pulled into a turning space just below the ridge and the hydraulic doors hissed open. Monroe was quickly on his feet, shuffling down the aisle with the tourists, stepping down on to the Kehlstein, using the crowd as cover to shadow the couple. Easy, Jack, he told himself, nice and easy! Close tail, that's the name of the game, but if Daniels makes you, could be finis!

They bought tickets at a kiosk for the final part of the ascent to the Eagle's Nest. Monroe slid his 3 DM under the glass window and took his ticket from the attendant, then followed the line down the long tunnel driven into the mountainside, making sure there were always plenty of people around him. Silently he counted off the hundred and twenty-four metres until the tunnel opened out into a bulbous chamber under the peak where a cavernous ornate lift was waiting to carry them up to the Kehlsteinhaus perched above them. It was unlike any other elevator Monroe had ever seen. Panelled in polished brass and inlaid with a huge oval Venetian mirror to overcome claustrophobia, the lift was capable of carrying twenty people at a time and Monroe made sure that he was among the first to enter, stationing himself inconspicuously in one corner as the lift quickly filled up and the operator closed the door. They rose upwards, and despite the confined space he was still sure that Daniels suspected nothing as he watched the fat man and his girlfriend at quarters too close for comfort. He knew he was taking one hell of a risk.

When the lift hummed smoothly to a halt Monroe loitered for a moment and then followed his fellow passengers outside. Up here on the summit the mountain air was appreciably colder and as he took his first look he realized that the view was quite stunning. Alpine peaks purple shadowed, wreathed in a lace of mist, as far as the eye could see. The sky was azure blue and a little powdery snow had gathered beside the pathway which led to a flight of steps guarded by a wooden handrail above which the shallow-pitched roof of the Eagle's Nest was visible. Monroe waited for a moment, fiddling with the adjustments on his camera, making sure that Daniels and the woman were on their way. Then as he followed up the steps approaching the Kehlsteinhaus he wondered if they were already getting any of this on the TV down below.

"How long now?"

"Twenty minutes." Wolfe read the time off the status line.

"He's not going to show," Rowley said.

"Give him a chance, there's still time."

"How're our friends doing?"

"Drinking chocolate, taking it easy, no problems."

"I'm getting bad vibes on this. Looks like it's going to be a no-show."

"Easy, give him a chance."

"How're our friends doing now?"

"Relaxed, having a drink, no problems."

Rowley grimaced. "It's going sour."

"Wait a minute," Wolfe said.

In front of them the TV screen revealed the interior of the Kehlsteinhaus. There was plenty of activity as busloads of tourists in gaudy hiking gear moved about, getting themselves drinks and snacks on plastic trays and finding tables. Daniels and the woman had found a place at the rear of the rather plain-looking restaurant. They had hot chocolate and brandy in front of them. The fat man smiled frequently, apparently at ease. Tracking off to the left, they found Monroe beside a granite windowsill, sipping from a tall glass of lemon tea and pretending to take pictures of the view with his Nikon.

"They're going to spot him any time now." Rowley voiced his anxiety, suddenly sharing Wolfe's misgivings. "I can see it coming."

But now that he had the SMART system functioning, Wolfe seemed to have dismissed his apprehension. "Maybe not," he said. "Maybe this

Ryker likes to take his time, weigh it all up, make absolutely sure before he moves."

"Passed it by, more likely," Rowley said glumly.

"Why should he do that?" Wolfe glanced up. "He's got no reason to suspect anything is wrong. Look at that, just another day at the Kehlsteinhaus, lots of happy trippers getting their money's worth. Let's just be patient, give it time. You've got to remember—"

Wolfe's voice broke off as he jerked upright, suddenly attentive. "Hey, wait a minute!"

Instinctively Rowley leaned forward. "What! What've you got?"

"See the woman there." Wolfe was excited as he pointed to the screen. "There, just come through the door, suede jacket, hair scraped back."

"Yeah, I see her, but who is she?" Rowley asked, puzzled by the BCI detective's sudden excitement.

"Wait till she turns . . . there!" Wolfe froze the frame. A pale oval face with slanted eyes and a wide mouth pulled down at the corners. Wolfe's fingers stroked the keypad and the screen divided, the cursor drawing another picture from the crime intelligence data bank. A mirror image of the woman's face appeared followed by a stutter of text which read: *Terrorist Target. Anna Dorfmund. Active with Baader-Meinhof Group, now with Red Brigades. Wanted on Federal warrants for questioning in connection with terrorist offences listed in appendix C. Alert! Dorfmund is an active and dangerous terrorist. Approach with extreme caution. Notify GSG9.*

"Red Anna!" Wolfe spat the name, flipping back to the video and tracking the woman. "If she's mixed up in this, then we've got a whole new dimension to consider."

"What's she doing, is there anybody with her?" Rowley asked. Wolfe's excitement was becoming infectious.

"Let's take a look." Wolfe tracked the shot. "Hey, there, she's moving towards our people. Look at that, Daniels's ladyfriend's recognized her. She's going over."

"Then where the hell's Ryker?" Rowley exclaimed.

"There!" Wolfe replied immediately. "See, there, brown coat and fur hat." The optics danced, trying to close in on the target and meet the demands Wolfe was placing on the system. "Just let me get in on his face. Turn, damn you!"

"Think that's him?"

"Got a good chance. Look at them. They know each other." He tapped the keyboard furiously. "That's got to be Ryker. Come on, turn around!"

"Where's Monroe?" Rowley asked.

Wolfe flipped to one of the subsidiary screens and focused on the DEA agent. "Right where he was before," he replied. "And what's this . . . uh-huh . . . now he's got company."

"Can we warn him?"

Wolfe kept his face perfectly straight as he looked up at the Yard DS. "Not a chance," he said. "He wanted it this way, now he's on his own."

Despite all his experience of undercover operations, Jack Monroe was growing nervous. Lighten up, he urged himself, you've done this a million times, no sweat. He sipped fragrant tea and allowed the minutes to tick by. There were enough people around in the Eagle's Nest to preserve his cover, and although he was still confident that Daniels was unaware of his presence, he couldn't throw off the jitters. Unconsciously the DEA agent slipped a hand inside his shirt and fingered the dog-tags nestling against his chest like a touchstone to help him relax. Ryker! He muttered the name to himself and once again glanced over at the table where Daniels and the woman were sitting, willing the mystery man to appear. Monroe turned to the window and regarded the spectacular view. "Come on Ryker," he murmured, "where the hell are you?" When he looked back, a girl was standing at his table watching him with quizzical interest. Her brown hair was braided into a plait and she was wearing a red ski jacket with an alpine motif, but her most dramatic feature was a pair of vivid green eyes.

"May I join you?" Her voice had a musical note.

"Sure," Monroe replied, grateful for the diversion, and the opportunity to improve his cover. Looking at the girl, he realized that the bright eyes had to be cosmetic contact lenses.

"American?" She raised an eyebrow.

Monroe nodded.

"Me too," she announced, pulling out a chair and positioning herself opposite him. "Ellie Kellerman, Eugene, Oregon."

"Jack Monroe," Monroe said. "Sweetbriar, Virginia."

"Small world."

"Yeah, small world."

"I'm on this tour." She shrugged. "The usual tourist drag, doing Europe. If it's Tuesday it must be Belgium." Laughter tinkled in her throat. "Actually this is the part I've been looking forward to. I'm a modern history buff actually, can't get enough of it." She looked around her. "I just had to see this place. Isn't it something?"

"Yeah, it's certainly something," Monroe said.

Bright eyes widened. "Did you ever think we could be them, you know. Adolf and Eva, Hitler and Eva Braun, sitting up here on the top of the world. Like a time-warp or something, making history?"

Before Monroe could reply she said, "Listen, screw up your eyes and imagine it. Sitting together on the window-ledge looking down on the eagles and the Reich, doesn't it bring you out in goose bumps?"

Laughing at her enthusiasm, Monroe felt himself disarmed by the careless familiarity of the American female abroad. The total lack of inhibition, the eagerness to impart newfound knowledge. As she prattled on, he found the encounter therapeutic.

"You know, Jack—you don't mind if I call you Jack?—they only came up here a dozen or so times and never for more than a couple of days at a time, isn't that fantastic, and she used to make home movies out there on the terrace. Right there. My stolen moments with the Führer. I'll bet they were a gas."

"I'll bet," Monroe agreed.

"Of course this was a house then, no Coca-Cola parasols. Did you know this was going to be his tomb? The Eagle's Nest? Hitler was going to lie here forever right opposite Charlemagne. Like a legend."

"Delusions of grandeur," Monroe suggested, sipping his tea and snatching another glance at Daniels.

"Now look at it," Brighteyes said. "Not a swastika in sight to remind you of those days. I poked around and all I could find was an iron fireback in one of the rooms in there with 1938 on it."

"That's the way it goes with history," Monroe said.

"They even say there was a U-Boat engine in the rock underneath us which could be used as a generator if the snows cut the power. I asked the guide if we could see it, but he just pretended he didn't understand. These Germans are so sensitive, don't you find that?"

"Maybe they've got something to be sensitive about."

"You know," she said, lowering her voice to impart a further treasure, "there was nearly no Eagle's Nest at all. Back in the fifties us.

Yanks wanted to blow it up, raze the whole lot, blow away a piece of history. Can you imagine that?"

"You know the folks back home," Monroe said. "Hollywood rewrites the history books every chance it gets. Who needs the real thing?" He grinned at his own smugness, raised the glass to his lips and took another peek across the room. The table was empty. Shit! He'd been lulled too deep. Quickly he scanned the room, but there was no sign of Daniels or his girlfriend.

"What's the matter, Jack?" the girl exclaimed. "You look like you just saw a ghost."

"I just remembered something." Monroe was on his feet, moving, trying not to draw attention to himself, cursing his own carelessness.

"Hey!" Brighteyes called after him. "I was only kidding!"

Smarting at his ineptitude, Monroe walked quickly through the crowded restaurant, working out the angles. There was only one route they could have gone, he determined, out on to the terrace. He dodged through the French doors, felt the chill of the mountain air like a slap in the face after the heavy warmth of the restaurant, crossed the flagstones to the guard rail for a better view, looked out, soaring above a diminished world, swung back to survey the shallow-pitched roof of the Kehlsteinhaus and swore viciously under his breath.

The second time around he spotted them, strolling down one of the pathways which crisscrossed the summit, raised the Nikon for a view through the zoom and fired off a couple of shots. There was a woman with them, sallow-faced, hair scraped back, and the glimpse of another figure in a corduroy coat and a fur hat. Ryker?

He let the motorwind run a few more frames as he cursed his own stupidity, then hurried after them, but by the time he reached the spot, they had disappeared. The path ended at a viewing platform poised over a sheer precipice. Beyond, the ridges of the mountains were sharply etched against the sky, breathing wispy trails of mist and cloud. They must have doubled back, Monroe reasoned, and he swung around, again using the Nikon's zoom to scan the scene until he caught sight of them in the distance, climbing the steps to return to the Kehlsteinhaus terrace. Angrily he fired off the rest of the film.

Abandoning caution, Monroe hurried back, only to discover that the fat man and his companions had again slipped away. Back on the terrace he forced himself to recover his composure. Were they putting on this game of hide-and-seek for his benefit? Had he been spotted?

Was this all some elaborate precaution to lose a tail? Anything was possible.

Carefully Monroe surveyed the crowd in the Kehlsteinhaus. A troupe in colourful Bavarian costume was entertaining the trippers. Bright cagoules and anoraks swirled in a kaleidoscope of colour. Then he spotted them in the crowd. Daniels's girlfriend and the second woman, heads close together in conversation. Desperately he looked around and caught sight of a door marked with a toilets sign swinging on its hinges. For Chrissake, it had to be!

A heavy-set man in costume was playing an accordion, squeezing out traditional mountain music as Monroe elbowed his way through the crush, pushed through the swing door and found himself in a blind corridor with further doors which led off into the toilets. He went through the one marked *Herren* and looked around, taking in the dazzling white tiles, the rows of cubicles, the urinals and the washbasins, the wide sinks which Wolfe had quaintly described as for use when "the food is falling out of the face." The tang of disinfectant stung his nostrils and the place shone with spotless German hygiene. But to his astonishment the washroom appeared deserted, and competing suddenly with his frustration, Monroe felt an overwhelming urgency to micturate. Suckered, he thought as he stepped up to the urinal and hurriedly began to relieve himself; somewhere along the line he had been suckered, but where?

Monroe was occupied with the problem, the ache in his bladder subsiding, when out of nowhere a forearm fastened around his throat in a grip like a steel bar. The shock of the attack was absolute and all Monroe's survival instincts immediately tripped into automatic, sending a jolt of adrenalin into his muscles. Instead of struggling against the throttling grip, he sagged forward, using his weight to throw his assailant off balance. Surprise caused the stranglehold to relax for an instant and sour breath brushed Monroe's cheek with a grunt of astonishment. That split second was all the DEA agent needed. He drew his right arm across his body, grasped the fist with his left hand and using the combined strength of both arms drove his elbow back with all the force he could muster. The pile-driver rammed home and produced a winded gasp. Monroe instantly transferred his weight to the ball of his left foot, spun around and delivered a karate kick, aiming high and blind, the heel of his shoe slamming into the face of his unseen attacker with a crunch of fractured cheekbone. A black cape flapped as the force of the piston kick sent the figure of a man cannoning off the wall to slide down on to the tiled floor, pawing at the soggy bloodsmeared mush of nose and mouth. Not a word had been exchanged and with the same mechanical efficiency Monroe followed up, grabbed a shock of blond hair and jerked the head up. The smashed face belonged to a man of no more than twenty, the staring eyes registering pain and disbelief. With a flick of his hand Monroe cracked the youth's head against the wall and saw consciousness fade from the eyes. Grabbing hold of the cape, he dragged his attacker across the floor, humped him into one of the cubicles and slammed the door. No more than ten seconds had elapsed. Monroe blinked as he regained control of himself and without looking back he zipped his fly and walked out.

In the Kehlsteinhaus the noise level was high and boisterous. Daniels and his girlfriend were back at their original table, talking and drinking. There was no sign of the other woman or the corduroy coat and fur hat which must have been Ryker. Monroe cursed himself. He went out on to the terrace and leaned against the guard rail, recovering his composure, staring at the purple mountains. Then despairingly he reached inside his body-warmer and yanked open the Velcro flap, fumbling for the hidden radio. Time to call it a day, the bird had flown the Eagle's Nest.

13

Wolfe drove the black Manta GTE in a fast dash down to Berchtesgaden, the Opel's tyres squealing on the winding alpine bends.

"You got yourself mugged," he told Monroe without bothering to disguise the irony in his voice. "That kid pegged you for an easy mark and hit you when you least expected it."

The DEA agent shook his head, still feeling a little groggy. "Just a mugger, huh." He rubbed his throat, which was still sore from the stranglehold. "Yeah, had to be. At first I thought it was one of their people, even Ryker himself. Until I saw his face."

Leaning forward from the back seat, Rowley said, "Lucky for you, Jack."

Monroe said, "Yeah, lucky for him too. If I'd had a piece I'd've wasted the little prick. I was on auto all the way."

"You do know you could've botched the whole operation, taking a risk like going up there on your own?" Rowley said. "One false move was all it needed."

Monroe turned to Wolfe. "Have you got an opinion on that too?" he asked defensively. "Might as well clear the air on that point right now."

But the BCI detective merely shot him an amused glance. "You don't think I was going to leave you to blunder around and screw up the works? We were tighter on you than your shadow, and you didn't know it, did you?"

He looked back to the road, taking the curves without slowing speed. "Only the kid in the cape hit you the one place we couldn't cover."

"How's that again?" Monroe asked in surprise.

But Wolfe merely chuckled. "You'll see," he replied mysteriously as he swung the Manta into the yard of the Polizei Inspektion at Berchtesgaden.

Inside the station cheerful shafts of sunlight slanted down on to parquet floors and pine panelling. The Kriminal Hauptkommissar greeted the uniformed man behind the desk and then led them through to the detectives' quarters at the rear of the station. In the main office a group of villainous-looking characters were gathered around the usual clutter of desks and from their midst a girl turned to look at them as they walked in. Brighteyes!

Monroe recognized her at once. "Well, well," he murmured. "The little lady from—where was it again—Oregon, wasn't it?"

It was Wolfe's turn to laugh. "Let me introduce you to your shadow," he said. "Kriminal Kommissar Lisa Weisbrodt, one of my best detectives."

"My apologies, Herr Monroe," the girl greeted him seriously. "I should have looked after you better." She no longer feigned an American accent. "But you took care of that boy without our help. By the time the paramedics got to him he had practically swallowed his face. He'll be eating lunch through a tube for a week or two." She shrugged eloquently. "You gave me a scare, though."

Monroe grinned a little sheepishly. "Tell you what, honey," he said, "with that act, any time you want a part on Broadway, give me a call. Where'd you get Eugene, Oregon?"

"One Flew Over the Cuckoo's Nest," the girl replied. "I'm a Ken Kesey fan."

Wolfe dismissed her with a few words of German and then sank into a leather chair, his face shining with good humour as his group formed an expectant semi-circle around him. They wore workmen's clothes or casual outfits, jeans and leather jerkins, and had a carefully contrived unkempt appearance about them, studded belts and wrist straps, earrings and bikers' boots. Wolfe took his time enjoying a pinch of snuff, the self-satisfied smile still playing around his mouth.

"Gentlemen," he began, "it would be unforgivable of me not to introduce you to our visiting firemen." He adopted Muller's expression with glee. "Today they have unwittingly done us a great service."

Monroe and Rowley exchanged uncomprehending glances as Wolfe waved a hand towards them. "Federal Agent Monroe from the United States Department of Justice Drug Enforcement Administration, and an English cousin, Detective-Sergeant Rowley from New Scotland Yard. Come along now, I'm sure you will wish to welcome our guests in Bavarian style!"

One of the group, a giant with a gleaming gold tooth and a shaggy black beard, produced a jug of apple brandy.

"Ah-ha," Wolfe exclaimed as generous slugs were sloshed into paper cups. "I'm glad to see you ruffians haven't lost all your manners." He raised the cup which was thrust into his hand. "As I said, our friends have today presented us with a gift in kind. While we were playing the gamekeeper with our SMART electronics and Herr Monroe there was indulging himself in a little unarmed combat, who should pop up?" He paused for dramatic effect, watching their expectant faces. "None other than Red Anna!"

They raised their cups in silence and toasted the name, tossing back an inch or so of fragrant firewater in one swallow.

Rowley followed suit, the jolt of raw spirit burning his throat and bringing tears to his eyes. Scowling at Wolfe, Monroe left his drink untouched.

"Drink, my friend!" Wolfe chided him. "While you were taking the air at the Eagle's Nest we were getting pictures of your man Ryker and his charming lady companion, Anna Dorfmund, who only happens to be one of our top terrorist targets. For the best part of a year we have been waiting for Red Anna to reappear and now, thanks to you, we have her in our sights once again and this time my group here will stick to her like a second skin. You have done a service to the noble State of Bavaria and we salute you!"

Slowly Monroe picked up his drink and toyed with the paper cup. "What about Ryker?"

"Ryker! You shall have your Ryker," said Wolfe airily. "Our little covert operation this morning has produced some excellent data for our crime computers. Now that we have the man who calls himself Ryker in our databank, I can tell you that he is identical to one Richard Ellman, a businessman with an American passport who moves freely in and out of our country. Now that we have identified him as a target, we can watch him with ease."

"What about the fat man?" Monroe asked. "Where does Daniels fit into your plan?"

"Do you care?"

"Look, I've invested time and trouble in his re-education. By rights he's mine."

Wolfe spread his hands. "Then you shall have him. He's of no particular interest to us. Apart from his unsavoury sexual activities, he's just a lightweight. As it was he who inadvertently led us to Red Anna, then he will be suitably rewarded. I shall recommend that we let him off the hook, drop all charges. He's earned it."

"Very generous," Monroe said. "But he's not finished yet."

Wolfe's lip curled. "No," he said, "you're quite right, he's not finished yet. But the game has changed. Now we have a new priority, a particularly ruthless terrorist."

"Didn't I say there'd be something in this for everybody?" Monroe said, choosing his words with care, playing the German's game. "What do you propose to do now?"

"Ah, we must be patient, my friend," Wolfe said. "Patient as the fox in winter. First we must examine the details. For instance, our analysis of the video of the Eagle's Nest has shown how the eye can be deceived. While you were preoccupied with Ryker and the fat man, it was the women who were completing the transaction. A floppy disk changed hands, no doubt containing coded computerized instructions. Soon enough Daniels will feed that disk into his IBM to learn what he must do next." Wolfe smirked. "But we shall know too. We have just installed a tap into his modem. His secrets are our secrets."

"Very neat." Monroe raised his paper cup to the BCI detective. "So what do you propose we do in the meantime?"

"Why, we go back to Dachau and prepare for busy days," Wolfe said. "As Muller promised, you have our hundred per cent cooperation. Now we are truly working together." Wolfe took a fresh slug of brandy. "But first"—he raised his paper cup to touch Monroe's—"you insult my group if you do not share a drink with us."

All eyes were on Monroe as he returned the gesture and brought the cup to his lips. For a second, Jack Monroe stared into Wolfe's eyes. The German was playing a crafty game, no doubt about that, and from now on he would need to tread warily.

Monroe raised his cup. "Here's to Balzac's noblest profession," he proposed the toast, and tipped the spirit back in one quick gulp.

"It's a funny thing, slick," Monroe reflected. "Just before that kid jumped me, just a fraction of a second, when I had his stinking breath on me, I went for my piece, you know, reflex, just reached straight for it. The stupid thing is I knew I hadn't got it, but I still went for it." The DEA agent shook his head. "That's what made me really mad, grabbing at air, knowing all the time that it was a dumb thing to do. Hopping around in the can with my dick hanging out, reaching for a piece I didn't have. That got me so mad I just kicked shit out of the creep." Monroe wagged his head again. "How you guys manage to do the job without weapons beats me, the kind of bugs crawling out of the woodwork these days."

"We're going down that road, Jack," Rowley said. "Carrying guns more and more these days. The thing is, if you don't have a gun, you've got to have a sense of humour, otherwise you're finished."

They were back at Dachau that evening reflecting upon the events of the day in the guesthouse off the cobbled square just around the corner from the police station. Sitting at a long wooden table in the low-beamed bar eating spicy sausage and drinking light Bavarian beer which reminded Rowley of Elderflower.

"We've always had this tradition where we don't want firearms," Rowley said, "only it's wearing thin these days. You're supposed to go through the whole rigmarole before you can carry a gun or get armed back-up. It's getting to be pretty much a farce, though. Mainly you don't bother with all the red tape, you've got a situation where you need a gun, you carry one anyway, unofficial and the hell with it. You know, Wolfe's got a Walther PPK in that leather purse he carries around. Pull the flap it jumps into your hand."

"I prefer the man-stopper," Monroe said. "Remington pump. Those toy pistols, you can put six rounds into the target area and he'll still be coming at you. One shell from the shotgun and the guy's stopped in his tracks. If you're going to do it, you might as well do it properly."

Monroe sipped his beer and Rowley changed the subject. "I had London on the blower. Drake wants to see some return on his investment. The way I read it, I'd say he's getting nervous and if he should get backed into a corner then he'll blow the whistle on the whole deal."

Monroe wiped his moustache with the back of his hand. "There's no way we can rush it now, slick, no way at all. We're going to have to give our fat man room to work. Jerk his chain and he'll come to pieces. Besides, we've got other problems."

Rowley raised an eyebrow.

"The Polizei are getting ready to dump us, I'd bet money on it. You see that keen look in Wolfe's eye? That Red Anna thing is just too convenient for my liking. We're being set up for a double-cross."

Rowley said, "You're imagining things, Jack. Wolfe does what he's told, and provided the fix is still in, where's the problem? It's Drake I'm worried about. If he decides to cut and run, then all the cooperation we've been getting is going to evaporate."

"Maybe I am imagining things," Monroe said, "but we're coming up to crunch time. If Daniels delivers, then Wolfe and his masters are going to want a slice of the cake. Why do you think they're making such a big deal out of this terrorist connection? Because if it comes down to it, they'll claim it takes priority. All previous agreements null and void. If they're as hot for Red Anna as Wolfe makes out, then when they make their move, everything else will go by the board. You know how it is over here, they are paranoid over enemies of the state."

Monroe leaned on the table. "All I'm saying is, when the fat man clinches the deal, we've got to keep an eye on Wolfe, because he's going to be watching us like a hawk. Look, why don't you see if you can keep Drake sweet for another day or two, because if we try to rush it now, we could lose everything."

"You still think the fat man's capable of delivering?" Rowley sounded doubtful.

"Well, he took us to Ryker, didn't he? I've got to admit that fancy gear Wolfe had going there produced some good identification on Ryker, Ellman, whatever he's calling himself. Now we've got him in the system, we can cramp his style any time we want to."

"I still don't like it," Rowley said. "The way Daniels was acting. Very casual, not like when he was with us, all screwed up. I've seen it with snouts before, personality disintegration. When the going gets too tough for them, they start to break up, become erratic. Then you might just as well forget it for what use they're going to be. All you're going to get from then on is fairy stories."

"Look," Monroe said, "we're still his best chance of coming out of this in one piece. He understands that. He knows what we can do to him if he fouls up. He's going to come through for us because he doesn't have any choice."

"I wouldn't bank on it." Rowley shrugged. "I still say that fat man could crack up."

"Well, what choice have I got?" Monroe's expression grew bleak. "There's people standing in line for a piece of my ass. I'm a long way from home, I've got no jurisdiction, and there's a bunch of good old boys with the light of glory shining in their eyes getting ready to rip me off." Monroe took a pull on his beer. "You want to trade places, slick? See if you could do better?"

Rowley leaned back. "Hell, no," he said, and grinned. "I'm only the minder, remember."

Later that night Jack Monroe slotted *Apocalypse Now* into the video player, stretched out on his cot in his room at the Dachau Inspektion and watched the picture materialize on the TV screen. It was near the end of the movie, or to be more precise, one of the several endings Coppola had experimented with. This was the cut they had printed. The Swift boat nosed through layers of mist banked down over the torpid river. White-daubed Montagnard tribesmen leaned on their spears, waist deep in the brown water, ghostly apparitions watching the boat creep past. Decadence and decay; silent brooding malevolence hung in the air. Willard leaped on to a ruined escarpment, devastation all around him, crumbling monuments, heads skewered on stakes. A lunatic combat correspondent with crazy eyes, his body festooned with cameras, took him to the hooch. In the deep gloom he could just make out the sweat-slicked Buddha inside. One bloodshot eye stared back at him.

Fingering the dog-tags around his neck, Monroe was transported back to Vietnam, to his perch in the massive tree overhanging the Song

Tra Bong. Time to saddle up, the green man told him, move down to the ville where the angel dust came and went. Time to get it done.

Monroe felt the deep thrill of anticipation as he followed his guide down the knotted limbs of the great ancient tree, humping his M16. On the ground the red clay clung to his boots. He steadied himself against a gnarled root as thick as his thigh, fitted a magazine to the assault rifle and drove it home with the heel of his hand. Lock and load.

The green man was watching him, berry-brown face under the filthy bandanna showing no expression. "Move out, Lieutenant," he drawled, "get it done." They edged down the trail in single file, moving into the deserted ville. The smell of cooking fires still hung in the air, wispy spirals of smoke. The hairs on the back of Monroe's neck began to bristle and his hands grew slippery on the black plastic grip of the rifle. It looked too damned easy.

As they went through the ville the green man indicated a bamboo hooch and motioned Monroe inside. It was dark in there. Entering from the sunlight, it took a few moments for his eyes to adjust. Dark shapes began to take form, piled high against the bamboo wall. Is this how they transported the dust, Monroe asked, part of him wanting to confirm the sight before his eyes, get the evidence, proof positive; part of him screaming, Get out! Run! Body bags, the green man confirmed casually. See, they boil the flesh, feed it to the pigs, grind down the bones, pack the empty body bags with angel dust, then ferry them up the river. Who's going to check? Just dead soldiers.

Monroe felt his skin crawl. Run, his conscience screamed, get the hell out of there, call in an air strike, bring in the Phantoms, diving in, avenging silver arrows dropping napalm. Radio the coordinates, wipe the filth off the face of the earth. Yet still he had to be certain.

The green man was reading his mind. He drew the bowie knife from the belt of leathery severed ears and offered it. Monroe took the knife as if in a dream, the last mind-screaming seconds of a nightmare before jolting awake. He stabbed the point into the nearest drab green bladder, pulled the knife back and a rivulet of white dust trickled out. Grade A cocaine, the green man said, Charlie's candy, angel dust, seven seconds to heaven.

Using his rifle for support, Monroe crouched down and watched the cascade form a pyramid on the dirt floor. Then it struck him. Not just the little people. There had to be Americans in this. Soldiers! He jerked his head up, exclaimed, "Hey! You know who's behind this!" Squinted.

The green man was in the doorway, just a silhouette against the harsh light, face hidden.

Monroe screwed up his eyes, squinted, saw only the TV screen. The face of the Buddha was taking shape in the gloom. He reached out and snapped off the set. Drenched in his own sweat despite the chill of the night, Monroe slumped back on to the cot, clutching the dog-tags in his fist. The old familiar ache gnawed at him. After a while he reached out with his free hand and groped for the airline bag, found the bottle of whisky, took a deep swig and waited for the alcohol to do its work and calm his shredded nerves.

14

Down below, the Bayern Motor Werke rose like a silver three-pack out of the urban sprawl, the initials BMW emblazoned on the clover leaf. Chunky glass and concrete office and apartment blocks melted into the red tile of the immediate suburbs. In the foreground the Georg-Brauchle-Ring rose on stilted flyovers and swooped through canyoned underpasses, feeding into loops of roadway around the landscaped lakes and meadows surrounding the Bedouin camp of the Olympic Stadium.

Cranked aloft on steel hawsers and strung between cigar-shaped pylons, a pewter metallic spider's web spread in peaks and troughs over a sculptured landscape crafted from World War Two rubble into the science fiction setting for the '73 Games. The area was now a leisure park presided over by the slender spire of the Olympic Tower.

A rocket ride in an express lift shied visitors up to the crow's nest restaurant and viewing deck perched above a bristle of communications antennae at the top of the sleek grey tower. The attraction was a perfect bird's eye view of the surrounding Olympiaberg and beyond the urban vista of metropolitan Munich.

Polizei Oberat Dieter Muller, dressed in fawn sports slacks and sheepskin jacket, leaned against the aluminium rail of the viewing deck and watched the mellow autumn sunlight glint off the gossamer web way below.

"You know, Rainer," Muller remarked, "Sunday mornings I used to bring the kids out here, here or the Englischer Garten, before they

grew up and became objectionable. Heidi in pigtails holding her dad-
dy's hand, begging for candyfloss. Now, you know what? She's got this
sound system puts out about a million decibels and her sole ambition in
life seems to be rupturing my eardrums." Muller shook his head.
"Happy days—where do they go, eh, Rainer?"

Wolfe lifted the shoulders of his blue reefer jacket in response. "You
want to think yourself lucky she's not blowing grass in your face or
staying out all night with a bunch of motorbike freaks who don't ever
wash or change their jeans."

Muller turned and gave the Hauptkommissar a smile. "So how'd our
cousins enjoy the show?"

"Outstanding," Wolfe replied.

Muller laughed. "Red Anna?"

"Who dreamed that one up?"

Muller rubbed his chin. "Well, the old man dropped a few hints,
nothing specific, you understand, and we took it from there."

"She's one of yours?"

"Sort of, Rainer, sort of. We had some help from Kristi Rosche,
bright lady, Kristi, she caught on quickly once we gave her some incen-
tive. All we needed was a look-alike we could feed in with Kristi, she's
got quite a creative imagination when she puts her mind to it."

Wolfe grinned. "Sounds like you've been sampling the wares."

"Who, me?" Muller feigned innocence. "Would I take advantage of
a situation like that? But I tell you something, Rainer, now we're getting somewhere with this drugs thing, now that it's shaping up into a
hard proposition, the old man's beginning to tack around with the
wind. He wants us in pole position if and when it comes off, but he
doesn't want us to go giving our friends across the water a slap in the
face, so you see we needed something that would give us priority. It
had to be anti-terrorism, scores the maximum points every time."

"What a devious web you weave," Wolfe remarked.

"It's the way of the world, Rainer. Anyway we slipped Anna's profile
into the Wiesbaden computer and you did the rest."

"I ought to tell my group it's all a leg-pull."

"No, you can't do that," Muller objected. "It's got to look a hundred
per cent kosher."

"Red Anna." Wolfe shook his head in amazement. "What if she
really puts in an appearance?"

"Not a chance," Muller replied. "We hear she's in Lebanon or somewhere out there where they eat bowls of sheep's eyes for breakfast, getting indoctrinated. We did our homework, Rainer."

"Yeah, but what if something changes and she does show up?"

"Wouldn't matter a damn. The facts are not what is important, the excuse is."

Wolfe looked out to the crescent escarpments of the Olympic village, which was now a honeycomb of apartments. "Whose idea was it to install Kristi Rosche in the Olympischesdorf?"

Muller smirked. "Modesty forbids," he replied. "Nice touch though, don't you think? Just the right ambiance, the informer and the whore, the terrorist and the drugs dealer."

"You ought to be writing soap operas for the TV," Wolfe replied. "You've missed your vocation."

Muller said, "All we have to do now is keep the heat turned up, keep everything simmering." He consulted his watch. "Damn, look at the time, got to pick the wife up at Schwabing, you've not met my Finni, have you, Rainer? Beats me what gets into a woman of her age, she's taken to wearing beads and kaftans, rebel without a cause. Keeps telling me I'm a stuffed shirt."

Wolfe said, "It happens with the ladies. At a certain time they all want to throw off their bras and become carefree hippies again. Got to be something to it."

"Yeah? Well, she's spending my stuffed shirt money like it's going out of fashion. So look, give me a quick rundown on the state of play and I'll be on my way."

Wolfe gestured towards the distant dorf. "Next thing I'm going to do is take our visiting firemen over there for a meeting with the fat man. No strain. He's going to tell them the story, draw 'em pictures if they want it. It's all set up."

"Don't forget, we've got to keep them sweet," Muller cautioned. "We certainly wouldn't want our good friends at the DEA or NSY to get any notion that we're selling them down the river."

"You mean it'll be pure coincidence when it suddenly meets all our specs," Wolfe said with a hint of sarcasm.

Muller ignored the jibe and continued to inspect the view. "There's another thing I've been meaning to ask you. Is Monroe still preoccupied with this Ryker character?"

"Oh yeah," Wolfe replied. "Every now and then I try playing pinball with him on that, throw Ryker into the conversation just to see how he reacts. Lights up every time, but tries not to show it."

"Now what would be behind that, do you suppose?"

"Search me," Wolfe said. "I don't have a crystal ball."

Muller frowned. "You don't think Ryker could be DEA, do you? On the inside?"

"Come on." Wolfe dismissed the idea scornfully. "Now you're getting into Hans Christian Andersen country."

Muller grinned. "I've got an over-active imagination, that's all."

"Definitely not recommended for police work," Wolfe said. "That way you either end up gobbling down the happy pills or nursing an ulcer."

Muller stretched, flexed his muscles and glanced at his watch again. "Jesus, I've got to run along. Keep in touch, Rainer. Anything comes up, I want to know about it. The old man's eager to see how this all works out."

Kriminal Hauptkommissar Rainer Wolfe drove his guests out along the Georg-Brauchle-Ring in his own undercover car, a black BMW 325i with special features not in the brochure which included light armour, interchangeable number plates which could be rotated automatically, a video surveillance system concealed under the nearside rear wing with a fibre optic lens hidden in the rear aerial which could be remotely focused, a voice-activated recording system which would both tape and transmit every word spoken hidden behind a St. Christopher motif on the dashboard, and a spring-loaded concealed compartment in the driver's door which held a Heckler and Koch machine-pistol.

Normally the BCI detective took considerable professional pride in showing off the car's capabilities, but today they were not uppermost in his mind as he swung into the underground car park at the Olympischesdorf, passing a telephone truck near the entrance which contained a troop of his own men who had swept the area for electronics prior to their arrival.

Narrowing his eyes, Wolfe felt his neck prickle as memories of this dimly lit place stirred in the recesses of his mind. He could actually see the drab olive bus waiting there as Black September brought their terrified hostages down from the village where the bloodbath had begun. In the shadows he could actually see Commissioner Schriber standing helplessly aside as the terrorists herded their hostages on to

the bus for the short ride to the waiting helicopters which would fly
them to the airport. The tension crackled like an electric charge as,
impotent spectators, the Polizei could only stand and watch. Wolfe had
to shake his head physically to clear the spectres from his thoughts and
concentrate on manoeuvring the car around the concrete pillars.

He drove slowly around the half-empty car park and stopped well out
of sight of the service road.

"You want to sit this one out?" Monroe suggested from the back
seat.

"Sure," Wolfe agreed amiably, taking a further moment to look
around, check the place out. "He's your guy." He glanced over his
shoulder at the DEA agent. "I'll stick here with the car just in case.
You can tell me about it afterwards."

"How about you, slick?" Monroe said to Rowley sitting beside him.

Rowley said, "We're the Siamese twins, remember. I'd hate you to
have a lapse of memory, Jack, forget a few details."

Wolfe looked into the rearview mirror, watching their expressions.

Monroe chewed on his moustache, then, making up his mind, said,
"Come on then, let's get on with it, see if our fat friend is ready to
graduate."

Monroe got out of the car and Rowley followed from the other side.
They closed the doors carefully, the snick of the locks echoing in the
silence, and then they walked slowly further into the gloomy recesses of
the car park. Up ahead a figure materialized from the shadows and they
recognized Gary Daniels standing there waiting for them to approach.
The fat man was wearing a grey three-piece business suit under a
smoke-grey trenchcoat and he looked remarkably cheerful and relaxed,
his fleshy face wreathed in smiles.

"Top of the morning!" he hailed the detectives as they reached him.

Monroe squinted into his face. "What's got you so chipper, hot
dog?"

Daniels laughed, slack-jawed. "Hey, come on . . ."

But Monroe's hand went out and grabbed the collar of his
trenchcoat, jerking the face up close. "Jesus! What did you do? You hit
the dust, didn't you! Got yourself a good mellow rush." He pushed
Daniels back against the rough concrete wall in disgust. "You stupid
bastard!"

Daniels said, "Hey!" and jerked himself free. "I took a little hit,
that's all."

"For Christ's sake." Monroe gave him a furious glare and balled one hand into a fist. "I ought to smack you in the mouth, you dummy."

"Hey, look, fellows," Daniels protested, his voice beginning to whine. "What'm I supposed to do? My nerves are coming unravelled, I swallowed your thing, so I can't even take a shit. I either fall apart or I get a little snort to keep myself on an even keel. Where's the harm?"

"You do your lines with your lady?" Monroe said. "Is that it? Your buddy Ryker handing out free samples?"

Daniels's eyes widened until the whites showed. "Ryker's gone," he mumbled. "It's all over."

Monroe grabbed the man's face, sinking his fingers into the pudgy cheeks. "Gone when . . . gone where?"

"Hey, look, I told you what was going to happen," Daniels said, "and it's happened just like I said it would. He took the morning flight to London, it's like I told you, leapfrogging ahead to the next stage."

Monroe turned and looked back at the parked BMW. Wolfe had sunk down in the driver's seat and had his head against the headrest. He didn't look at them.

Monroe turned back to Daniels. "Terrific." He ground out the word. "Looks like we're tagging along on your coat-tails, fat man. I ought to ream your ass."

Rowley placed a restraining hand on Monroe's arm. "Jack, what's the problem? So Ryker's gone, so what? All it means is the shipment's moving and nobody can stop it now. Isn't that right, Gary?"

Daniels nodded. "That's right," he confirmed. "That's what I came here to tell you." He straightened his coat and tried to look offended. "I'm here to complete my end of the deal. I've done everything you asked for. You don't have to give me a hard time any more. I'm delivering."

"Yeah?" Monroe sneered. "You want to be a junkie, be my guest. You want to freebase cocaine, let the angel dust addle your brain, that's your business, fat man, whatever makes your day. So let's hear it, what've you got for me?"

Daniels's cherubic features took on a crafty expression. "Before we get down to business," he said, "I've got to have some guarantees. When do I get my ticket out of this mess?"

"You've got the price, you get the ride," Monroe said.

Daniels looked at Rowley. "I want to go to New Zealand. What do you think?"

"You heard the man." Rowley shrugged. "You've got to make it worth our while, Gary, you know that."

Daniels's lips began to quiver and Rowley said, "Look, you're among friends here. We can work it out."

"Well—" Daniels breathed the word like a sigh of relief. "This is it. Ryker's gone and the shipment's on the move, Colombian mountain hundred per cent pure grade A cocaine." He giggled nervously. "That's the stuff dreams are made of. That hits the streets back home, there'll be no stopping it."

"But it won't, will it," Rowley reminded him. "Because right now you're the knight in shining armour, Gary. You're the hero who's going to stop it in exchange for a new life."

"What more do you want, fat man?" Monroe said. "A Purple Heart?"

Daniels shrank back from the rebuke, the heavy flesh of his face sagging into his jowls. "All I want is out," he replied.

"That's the deal," Monroe confirmed.

"And I want Kristi out too," Daniels blurted the request. "Otherwise no deal. It's off."

Monroe glanced at Rowley. "Touching, isn't it?" he said.

Rowley said, "You're all heart, Gary."

"With a cock for a brain," Monroe added.

"You've got to give me your word," Daniels persisted. "Me and Kristi. New names, new papers, New Zealand."

"You're jumping the gun," Monroe said. "But if this comes off, I'll make the reservations for the two of you myself, courtesy of Uncle."

Daniels turned to Rowley. "You heard what he just said? You're my witness on that."

Monroe shook his head in disbelief. "What d'you want, fat man? You want me to swear on the Bible? You want to get a lawyer down here and draw up a contract?" He jabbed a finger into Daniels's chest. "There comes a time when the music stops and you have to quit all this horsing around and actually do it. You've just reached that time. Now you either give what you've promised to give, or you take your lumps."

Daniels sagged back against the concrete wall. "What if—"

"No whats, no ifs," Monroe cut him off. "This is the time and this is the place. You're either in where we can help you, or you're out where we can cut your balls off."

Daniels sighed. "OK, OK. There's an airstrip," he began. "Down near Bad Tolz, out of the way down there. There's a plane, comes and goes all the time, nobody takes any notice of it. Twin-engined, Italian plane, blue and white, fitted with long-range tanks. If anybody does get curious and checks it out, they'll find it belongs to Blue Water Trust, a conservation trust on the face of it, but really another front for The Enterprise. Even if you read the logs all you'd see is Blue Water chartering all over the place, surveys, that kind of thing, filing all the necessary flight plans, everything above board."

He drew a deep breath and regarded the detectives, the sniff of coke he had taken to reinforce his courage still propping him up. "So this is the plan. Tomorrow, at noon, this plane takes off on another routine charter, flies up to Munich Riem, refuels in the aeropark and files a flight plan for a maritime oil pollution patrol. No one raises an eyebrow. Just Blue Water on its usual hobby horse, protecting marine life from oil slicks. So they take off and fly down the coast and out into the Channel."

"Guardians of the environment," Monroe said. "Just another bunch of ecology nuts. That's a cute move."

"These are very cautious people," Daniels said. "All the risks are compensated out."

"Yeah, but what about when they appear on our side of the Channel?" Rowley said. "They're going to have the coastguard, air traffic and possibly the military breathing down their necks. You can't just pop up in UK airspace. Once they cross the coast, lots of people are going to be asking questions and taking a hard look at them."

A secret smile formed on Daniels's lips. "They don't have to," he said. "You see, that's it, that's the clever part, they don't go near the coast."

Monroe's eyes narrowed. "How's that again?"

"They don't go near the coast," Daniels repeated. "That's the trick."

"You're going to tell me they go to all this trouble, then jettison the stuff into the ocean?"

"You've got it in one." Daniels snapped his fingers. "That's exactly what they're going to do. They come down low, like they're tracking a slick, some tanker's been clearing its tanks, that's what they're saying over the radio in case anyone's listening. The cocaine is sealed in a watertight container and when they're down on the waves they drop it into the sea five miles out and then head for home. Another Blue Water save the mackerel mercy mission accomplished."

"You're going to tell us they've trained a shoal of these mackerel to tow it ashore?" Monroe demanded.

"Oh, better than that." Daniels smirked. "Much better. There's a ship. Are you ready for this? When they drop the container into the sea the ship puts out a boat and picks it up and it's all over."

Rowley shook his head. "There's no way they could do that. The coastguard would be on to them. They'd be tracking a ship on radar, and besides—"

"Not this one," Daniels cut him short, suddenly eager to impart his secrets. "You see, this ship is like part of the scenery, nobody watches it because it doesn't go anywhere, it hasn't moved in months. Nobody takes any notice of it."

Monroe was losing patience. "Fat man, if you're jerking me off—"

"No," Daniels protested, taking perverse delight in their sceptical expressions. "There's a place off the coast, the coast of South Devon, called Torbay, five miles out from Start Point. It's called the tanker nest. It's where the big oil tankers lay up. What happens is, the oil companies have their tankers go into Rotterdam, they buy when the spot market's low, fill up with petroleum products, move the ship to the next, pay off the crew and just sit there as long as it takes for the market to rise, then they move in to a refinery and make their killing. Could be a year, could be two, sitting out there in the tanker nest with just a couple of crewmen and an engineer to keep things ticking over. Better than money in the bank."

The detectives exchanged glances, felt the spark of excitement rekindled. All of a sudden Daniels's story had the ring of authenticity about it.

"The Enterprise got on to this," Daniels told them. "Saw how they could exploit the possibility of using a tanker as a staging-post. Put their own people in, seamen and engineer, a chemist and lab technician to process the product and there they've got an offshore dope-processing plant. Drop the shipments in by air, then ferry street-cut supplies ashore piecemeal using the service tender which Customs don't bother about because it doesn't go anywhere. Familiarity is the key, and as I told you, these people are like the magic circle."

"This ship," Monroe said. "Does it have a name?"

"The *Petroqueen*," Daniels said. "Panamanian registered, been sitting in the nest for the best part of a year, just part of the scenery."

"Well, that sounds like some sweet set-up," Monroe concluded.

Now it was Daniels's turn to crow. "All you've got to do is sit there and wait for Blue Water to come in and unload into your lap and you've got The Enterprise." Elation shone in his eyes. "So does that do it? Do I get my tickets?"

Monroe said, "If this works out, you're on your way. We'll have our good friend Wolfe babysit you until it all goes down." He gave Daniels a playful slap on the cheek. "You can relax now, fat man, take your girl out to dinner, have a good time, you're on the payroll. You've just got yourself a new uncle."

Daniels extended his hand to Rowley. "Can we shake on that?" he asked. "Would make me feel better."

Rowley took the hand and Daniels clung on. "I've stuck my neck right out for you. I hope you realize what it's cost me."

Rowley said, "You did all right, Gary." He extricated his hand. "You kept your promise. Don't worry about a thing now, we'll take care of you."

They left Daniels and walked back to Wolfe's car. On the way Rowley said, "What d'you think, Jack?"

Monroe said, "Only one way to find out, slick, and that's check it out, see how it stacks up. Can your people put something together without making waves?"

"Shouldn't be a problem for a man of Commander Drake's ingenuity," Rowley said. "Only what about Wolfe, will he go along with this?"

"What he doesn't know he won't grieve about," Monroe said. "We'll get him to nursemaid our fat friend while we check this out, and if it happens the way Daniels says it's going to happen, we'll give him this end of the operation."

"You think he'll settle for that?"

"What else is he going to do? If it runs according to the timetable, he's going to be left behind anyway."

They got back into the car and Wolfe said, "How'd it go?"

Monroe said, "Good. The ball's rolling and we're right on top of it. We're going to have to get back to London and make some arrangements. Can you check on the flights?"

"No problem," Wolfe said. "There's a Lufthansa out every afternoon. I'll radio the airport, get a couple of seats reserved. Anything else I can do for you?"

"We'll fill you in on the detail on the way to the airport," Monroe said. "But if it all goes according to plan, you can get yourself ready to grab some bad men. They're falling into our hands."

Wolfe kept his own counsel as he started the BMW, eased the car out of the car park and began to drive back into the city. He could see no useful purpose in informing the visiting firemen that he already knew all the details they had just gleaned from Daniels because Kristabel Rosche had passed the information to Muller in return for a package of official favours. He could see no advantage in advising them that the world was full of cunning, self-serving schemers who would pull the rug from under the feet of their best friends without a second's hesitation if it suited their book. He presumed they understood the machinations of the power game, and cared as little for the dubious dealings of the hierarchy as he did. After all, they were just like himself, street cops, just doing their job.

15

Off Berry Head, under the shadow of the tall cliffs, the Customs cutter *Jezebel*, diesels idling, began to roll viciously in the choppy swell running in across the wide horseshoe of Torbay.

The seesaw motion of the naval-grey patrol boat did not unduly perturb the crew as they prepared to launch a raider inflatable from the port quarter, but in the spit-and-polish wheelhouse, clinging to a chromed stanchion as sea and sky wildly alternated, Detective-Sergeant Tony Rowley found himself growing decidedly queasy.

Concentrate on something else, he told himself, in an effort to ignore the churnings of his stomach, and eyes closed against the nausea, he began to review the events which had brought him to the rolling deck of the *Jezebel*. Wolfe had driven them out to Dachau to collect their gear and had then taken them directly to the airport and they had departed from Munich on the afternoon flight. At Heathrow there had been a hurried briefing before they travelled west to Devon, where under cover of darkness a combined police and customs raiding party had slipped out to the Torbay tanker nest and had boarded the *Petro-queen*. There had been no opposition from the skeleton crew, and the searchers had quickly found quarters in the crew island, which had been converted into a drugs processing plant with the capability of converting pure cocaine into crack, rock and a variety of designer drugs.

At first light Commander Larry Drake and a NEL task force had been ferried out to the tanker by Navy Sea King and everything was set up for the big bust. For his part, jet airliner, fast car and now the swaying deck of the Customs cutter had conspired to induce a sense of unreality which left Rowley light-headed.

Beside him, struggling to pull an orange immersion suit over the bulk of a borrowed pullover, DEA agent Jack Monroe glowered at the stocky coxwain, who seemed impervious to their discomfort and complained, "This is stupid, you know! Whose idea was this? Why couldn't you have taken us all the way out to that goddamned tanker instead of bucketing around here like the Texas navy?"

The coxwain gave Monroe a salty grin. "Orders, old son," he replied. "Lay up here, out of sight, and then put you across in the Gemini."

"Whose orders?" Rowley asked weakly.

The coxwain glanced at a scribbled note in the log. "Commander somebody . . . yeah, here it is, Commander Drake." He raised an eyebrow. "One of yours?"

Oh yes, Rowley thought, one of ours all right. If Commander Drake had materialized in front of him there and then he would have cheerfully grabbed him by the throat and throttled the life out of him, so acute was his seemingly needless discomfort, swaddled in his gaudy nylon suit.

The coxwain gestured through the spray-speckled windshield and said, "Your man Drake, good name for him, does he think he's going out after the Armada or something? All I could get from my people was a whole lot of special operations eyewash. We've been mucking around all night and all day running errands. Nobody knows what the hell's going on. Now they tell me lay up against the cliffs where you can't be seen and use the inflatable because it won't show up on the scopes against the sea return." He peered at the detectives as though inspecting something unpleasant. "What have you got on that tub out there that's so important anyway? You've kidnapped Gadaffi? The Russians invading?"

Monroe gritted his teeth, chewed on his moustache and tugged the zip of his suit up under his chin. "Let's just get on with it, skipper," he replied. "Before I throw my cookies all over your nice clean little boat, huh?"

The coxwain's grin turned malicious. "Be my pleasure, gentlemen." He shot a glance at the boiling rocks where the waves crashed against the foot of cliffs, which now seemed alarmingly close at hand, checked aft to ensure that the Gemini was in the water and gave his charges a mocking salute. "Your cab is waiting, my friends, and the meter's running."

They went down to the pitching aft deck, where practised hands were waiting to bundle them unceremoniously into the rubber boat which leaped and bucked against the side of the cutter as though determined to smash itself to pieces. The outboard barked into life, and leaning out from the wheelhouse rail, the coxwain called after them, "Give Commander Drake my compliments and tell him next time he wants to play silly buggers count me out!"

But the Gemini leaped away, guided by a hunched helmsman, and Monroe's obscene rejoinder was lost on the wind. Within seconds, before either Rowley or Monroe could recover their equilibrium, the inflatable was scorching across the waves, rearing like a demented bronco as it smashed into solid ridges of sea in bone-jarring leaps and bounds which drove the breath from their bodies. Paralysed with fright, the detectives could only crouch awkwardly and cling to the rope grab rails as the blunt rubber bow delivered its hammer blows to the unyielding rollers, duck their faces away from the stinging spray and heap fearful curses on the head of the lunatic responsible for their predicament.

In desperation, Rowley found himself muttering the lines of half-remembered prayers, but there was worse to come. When their nerve-ends shrieked with the certainty of imminent destruction, the helmsman expertly flipped the Gemini through a wide carooming arc and the outline of a ship, long and low, stretching back to a high stern island, abruptly came into sight, the unmistakable profile of an oil tanker. Larger and larger the ship loomed as they raced the last quarter of a mile, cutting a frothy white swathe across the undulating sea until, at the very last moment when collision with the rearing rusty hull seemed inevitable, the screaming outboard was throttled back and they swept alongside the towering red iron wall which threatened to swamp their puny rubber boat dancing in the ten-foot swell.

Petrified, Rowley could only stare at the rust-streaked hull, his mind refusing to function. A spindly scaling ladder swam into his field of vision, wooden treads lashed with rope, and as the last few feet of oily swell narrowed, he realized with a flash of dread that he was expected to climb this precarious stairway thirty feet up the vertical flank of the *Petroqueen.* The very idea terrified him, but as the helmsman skilfully manoeuvred the inflatable, Rowley realized there was no alternative but to leap for the flimsy ladder snaking upwards. But what if he missed? What if he fell? Rowley chanted his prayer faster, willing his muscles to respond, then glanced at Monroe for moral support. The American's narrowed eyes were also fixed on the ladder as he went through the same agonies, gauging the jump, beads of spray glistening in his moustache.

Faster and faster Rowley chanted, the words running into each other in a meaningless litany. The ladder swung towards him as the Gemini reared up and hung motionless for a split second. Now! He grabbed a rung and clung on as the inflatable dropped away, leaving him suspended, clinging with aching arms, babbling his incoherent prayer, scrabbling for a foothold as he bumped against the rusty iron.

Rowley began to climb frantically, hand over hand, self-preservation spurring him upwards, no time to stop, no time to think or he would have been finished: scrambling thirty feet up to the deck above his head, where hands hauled him aboard the *Petroqueen.* Relief flooded through him, blurring his first impressions: Larry Drake's theatrical greeting, a second face, vaguely familiar, peering at him with a patrician smile. Drake's lips moving but only snatches of what was being said making any sense. Rowley blinked and people were swarming around him, Drake clutching his arm, then thumping him on the back. Behind, Monroe was being hauled aboard for the same treatment. Nothing made any sense . . .

It was then, through his bewildered state, that Rowley spotted the television cameras, the hand-held lights flaring in his face. Instinctively he raised a hand to shield his eyes from the glare as he was propelled across the well deck and through an open hatch in the island and into a passageway which reeked of oil and made his stomach churn all over again.

In the bowels of the tanker the two detectives clambered out of their immersion suits and were then escorted up to the captain's stateroom, which had been commandeered to serve as the nerve-centre of the police operation.

It immediately became apparent that the ship was crawling with officers from the Narcotics Enforcement Liaison task force and at the same time Rowley recalled the identity of the face he had glimpsed on deck, the wan complexion, the lick of dark hair . . . and trailing a gaggle of TV crews! What the hell was going on?

Inside the stateroom Commander Larry Drake was waiting for them.

"Well, hail the conquering heroes!" The drugs chief grabbed each of them in turn and began pumping their hands. Drake was his usual urbane self despite the austere surroundings of the mothballed cabin. His chalk-striped Savile Row suit was immaculate and complemented by a maroon tie with matching show handkerchief spilling from the breast pocket. "Congratulations, congratulations," he enthused. "Sorry about the boat ride." His expression grew apologetic. "I said no way, but the telly boys insisted. Always got to have some drama, and you were the best we could rustle up in the circumstances." He spread his palms in a gesture of contrition.

"What in the name of Christ are they doing here anyway?" Monroe ground out the question, his voice menacingly low.

"Jack, Jack." Drake became soothing. "Trust me, OK? We didn't have a whole lot of choice. It was either a Press pool, or blow the whistle on that little *faux pas* of yours. Relax, they're hand-picked, people we can trust."

"In a pig's eye!" Monroe snarled. "Are you out of your mind? I give you The Enterprise on a plate and you're going to turn it into a fucking B-movie."

Drake sighed, concern furrowing his brow. "Jack, calm down. I can see how you might see it that way, but we've been running into stormy waters over that Helen Linden thing. You remember that, don't you? Pretty little thing. Heroine undercover policewoman cut down in the bloom of youth, just because some gung-ho narc got careless. That's the way the Press would interpret it, you know what they're like." Drake shook his head sorrowfully. "Remember I pulled your ass off the griddle on that one? But nothing lasts forever. Sometime or another you have to trade what you've got for what you don't want to see in print. This is it."

Monroe stood still, eyes blazing, fists clenched dangerously.

"Jack, grow up," Drake appealed. "This is the real world. You've got to give and take if you want to stay ahead in this game, these days. Nobody likes doing it, but in the end there's no other way." He smiled. "Look, just trust me on this. You and Tony there, you both did a grade A job setting this up. Nobody's losing sight of that, believe me. Nobody's taking any of that away from you. Only now it's a different ball game." Drake tapped his chest. "This end of it's my show, a hundred per cent NEL operation. This is where we make our reputations, and like it or not, these days that means publicity. Think of the image, Jack, the biggest cocaine bust of all time. It'll go around the world. You're going to be a folk hero instead of a cop-killing fuck-up."

Monroe looked over at Rowley, disbelief on his face. "Is this guy for real? Is this what we've just worked our tails off for, an all-channels TV special?"

But Rowley was staring at Commander Drake with the dawning of another realization. "Guv'nor, wasn't that Peter Ashworth, the MP, I saw up there?"

Drake turned on an artful smile. "Stamped with the government's seal of approval. Peter is our sponsor. Who d'you think's been keeping this sweet with the Germans? Freebase cocaine, that's the name of the game."

Monroe went white with anger. "We've been sapped, slick," he told Rowley bitterly. "Set up and sucker-sapped."

Unconcerned at the DEA agent's outburst, Commander Drake drew back a pristine white cuff and glanced at his gold Rolex. "Well, if you boys will excuse me," he said, "I'd better get back up to the bridge. Our friends should be up and running any time now." He rubbed his hands together and then added magnanimously, "Better still, why don't you join us? I've had some smoked salmon and canapés brought out with a few bottles of nicely chilled Chablis."

He gave Monroe a triumphant smile. "Spot of lunch might improve your health and temper, Jack. Besides, Peter is just dying to hear about your exploits."

Time was running out at Munich Riem. As the final minutes ticked by, Kriminal Hauptkommissar Rainer Wolfe felt the tension wind up inside him, tightening like a clock spring.

For two hours they had been watching a blue and white Partenavia P68C registered to the Blue Water Conservation Trust as the high-

winged twin-engined monoplane routinely took on fuel in the light
commercial park. Wolfe had waited for the plane to arrive from Bad
Tolz before deploying his forces.

A hand-picked team from his own group together with a troop of
GSG9 commandos had slipped out in an airport van under cover of a
taxiing Lufthansa 737 and had gone to ground in the long grass on the
far side of the commercial park.

Wolfe was sitting in a Grenzpolizei Edelweiss on the heli-pad beside
the airport police station from which he could unobtrusively keep
watch on the sleek Italian light transport. He was wearing a flying suit
and bone dome with internal radio linked to his men and also patched
into a secure telephone line to Polizei Oberat Dieter Muller at the
Ministry of the Interior in Munich.

The side cabin door of the Bolkow had been slid back and beside
him the helicopter pilot sat with his hands resting lightly on the controls ready to fire up the twin jet turbines. Across the airfield, behind a
fifty-foot perimeter cyclone fence, two dark-hulled Pumas of the
Bundesgrenzschutz were lurking, awaiting his command. The trap was
set. All Wolfe needed was the authority to issue the orders.

Through his binoculars Wolfe could see that the Partenavia was
preparing for take-off. For the hundredth time he thumbed the talk
button isolating his line to Muller.

"Any word from the old man yet?"

"Patience, Rainer, he's still giving it some thought." Muller's casual
response echoed in the earpiece of his helmet.

"Better make it fast, otherwise it's going to be too late."

"Listen, Rainer," Muller said, "you might not get a direct order on
this, you know. There's all sorts of diplomatic etiquette to consider
here. It's a fine line."

"Yeah, and there's big K's of cocaine out here, about to fly away."

"Well, you've still got the anti-terrorist angle."

"You want me to do it, then?"

"Hey, not so hasty! I didn't say that. Look, probably the best the old
man can do is give us a nod one way or the other. That's the most we
can expect."

"Well, he'd better hurry."

"The lines are open. I'm working on it."

Through his binoculars Wolfe saw the puff of exhaust smoke as the

Partenavia's twin Lycomings started up. Slowly the blue and white plane began to manoeuvre out of the parking area.

His thumb stabbed the talk button.

"They're moving. What do I do?"

"There's no word yet."

"Make up your mind."

"Look, Rainer, I'm going to go in there, see if I can get some indication, OK?"

"Be too late," Wolfe said urgently. "They'll be long gone any minute."

"Hang on."

On his own initiative Wolfe jerked a thumb to the pilot to start up and through the padding of his helmet he heard the swish of the blades as the starter whined and the turbines caught with a deeper roar. The pilot returned the thumbs up and Wolfe signalled him to wait, holding the button down again, straining for Muller's decision.

Out on the field the Partenavia began to taxi to the holding point.

"They're going," Wolfe said into the radio. "It's now or never, make up your mind or kiss 'em goodbye. Do you want me to do it or what?"

"I don't know," Muller said.

"What!"

"I just don't know. Do what you can, OK?"

"What do you mean? Shadow him?"

"Can you do that?"

"I suppose."

"Can you give me another minute? I'm going in there. See the old man."

Wolfe released the button. Mentally he cursed Muller and his chickenshit kind, mincing around without the balls to give the order. It hurt his pride to think of a big drugs shipment slipping out right under their noses while they watched it happen and did nothing just because some politicians had traded favours. It stuck in his craw.

The Bolkow spooled up and lifted into a low hover. Wolfe could see the blue and white Partenavia turn at the holding point and wait, running up the engines.

Over the command net he instructed his men to lie low and then gave his pilot brisk instructions. The face turned towards him, framed in the bone dome, expression questioning. Gritting his teeth, Wolfe told the pilot to get it done. The Grenzpolizei aviator returned his attention to the controls and the Edelweiss began to skim across the airfield, the slipstream snatching at Wolfe's flying suit as he reached behind him and took a Heckler and Koch machine-gun from its stowage clip, slotted a magazine into place and thumbed off the safety-catch.

When Wolfe looked back he could see the Partenavia was now travelling down the runway, picking up speed, but they were fast closing the tangent, and still without any clear idea of what he would do next, Wolfe buckled himself on to the abseil safety line and stepped out on to the skid as they came abreast of the moving plane. So close he could see into the windows below the high wing, could see faces, just pale blobs, staring back at him. He held the machine-gun across his chest in a warning gesture, but the Partenavia kept going. Wolfe cursed the ominous silence on the radio. No command was forthcoming. Muller had opted out.

Then it happened. Beyond the sleek fuselage of the Partenavia the olive green Bundesgrenzschutz Pumas suddenly popped up over the perimeter fence, the imagery so powerful that Wolfe's mind was snapped back to the memory of that fateful day when Black September had castrated the cream of the Bavarian police, right there, at this very spot. Blinking, he thought he saw a muzzle flash from the window under the shadow of the Partenavia's wing, half realized that it was impossible, just a trick of the light, but rationale had fled, so powerful was his inner rage. Instead the machine-gun was shuddering in his hands as he emptied the magazine into the streamlined wheelpods of the drug smugglers' aircraft, saw the wing dip as the tyres blew out and the Partenavia veered off the runway, slewed around, a wing tip digging into the grass, sending the plane cartwheeling in a shower of debris.

Wolfe snapped back to reality and stared in amazement at the now empty machine-gun in his hands, realized the enormity of his action and calmly ordered his men to close in on the wreck. Then he pressed the button to call Muller.

"What happened?" the Polizei Oberat wanted to know from the sanctuary of his booklined office at the Ministry. Wolfe told him.

"Must have looked like terrorist activity," Muller suggested. "Red Army Faction."

Something like that, Wolfe agreed as the Bolkow circled the crippled Partenavia.

"Well, you were there," Muller said. "You had to make the decision." He sounded relieved.

Would the old man back him, Wolfe wanted to know.

"Hard to tell," Muller said. "Depends how it all turns out."

In the orbiting helicopter Wolfe fell silent.

"Rainer! You still there?" Muller called out over the radio.

Wolfe said yes, he was still there.

"Welcome to the club," Muller told him.

Aboard the *Petroqueen*, Commander Larry Drake's Press corps, still unable to believe their good fortune at being on the inside of a multi-million-pound drug bust, strained their eyes out to see from their concealed vantage-point on the tanker's superstructure and allowed their collective imagination to run riot.

Below, locked in an airless mess deck, the skeleton crew of four seamen and an engineer still found it hard to believe their misfortune at having been jumped by the law. The two men they knew only as the mechanic and the chemist who had assured them that there was no risk whatsoever were incarcerated with them but had suddenly become totally uncommunicative. Guarded by jubilant NEL detectives and the Customs' rummage team, they chainsmoked and morosely awaited the next turn of events, which could only be bad.

Up on the bridge, the debris of a Fortnum and Mason's picnic scattered around them, Drake and his entourage preened themselves in party spirits. The unctuous Home Office Minister, Peter Ashworth, smiled and nodded frequently as he offered conversational titbits on the government's drugs policy. In the chartroom a secure S Band communications link had been established by satellite with the West German end of the operation, but when the appointed hour came without sight of the Blue Water aircraft and the euphoria began to wear thin, the telecom link became curiously silent.

In the radar room behind the bridge Rowley found Jack Monroe leaning against a corroded bulkhead. The DEA agent scraped the paint with a fingernail and a flake fluttered off. The creeping rust was winning.

"How much crude d'you think they've got floating on this rust bucket, slick?" he asked idly.

"I dunno," the Yard DS replied. "Got to be worth it, though, sitting out here waiting for the price at the pumps to go sky high."

"Yeah, if the old tub doesn't rust away and sink first." Monroe scraped at the rust. "How are the fat cats doing out there?"

Rowley said, "Still having a ball."

Monroe chewed at his moustache and looked at his watch.

"What do you think, Jack?" Rowley asked.

The American continued to pick at the paint. "About what?"

"Come on," Rowley said. "You know what I mean. That plane hasn't come when the fat man said it was going to come."

"Could be a million reasons," Monroe said, "headwinds, something like that." He didn't sound convinced.

"You know what I'm saying." Rowley voiced his doubts. "I'm saying maybe we were taken for a ride over there."

"By Daniels?"

"By somebody."

Monroe smiled. "You win the Kewpie doll." He stared out at the expanse of sea. It had been a misty grey, but now the sun was burning through in a brassy haze and it was hard to tell any more where sea met sky.

"That plane's not going to show, is it?" Rowley persisted, feeling it but not yet knowing it.

Monroe turned, leaned against the rust-encrusted bulkhead, the dead radar scopes sitting there like so much junk. "You want my opinion, slick? My best shot? If that plane didn't show when the fat man said it was going to show, then it's not coming, not ever. And the thing is, the question we've got to put our minds to, is why not? That's the sixty-four-thousand-dollar question."

"Drake'll go ape," Rowley predicted.

"Serve him right," Monroe said. "He's the superstar now. Like the man said, we did our party piece, now it's his turn to pull rabbits out of the hat. This is the way he wanted it."

And so they waited. Time began to run down in slow motion, each minute dragging by. By mid afternoon when it was becoming embarrassing, three hours after the blue and white Partenavia of the Blue Water Trust had been intercepted and prevented from leaving Munich Riem, they got the word.

Commander Larry Drake, his face taut with fury, his lips compressed into a bloodless line, rounded on his patron, Peter Ashworth, the political deal-maker.

"Peter, for Christ's sake, you said your guy over there in the Ministry, the top Kraut over there, was a hundred per cent on this!"

Ashworth stared at him.

"You said the guy went along with our game plan. You guaranteed it. You said we had a watertight deal on this. Jesus, Peter, they shot the bastard down! They grabbed it all for themselves!"

Ashworth's lizard expression remained unmoved by Drake's tirade. The junior minister didn't even blink.

Drake put a hand on his arm, shaking his sleeve. "A hundred per cent, Peter, that's what you promised! Now you'd better get on the horn and you'd better tell that wanker his fortune. You'd better tell your tame Kraut over there that he's just made a laughing-stock out of the Metropolitan Police and we don't stand still for a stroke like that. You know what I've got? I've got the Carabinieri, Brigade Territoriale, the whole fucking NEL operation about to come down around my neck. I've got my own promises to keep. For Christ's sake, Peter, I've got the media out there . . ."

The Under Secretary of State, Home Office, pulled his sleeve free with undisguised distaste. "If you don't mind, Larry," he said in a tone dry as dust, "I've got a meeting with the PM, aid to Colombia, see if we can't persuade the peasants to burn the coca harvest and save us a lot of grief. So I think the less said about this little fiasco of yours the better. Oh, I'll send our good friends in Germany a message of congratulations on behalf of Her Majesty's Government. The international war on drugs goes from strength to strength, that sort of sentiment. Important to strike just the right note."

"Peter, you're not listening!" Drake was becoming frantic, beside himself with rage and frustration. "The Krauts just kicked us in the teeth, you can't let them get away with that!"

But Peter Ashworth MP was already distancing himself from failure. "If you don't mind, Larry," he told Drake, "I think I'd better be getting back ashore now. I've got a very busy schedule and it doesn't do to keep the PM waiting. If you would be so kind . . ."

"So what the Christ do I do now?" Drake protested bitterly. "I'm going to get crucified!"

"Oh, surely not." The merest hint of a smile touched the politician's lips, his manner far away as his eyes roved over the luncheon debris. "Crack another bottle of vino, old man, I'm sure you'll think of something."

16

The full extent of the German anti-terrorist subterfuge did not become apparent until the next day, reading between the lines of the carefully worded account on the Interpol telex. The terrorist justification was as transparent as it was unassailable and deep inside the glass and concrete tower of New Scotland Yard, the Narcotics Enforcement Liaison command centre was already in turmoil as recrimination flared and internecine squabbling threatened the fragile strands of European cooperation.

French and Italian rivals joined forces for the common purpose of challenging the British leadership, demanding that NEL headquarters should be immediately transferred to Paris or Rome. Treated to such screaming tabloid headlines as DRUGS SUPREMO BUNGLES CRACK BUST, Commander Larry Drake found himself fighting a bitter rearguard action at a succession of hastily convened crisis meetings. With the cunning of a hunting pack on the scent of a wounded prey, the power blocks within the Yard's hierarchy had also combined to savage the drugs chief. Isolated, his back to the wall, Drake was fighting for professional survival. In the deep waters of the dream factory he was swimming naked with the sharks.

Momentarily ignored on the fringes of this gladiatorial combat, the pawns in the game went about their business with one eye cocked for the white smoke which would signal a victor.

Back on his home ground, Detective-Sergeant Tony Rowley did his best to stay invisible. There were still things to do, and giving the NEL operation a wide berth, Rowley took Jack Monroe up to the fourth-floor offices of SO11, where he reclaimed his old desk. While Monroe composed a wire to update his Washington office, Rowley dictated his own report on the Bavarian interlude into a pocket memo and dropped the tape into the squad's out-tray. For the time being, self-preservation had become the overriding priority.

Monroe put in several calls on the intercontinental but could get no joy from the Bavarian BCI on the whereabouts of a certain Kriminal Hauptkommissar. It seemed that Wolfe had gone to ground. While

Monroe was slumped behind the desk, telephone cradled to his ear, Rowley went down the corridor to the squad's duty room and ran an eye over the current surveillance scheme. When he found the item he was looking for, he slipped into the DI's cubbyhole, sat down at the computer console and tapped in the code of the day to access the METCOMCON command and control database. Scrolling quickly through the lists of targets, he discovered Ryker's alias, memorized the details and logged off.

When Rowley returned to the office, the DEA agent was off the phone. Monroe looked dispirited.

"No luck on Wolfe?"

"Nah," Monroe replied, "they're giving me the runaround. Looks like Wolfe's deliberately keeping his head down."

Rowley lowered his voice. "They're watching Ryker. I just took a squint at the surveillance dope."

Monroe perked up immediately. "Are you getting ideas, slick?"

"Well, anything'd be better than sitting around waiting for the wrath of God."

"What d'you have in mind?"

"The guy's using the Ellman alias. He's in a residential hotel over in Battersea with one DC sitting on him."

"You think we might take a look?"

"Well," Rowley said, "it so happens the D who's minding the store over there is an old pal of mine from way back. It wouldn't be a problem."

Monroe got to his feet and scooped his sports coat from the back of the chair. "So what are we waiting for!"

They took a cab across the river and had the taxi drop them on the corner of Albert Road, Battersea, well down from the Gladstone Hotel. The street was choked with parked cars and the detectives had no trouble in reaching the hotel without drawing attention to themselves. The place was a gloomy rabbit warren, cobbled together from a series of old buildings connected by corridors and stairways, each twist and turn protected by heavy firedoors. They went through the cheaply furnished lobby and Rowley led the way up to the top floor, where he found the door number he was looking for and rapped softly on the panel. There was the sound of movement inside the room.

"What d'you want?" A gravelly voice posed the muffled question.

Rowley leaned against the door. "Rocky," he said, "it's the job. Tony Rowley."

"Yeah?" The voice was unhurried. "You want to maybe slide something under the door?"

Rowley took his warrant card out of his wallet and, crouching down, slid it under the door.

A crack appeared as the door opened an inch, revealing a slice of face. The door swung open. "Hey, Tony!" The face was beaming. It belonged to a big paunchy man, a few strands of dark hair scraped across an otherwise bald head. The face was florid, a lump of a nose tinged purple from broken capillaries.

Detective-Constable Rocky Stone, an old-timer sitting it out to the pension, tugged red braces up over his meaty shoulders and slapped a paw into Rowley's outstretched hand. "Hey, skip, last time I saw you was Dad's funeral, right? When you were Dad's skipper. Jesus, that was a heartbreaker."

Rowley said, "How's it going, Rocky?"

"Ah, same as ever. Just as long as you don't let the bastards grind you down. Another eight months and I kiss all this malarky goodbye."

Stone looked beyond Rowley, a question in his eyes.

"Oh, this is Jack Monroe," Rowley said, recognizing the look. "Jack, shake hands with one of London's last real thief-takers."

"Glad to know you, Rocky," Monroe said.

"Yank?" Stone asked.

"Yeah."

"In the job?"

"DEA," Monroe said. "Federal agent."

"You mean like Elliot Ness and the Untouchables?"

Monroe smiled. "Something like that."

Stone looked back to Rowley. "This a social call, Tony? You just passing or what?"

"We've got an interest, Rocky," Rowley said. "Mind if we come in?"

Stone stepped aside. "Be my guest, skip." He frowned. "This official?"

Rowley shook his head. "Not so you'd notice."

"Well, don't let my pratt of a DI find out. Aggravation I can do without."

"We'll only be a couple of minutes, Rocky," Rowley said. "Be no sweat."

"Glad to hear it," Stone said, turning back into the hotel room as they followed him inside, closing the door behind them. Across the room beside the window a video camera with a zoom lens was set up on an aluminium tripod. On the bedside table a digital voice scanner hooked into a standard phone tap blinked monotonously. On the bed, a briefcase lay open, exposing a data terminal which was connected to the phone. It was a standard surveillance set-up.

Stone hooked a thumb into his braces and gave Rowley an offhand shrug. "Mickey Mouse stuff." He nodded at the equipment. "I tell you, Dad's well out of it, the way the job's going. No skill these days. Me, I'm like he was, from another time when you did surveillance on shoe leather and on your wits, not twiddling a bunch of gizmoes." He shook his head and then his expression grew quizzical. "This interest, you want to tell me about it?"

"We're curious about Ellman," Rowley said. "He figures in something we're involved in."

"I'm not surprised," Stone said. "You want to know about him?"

"That's the size of it, Rocky."

"This just between us?"

"You can count on it."

"Well, if you were anybody else, Tony, I'd tell you to take a jump. The job these days, all the ducking and diving, you don't know who's going to be sticking one on you next, CIB, anybody. Only seeing as it was Dad marked your card back in the good old days, I'm going to give all that eyewash a miss. What can I tell you about Mr. Ellman? Well, for a start he's like a walking telephone directory." Rocky Stone motioned them over to the window, which looked out on an air shaft. Two floors below, a glazed skylight was encrusted with bird droppings and a couple of pigeons were strutting on the sill of a window opposite. An iron drain pipe was leaking rusty water.

The DC pointed to a window below them and across the air shaft. "He's got a room over there. Been in this rat-hole these past three days, only he's a mover, here, there and everywhere, a very industrious fellow, Mr. Ellman. Putting himself about a fair bit."

"What d'you figure he's up to, Rocky?" Rowley asked.

"The usual thing," Stone said. "Wheeler-dealer dope merchant. He's teeing up his market, ready to get weaving. Drumming up business, talking on the phone, all sorts of people."

"You've got him on tape?" Monroe asked.

Stone gave the American a deprecating glance. "This is the Rocky Stone show, Mr. Elliot Ness. I've got him on sound and I've got him on vision, enough footage to star in a couple of full feature epics. If he so much as belches over there, I've got him, timed to the second. What d'you think I'm doing in this dump, taking a health cure?"

Rowley laughed. "I can tell you worked with Dad, Rocky."

"How d'you know that?"

"You've got the repartee. Can we take a squint at your stuff on Ellman?"

"Sure," Stone said. "Help yourself, only for Christ's sake don't wipe anything. It's all time and date logged. Push the wrong button and it's my arse in a sling."

"Just one other favour," Rowley said. "Can you keep us posted on developments without showing out?"

"No problem."

Rowley patted his arm. "I owe you one, Rocky."

But Stone was indignant at the suggestion. "It's on the house," he replied emphatically. "In loving memory of Dad Garratt, one of the all-time greats."

Later, back at the yard, Monroe finally got through to Rainer Wolfe. On the other end of the phone the Kriminal Hauptkommissar sounded distant and on his guard.

"No hard feelings this end, old buddy," Monroe reassured him. "You had to do what you had to do. Nobody's blaming you."

"I didn't have a choice," Wolfe said, still on the defensive, but a little less frosty. "It could have been Red Anna on that plane. We couldn't take the chance."

"Sure you couldn't," Monroe soothed him. "I'd have done the same in your shoes."

"I had to do what I was told. Orders."

"Well, anyway, between us we bagged twenty million in angel dust, so what's it matter. We stopped it, that's what counts in the long run."

"Yeah," Wolfe said apologetically. "We did that all right."

"Only we've still got the fat man dangling," Monroe said. "That's the problem now."

"Do you want me to take care of him?" Wolfe asked, grasping the opportunity to make amends.

"Well, look now," Monroe said, "we don't want to put you to any trouble. I mean, Daniels is not your snitch or anything, you don't owe him anything, you don't have to feel obligated. But he did come through for us, Wolfe. I mean, there's certain promises unfulfilled, and the way it's gone, there's going to be one worried fat man out there in the cold."

"I could pull him in again," Wolfe suggested. "That vice thing is still outstanding. That way he'd be in protective custody."

"Nah, be too risky," Monroe said. "People over here might take a different view. There's a few noses out of joint. They might get vindictive and go for extradition, then he'd be worse off than he is now. Be much better if he disappeared for a while, but not so that we couldn't find him again if we wanted to. What do you think?"

"I could probably manage that," Wolfe said. "Keep him out of harm's way."

"Well, we wouldn't want any of your urban terrorists taking it out of his hide, now would we?"

"No," Wolfe said. "That would be most unfortunate."

"Hard to explain too," Monroe said with just a hint of irony.

"I think we understand each other," Wolfe said. "It will be better if I have my group keep an eye on him."

"And you'll keep us advised?"

"It's the least I can do."

Monroe put the phone down and looked at Rowley with some satisfaction. "Wolfe'll play ball. His conscience is bothering him. Once this is all over we can start picking up the pieces again."

"That's going to be difficult, Jack," Rowley said. "The way the brass here see it, we scored an own goal. We won't get a second chance. And you know what that means? You and me, we're vulnerable."

Monroe nodded his agreement. "It's like the priest said to the virgin on her wedding-day. It doesn't matter what you do or what you say, the one thing that's for certain is you're going to get screwed."

At that moment Andy Barnes, a Detective-Superintendent from the National Drugs Intelligence Unit, poked his head around the door. "So this is where you two are tucked up!" He ran a hand through his hair in a harassed gesture. "Look, fellows, let me give you a piece of advice, OK? The guv'nor's getting his arse chewed from the Commissioner down to the backhall doorman. And as if that wasn't bad enough, we just got the glad tidings from our good friends in the Crown Prosecution Service that they're not going to proceed against those jokers off the ship, too circumstantial. The DAC's doing his crust and all the surveillance has been lifted. Not to put too fine a point on it, we're wiped out." He regarded them for a moment, shaking his head in disbelief. "You want a tip?" he said at last. "Make yourselves scarce for the time being."

After Barnes left, Rowley looked across at Monroe. The DEA agent was scowling and chewing his moustache. "What d'you think, Jack? What do we do, stick around and face the music or take his advice?"

"I've got a better idea, slick," Monroe growled. "Let's get drunk."

17

They began in the glitzy clubs of the West End, which suited their pensive mood. The dimly lit caverns were teeming with Arabs on afternoon binges, big spenders trailing fawning coteries, ogling the topless dancers under the strobes and tying up all the fixed-smile cocktail waitresses who inveigled them into buying exotic multi-hued drinks at rip-off prices. After a while Rowley and Monroe moved on to the hotel bars but the scene was equally frenetic, and by early evening when their spirits had mellowed they drifted into Soho. Just off Dean Street, under a neon sign fashioned in the shape of a brightly spangled pantomime character complete with visor and magic wand, Rowley found the place he was looking for: the Harlequin Health Club.

He showed the doorman his warrant card, palmed the man a tenner to circumvent the formalities of membership and the two detectives were soon exuding booze from their pores in the steam room and then submitting to the ministrations of a pair of Amazonian masseuses with paint-on tans and punk hairstyles.

Later, in the dry heat of the sauna, as they squatted on slatted wooden benches, towels around their waists, Rowley couldn't help remarking on the puckered purple scars which ran across the DEA agent's chest. "What the hell happened to you, Jack?"

Monroe ran a forefinger over the scar tissue as though reminding himself, touched the old dog-tags nestling against his chest and replied, "Long time ago, slick, I was a mean Marine." He gave a mirthless chuckle and flicked beads of moisture from his moustache. "One of the

Corps' few good men." Softly he chanted a marching cadence, "Hup, hoop, hreep, hoor, lift you head and hold it high, Mighty Mike is passing by." He tipped his head back and laughed. "Oh yeah, a mean Marine. You know something, slick? I was also stupid. I had my career in law enforcement all mapped out, kid college, pretty wife on my arm, everything going for me. John Jay and then the FBI Academy, that was the plan. Hotshot Federal agent on his way to Assistant Director at the very least, maybe even old J. Edgar's chair. Only before I could get started I got a bad attack of patriotism, rally to the flag, roll back the yellow peril." Monroe shook his head, sending out a spray of moisture. "Stupid. I volunteered for Nam, can you believe that? And because of my qualifications they made me a CID investigator, told me I was Wyatt Earp hunting down the bad men. They made me a brownbar grunt and sent me out into the boonies, oh, not to fight the VC, not to wage righteous war on the arch enemies of democracy. Oh no. They told me to snoop on my own kind, the dumb grunts."

Monroe began the chant again, "Hup, hoop, hreep, hoor, bustin' ass to win the war." He grinned at Rowley. "See, there were no rules out there in the jungle, no Miranda, no due process, not even the code of military justice. Out there, everything was crazy and you survived on your wits and your luck. I was near the end of my tour, in fact I was so short I was practically gone, when they handed me one last mission. Came down from the General himself. Pin on the star one last time, Marshal, you're the best we've got. Get us the bad men and then you can hang up your six-shooters." Monroe fingered the dog-tags, eyes aflame. "And that, slick, is when Lady Luck ran out on me."

He blinked back into focus, hitched the towel up around his shoulders and stood up, drawing the towel around him like a toga. "Tell you what"—Monroe changed the subject abruptly—"I've got a hankering for some female company. There's this little girl I got friendly with over here, works in the TWA office. We're both from Virginia, practically cousins. Kissing cousins. Thought I might give her a call, look her up. You don't mind if I duck out on you, slick?"

Rowley shook his head. "Just as long as you don't get yourself into any trouble, Jack. I'm still your minder, remember."

"Oh, I'll behave myself," Monroe replied. "I'll be back in the morning all bright-eyed and bushy-tailed."

Rowley said, "We'll meet at the factory, then. We'd better put in an appearance and make sure the dust has settled."

They went out to the members' lounge and made phone calls, sipping tall glasses of vodka and unsweetened orange juice. Rowley packed Monroe off in a minicab, and when the DEA agent had gone, he felt the same yearning. After a moment's struggle with his conscience, he picked up the phone again and called Cindy Miller.

Strap-hanging on the tube, Rowley almost decided to cancel the date, get off the train, call her again, make some excuse. Guilt burned inside him but here he was again, leaning on the girl who had helped him get over Dad Garratt's death and had brought him through the traumatic aftermath of the car bombing, but could not restore his shattered manhood. The impotent detective and the Intensive Care Unit nurse, thrown together by the memory of a man who loomed larger than life. Theirs was a strange relationship. After his patrol car had been ripped apart by the bomb that was meant for him, Rowley had sought refuge with Cindy, had used her as a hunted animal might seek a bolt hole in which to hide, had cynically exposed her to the wrath of contract killers who would have taken her life without a second thought if she happened to get in their way. Cindy had asked nothing from him and he had given nothing in return for her friendship. There lay the exposed kernel of his guilt. When he had phoned her from the Harlequin she had invited him to her flat without question, and it was at times like this that Rowley began to despise himself.

From the tube station he walked the last quarter of a mile to the familiar block of apartments, dawdling over the last few yards. In the lobby the guilt continued to assail him and outside her door he vividly recalled his last visit, slinking into her bed in the early hours after his nocturnal encounter with the capo. He had wanted only comfort and here he was, the same emotional cripple about to exploit her again. Just a selfish bastard taking advantage of her generosity.

As he pressed her doorbell, Rowley vowed that he would tell her everything, the truth about Dad Garratt, how the old DI had set up the Twins, the deal he had struck with Spinelli to save his own skin and the abortive trip to Germany with Jack Monroe. He would hold nothing back.

The door swung open and there she was, her face coming alive at the sight of him, her mouth smiling in recognition. The tight frizz of her Afro was pulled back with a ribbon and she was wearing a pale pink wrap tied with a sash at her waist. Cindy Miller, standing barefoot on her hall carpet.

"Cindy," Rowley said, "Cindy, look we've got to talk."

But she grabbed his hands and pulled him inside.

"Hey!" Rowley exclaimed. "What is this . . ."

She went up on her toes, her face close to his. "The treatment," she said.

"What?"

Before he could say any more she kissed him vigorously, her tongue darting into his mouth.

"Hey!"

Cindy rocked back and clamped a hand over his mouth.

"Shut up, you stupid man. I don't want to hear another word until I've finished with you."

Deftly she twisted his arm behind his back and marched him into the bedroom, where the curtains were drawn and the lights were dimmed. "Man," she breathed into his ear, "I got sick of you giving me all that jive about us girls from St. Kitts, all that hot passionate blood. I got sick of you feeling sorry for yourself, so this is the rape scene, lover. Now you take the nurse's advice, lie back and enjoy it."

She threw him down on to the bed, unfastened the sash at her waist and let the wrap fall open, shrugging out of it. Cindy was naked underneath, and as she flung herself on to him, her breasts poured out like molasses as she used her weight to pin him down on the soft duvet.

Rowley tried to cry out but she stifled him as she tore off his clothes. Thrown off guard, Rowley was powerless to resist. He was familiar with her, for they had attempted lovemaking many times before, always humiliatingly unsuccessful on his part, always culminating in his bitter self-recrimination. But never, never like this!

"Hush now," she breathed in his ear. "You're in intensive care!"

The realization that Cindy was ravishing him sent a thrill stabbing through him and he felt the first stirrings of arousal since the car bomb had castrated him.

As he tried to take control she sank her teeth into his shoulder and pushed him down again. Her mouth was over his, lips moving, kissing him passionately, her tongue probing deeper and deeper until he felt he would suffocate, her body rippling against him, breasts, belly, thighs, arousing him beyond belief.

A choking wave of emotion engulfed Tony Rowley. He lost his fragile grip over his feelings and began to sob uncontrollably, his chest heaving as a warm flood of relief swept over him. Tears streamed down his face as he realized that the spell was broken. Cindy had made him a man again and he clung to her as she stroked his hair and murmured soothing words of comfort.

They lay together for a long time without talking, just dozing in each other's arms. Once Cindy opened her eyes and imagined she saw Dad Garratt standing in the shadow at the foot of the bed smiling approvingly down at them.

It was past midnight and the yellow glow of the street lights made little impression upon the darkness of the night in the shabby surroundings of Albert Street, Battersea. In deep shadow cast by a peeling hoarding, the figure of a man leaning against the timber frame was concealed from view. Across the street the Gladstone Hotel was closed down. Dim nightlights burned in the lobby where the night porter had taken over from the girl receptionists and now sat at the desk, reading a paperback. The sprawling rabbit warren of an hotel had settled down for the night. Across the street in the shadows the watcher shrugged deeper into his coat and continued his vigil. Every now and then he succumbed to a nervous habit and chewed at the ends of his drooping moustache.

18

"Sergeant Rowley!"

Rowley had reported to the NEL centre the following morning and was looking for Monroe when the voice called him back. He turned to find Andy Barnes, the detective-superintendent who had given them the gypsy's warning, beckoning to him from his office.

"What's up, guv'nor?"

"Step inside, Tony," Barnes said. "Oh, and if you're looking for Monroe, he had to go over to the U.S. Embassy, sort out a couple of things. Should be back in a minute." Barnes closed the door behind them. "In the meantime, take a pew."

He gestured Rowley to a chair and moved behind the desk, taking off his jacket and slipping it over the back of his chair. A computer terminal sat on one side of the desk and a Swiss cheese plant on the other. In between in neat piles was the usual stack of files and concertina print-outs together with a brass shell cap which held a selection of pipes. Barnes chose one and took some time filling it from his pouch, tamping down the bowl with his thumb before striking a match and lighting up.

Puffing on his pipe, Barnes wagged his head from side to side. "What am I going to do with you two characters?" He posed the question rhetorically without taking the pipe from his mouth so that the words came out strangled.

"Guv'nor?" Rowley feigned innocence, perched uneasily on the edge of his chair.

"You and the 'Cisco Kid dropped yourselves in it with your eyes wide open so I suppose I ought to let you stew in your own juice." Barnes smoked speculatively, blowing clouds of aromatic smoke. His eyes twinkled. "On the other hand, if I were to mark your card, maybe between us we could salvage something from this fiasco."

Rowley blinked, still playing dumb. "How d'you mean, guv?"

Barnes leaned back. "Commander Drake, our revered leader, has gone. He got the bullet last night."

Rowley squirmed on the edge of his chair.

"Relieved of his duties on direct orders of the Deputy Commissioner. Flagrant disregard of operational procedures. Cleared his desk and slipped away with his tail between his legs. For the record he's on extended leave." Barnes waved a hand. "Oh, when this has all blown over I've no doubt he'll be quietly shipped out to a district and buried. It's a hard life, Tony, especially when you make promises and then don't deliver. Piranhas got nothing on this firm." He smiled at Rowley through a wreath of smoke. "But then you'd know all about that, wouldn't you? You and Monroe were working direct to our newly disgraced Commander." He tapped his teeth with his pipe stem. "Which puts your dick right in the wringer, so to speak."

"I don't know anything about it, guv'nor," Rowley said.

"Of course not," Barnes agreed mildly. "I believe you. I just hope CIB does too, for your sake."

Barnes took the pipe out of his mouth and examined it. "But they might not. You see, we had another kick in the teeth courtesy of your rabbi Commander Drake. Our good friends the Germans are taking over NEL." He delivered this bombshell matter of factly, with just a flick of the eyebrows. "Now isn't that a turn-up for the book. They pull off a big drugs stunt which by rights should have been ours and they get the jackpot. It's what's known as political expedient. A couple of their hotshots are coming over to advise Deputy Assistant Commissioner Moss and as you can imagine he's not exactly over the moon about that. Apparently that limp-wrister at the Home Office, Peter Ashworth, has pulled the stroke to save his own credibility, you know how it goes, the European dimension, all that crap. Moss had to go along. It was the only way to stop NEL falling apart."

Genuinely dismayed, Rowley said, "Look, guv'nor, I'm only a humble DS, I just do what I'm told."

"Oh, very commendable, Sergeant," Barnes said. "Don't take any of this personally. When you're out walking the streets again in the blue serge, you'll have plenty of time to work out where you went wrong."

Barnes squinted into the bowl of his pipe, tapped dottle into the shell case and picked up a reamer which he pointed at Rowley to emphasize his next point. "The thing is, Tony, these super sleuths coming over from Munich are called Muller and Wolfe. I believe you're acquainted with them."

Rowley swallowed. "We worked with them, Jack and me, when we were over there, guv'nor. Monroe made all the running, I just carried the bags."

Barnes scoured carbon from the bowl and began carefully to repack the pipe, lighting up again. He pursed his lips. "You see how it looks though, Tony. With Drake out of the frame, the hounds are scouting around, baying for blood. Loss of face all round. It's Pontius Pilate time." Barnes sighed at the prospect. "And the way it usually ends up is people like me picking up the pieces and people like you carrying the can. Natural justice doesn't come into it, not inside the job. It's dog eat dog."

He gave Rowley a knowing look. "That's why I'm marking your card. I was a DS once so I know what it's like when the roof caves in. You want to give it some hard thought, work out how to look after yourself."

"How could I do that?" Rowley asked hesitantly, having trouble absorbing the enormity of the disaster.

"Oh, just keep your head down for the time being," Barnes advised. "I'll see what I can do to vouch for you, might even pull you on to my team where I can keep you under my wing. I'm short of a good skipper and if you play your cards right you might just throw the pack off the scent. Only I'm going to need something in return."

Here we are again, Rowley thought miserably. "What sort of something, guv?" he asked carefully.

Barnes puffed contentedly on his pipe. "Well, the way I see it—and I'm merely speculating now, you understand—this drugs shambles has got to blow over, given time. It's all in the family, so we can take care of it. No, it's the other thing that's going to drop us right in it, that business with Helen Linden. That's going to blow up into a storm. Apparently the Coroner down there in Devon is mightily pissed off, thinks we've been brushing it under the carpet, and he's not far wrong, so we're getting to the stage where we can't expect to exert much more influence down there. Now it only takes a few people to get the bit between their teeth and we'll be lumbered with washing our dirty linen in public. For instance, Monroe's snout. That Coroner could swear out a subpoena and the next thing we'd know is there'd be questions in the House, questions like 'Why didn't the Metropolitan Police make any moves to extradite a cop-killer?' Now that could be a real tear jerker, very bad news." Barnes inclined his head. "Wouldn't do your pal Monroe much good, would it, if he was to get a witness summons. Very bad for the image."

"What're you trying to say, guv'nor?" Rowley asked.

"Watch this." Barnes took the pipe from his mouth, set it in the ashtray and turned to the computer terminal. He tapped away on the key pad and after a moment Gary Daniels's details flashed up on the screen. "You don't have to tell me that's Monroe's snout. I did the rubber heel job down in Devon and I got that far from my own inquiries before I was told to lay off. I've got enough to charge Daniels with conspiracy to cause an explosion at minimum, might even stretch it all the way up to conspiracy to murder, depending on the DPP, but there's certainly enough to put him on the sheet. That'd take the pressure off, now wouldn't it? Might get us off the hook, don't you think?"

Rowley nodded at the logic of the suggestion.

"All I need is the body," Barnes went on. "I can't get him through the official channels, would take too long, and anyway the Germans might not want to play ball, not now. But Monroe could reach him, couldn't he, Tony? Get him back over here, no questions asked."

"Leave it out, guv'nor," Rowley protested. "That'd be a diabolical liberty."

Barnes got up and strolled around the desk. "Your mate Monroe owes us one. If he was in this force he'd be roasted alive by now and out on his ear. I'd see to it personally. It was his stupidity got that girl killed. He owes us all right."

Rowley said, "You think he doesn't know that."

"Then get him to give us Daniels, clear the slate."

Rowley thought about it for a moment. Then he said, "Have you got the current surveillance targets on that machine, guv'nor?" He nodded towards the computer terminal.

Barnes replied, "Sure, why?"

"Can you tell me if there's a face calling himself Ellman still in the system? We've got him as Richard Ellman."

Barnes reached back over the desk, tapped the keys and scrolled back through the data. Ellman came up with a short action report and an NFA conclusion. "There you are," Barnes said. "He was on, but he was scrubbed last night along with the other NEL targets. What's that all about?"

"Just a thought about what you were saying," Rowley said. "I might have an idea, that's all."

Barnes placed a paternal hand on Rowley's shoulder. "Time to start counting your friends, son," he said. "See what you can do with Monroe on the quiet and then get back to me, OK?"

Rowley went down to the foyer of the Yard and hung around. He intercepted the DEA agent as Monroe came through the revolving door. His face was grim. "Recalled to Washington," he told Rowley flatly. "And to make sure I got the message, they sent it by diplomatic bag to the security chief at the Embassy." Monroe gave a harsh laugh. "Guy thinks I must be screwing the President's daughter to get a rocket like that."

Rowley said, "Let's take a walk, Jack. There are some things I've got to tell you, we can't talk about in here."

He steered the American back outside and as they walked up Buckingham Gate Rowley began to recount the latest twists in the story. They crossed in front of the Palace, where the usual crowd of sightseers had their faces pushed to the railings, and went over to Green Park, ablaze with the russets and gold of autumn. Falling leaves swirled around them as they strolled under the trees deep in conversation.

When they returned to the Yard, Rowley found an empty office on the CID floor and a deflated Jack Monroe put in a call to Munich. This

time Kriminal Hauptkommissar Rainer Wolfe came on the line immediately. He said he'd been trying to reach Monroe all morning.

"The fat man's dead," Wolfe said.

"What!" Monroe gripped the phone, his knuckles turning white.

"Daniels," Wolfe said, thinking the DEA agent hadn't heard him.
"Daniels is dead."

There was a long silence against the twitter of the continental phone
line.

Wolfe said, "Monroe? Are you still there?"

"Yeah." Monroe sighed. "I'm still here, Wolfe. Tell me about it."

"The traffic police found him," Wolfe said. "Pulled off the autobahn
in that white Jaguar of his. Slumped over the wheel, stone cold dead."

"What got him?" Monroe asked.

"Natural causes," Wolfe said. "When they IDd him the traffic boys
called us and in the circumstances we had the medical examiner go
over him with a fine-tooth comb. Turned out to be a brain haemor-
rhage."

"When was this?"

"Yesterday afternoon," Wolfe said. "About four o'clock. We figured
that right after he heard the news of the drugs bust he panicked and
ran. Was heading for the Austrian border when he popped his rivets."

"Terrific." Monroe exhaled the word.

"Must've been the excitement," Wolfe surmised. "According to the
doctor it could have happened any time. Cerebral haematoma."

"Where is he now?"

"They brought him up to the mortuary here in Munich and went
through the usual procedures, contacting next of kin, that sort of thing.
There was no reason for us to hold on to him so they've claimed the
body. There's a mortician making arrangements to fly him home."

Monroe frowned. "Here?"

"That's right," Wolfe said. "Flying out this afternoon, coming into
Heathrow. I kept tabs on that myself, that's what I wanted to tell you.
The fat man's out of it."

"Thanks," Monroe said.

There was another silence on the phone.

"Monroe?"

"Yeah."

"You know I'm coming over there, with Muller?"

"We heard. Congratulations."

"You want to do me a favour?"

"What sort of favour, Wolfe?"

"Meet me at the airport. I've booked myself on the same flight as Daniels's body. It'll be like a reunion."

"*Wunderbar,*" Monroe said.

The line fell silent again.

Wolfe said, "Monroe, you still there?"

"Yeah, I'm still here."

"Don't blame yourself," Wolfe said. "It wasn't anybody's fault. That fat man was on borrowed time. Could have dropped dead anytime."

19

Heathrow Airport, sky city at the end of a road and rail umbilical west of the capital; terminals seething with humanity in transit, all eyes turned to the departure screens: "New York, Ottawa, Cairo, Nairobi, Bangkok, Buenos Aires" twitching every few minutes like an electronic geography quiz; computer displays blinking beside the check-in desks, jet-lagged passengers shuffling through customs and passport controls; muffled thunder of departing Jumbos and incoming TriStars.

Rowley left the silver Capri Laser he had borrowed from the Yard's CID pool in a "Police Personnel Only" parking slot at the T Division station inside the airport complex, made his number with the duty DI and caught up with Monroe in Arrivals as the Boeing 737 from Munich breasted up to the gate. Wolfe came off the plane carrying a grip.

"Where's your boss?" Rowley asked, expecting to see Muller accompanying the BCI detective.

"He won't be over until tomorrow," Wolfe said. "I'm the advance guard, got to make sure the beds are comfortable and the sheets are clean before His Majesty arrives." He dropped the bag at his feet and added, "It suited me this way. Gives me an opportunity to make my peace with you guys."

They went up to one of the VIP lounges, where Rowley used the phone to make arrangements with a contact in Customs SIB. They drank coffee and talked over the events at Munich Riem, Wolfe sketching in the details. Then they moved on to the fat man.

Monroe said, "Hell of a thing, Daniels buying the farm like that."

"Weak artery in the brain," Wolfe said. "Could pop when you least expect it." He dug into his pocket, produced a sheaf of papers and explained, "I pulled a copy of everything we'd got on Daniels just in case it'd be helpful when you're tidying up the other thing"—he glanced at Rowley—"the policewoman who got killed."

"Who claimed the body?" Monroe asked.

"Some lawyer with power of attorney," Wolfe replied, "acting on behalf of the next of kin. They even flew a coffin over to speed things up."

"Kind of a hurry, wasn't it?"

Wolfe gave them a smile. "You want to know who shipped him? His own funny firm, Fricker Freight. Even now he's dead, they're keeping him in the family."

Monroe turned to Rowley. "How'd you make out with Customs, slick? I want to see that fat man one last time. I want to see if he died with a smile on his face."

They went out to the Capri and dropped Wolfe's bag in the boot. Rowley started the car and began to follow the labyrinth of internal roads around the airport, familiar with the route from the time he had spent there with Dad Garratt investigating the armed robbery at the bonded strongroom, the Nigerian bullion blag which had started off the carousel which now seemed to be swinging full circle. Dad would have appreciated the irony.

Rowley pulled on to an access ramp at the rear of a warehouse, where a stocky man with a crumpled face was waiting for them. The Yard DS introduced Jimmy Nicholson, the Customs investigator who had worked with them on the bullion case. Nicholson gripped his hand. "Always a pleasure to do a favour for a friend with a good memory, Tony. This official?"

Rowley shook his head. "We did some business with the guy, Jimmy, that's all. Just want to pay our respects."

Nicholson said, "I was sorry about Dad Garratt. He was one of the best and there's precious few left."

"And getting fewer," Rowley added.

Nicholson led them through the freight warehouse, which was stacked high with crates and containers. More air freight was trundling in on a conveyor belt and baggage handlers were working with a fork lift, unloading the boxes. "You ever wonder why contraband comes through here like an express train," Nicholson remarked. "You think I'm going to have the lads jemmy open every case and go rummaging around for the Colorado beetle, a gross of pet tortoise, some spider monkeys, exotic flora and fauna or otherwise prohibited species? Look at this lot, you tried to do the job properly, nothing'd move until next Christmas. We don't even scratch the surface."

The Customs investigator took them through a white-walled passageway into a tiled room with marble slabs and gutters running across the floor to a central drain. Out of habit he put a cigar in his mouth and lit up. "This is the mortuary," he said. "All the stiffs come in here so that we can make sure they enjoyed their flight, check out the paperwork and then hand them over to their nearest and dearest."

He gestured towards a coffin standing on a metal trolley. "Just your friend in today, one satisfied passenger who flew the flag." Nicholson chewed on the end of his cigar. "You want to take a look?"

They went over to the coffin and Monroe said, "Do you open it up?"

"No need," Nicholson replied. "Airfreight regulations require coffins to be zinc lined and sealed. We just lift the lid, like so." He demonstrated by sliding the unscrewed coffin lid to one side. "Make sure it's not been tampered with in transit." He ran a hand over the dull metal interior, checking the Customs-seals on the clips, and then pointed out the perspex window over the face. "Take a gander inside to make sure he's all nice and comfy." Nicholson looked into the window, nodded his satisfaction and stepped back.

"You want to take a look?" He repeated his offer.

Monroe approached the coffin and looked down through the perspex. Daniels's face stared back at him, swollen red lips slightly parted. The DEA agent gnawed at his moustache. So long, fat man, he said to himself and stepped back.

Rowley took a look into the coffin, felt his memory stir with some elusive fragment of recollection and drew back, frowning as Wolfe took his place, touching his brow in a salute, murmuring a word of German.

"You want to tell me about this guy, Tony?" Nicholson asked, his curiosity aroused.

"Ah, just somebody who helped us out, Jimmy, you know what I mean." Rowley's brow knitted. There was something he couldn't pin down.

"Oh yeah?" Nicholson laughed. "Where have I heard that one before." He reached for a metal clipboard hanging on a wall peg and thumbed through the paperwork. "Gary Daniels. Should that name mean something to me?"

Rowley shook his head. "No, not a thing. He was nobody special. What happens to him now?"

"Hearse comes up, my guy checks the death certificate's in order and the undertaker loads him up and wheels him away." Nicholson shot them an intrigued glance and then said, "Hey, come on. Here I've got the Yard, DEA and the Kriminal Polizei wishing some stiff *bon voyage* and I'm thinking to myself: There's got to be more to this. So who's going to tell me the story?"

Monroe said, "It's cool, that's all. Just a fat man taking his last trip."

The Customs investigator read from the clipboard. "Fat man is right," he remarked. "This guy's carrying excess freight. Got to be eighteen stone of fat man in there."

Rowley snapped his fingers as a thought struck him. "Hey, wait a minute! What did you say?"

"Who, me?" Nicholson looked puzzled. "Eighteen stone of fat man. That's what I said."

Monroe and Wolfe were watching Rowley, questions in their eyes.

"That can't be right," Rowley said, an edge of suspicion in his voice as he turned to Wolfe and added, "Those copies you've got, do they include the original arrest form, the one with the physical description?"

"Sure." Wolfe pulled the sheaf out of his pocket. "What about it?"

"What have you got for his weight?" Rowley asked.

Wolfe ran down the notations on the arrest sheet and read out the figure in kilos.

Rowley did the conversion in his head and then said to the others, "So who's got any ideas how our fat friend succeeded in putting on the best part of fourteen pounds after he was dead."

"Are you kidding!" Monroe snapped excitedly, taking the rap sheet from Wolfe's hand to check for himself.

Their eyes met. "Jack," Rowley said, "are you thinking what I'm thinking?"

"You're goddamned right I am," Monroe replied.

Wolfe caught on too, whistled through his teeth and exclaimed, "That's not possible."

Glancing from one to the other, Nicholson said, "This a private party or can anybody join in? You guys mind telling me what's going on here?"

"Can you open it up, Jimmy?" Rowley asked.

"Hey, wait a minute." The Customs man balked at the suggestion. "First you're telling me this is unofficial, just a favour among friends. Now all of a sudden you're into body-snatching. What is this?"

"Buddy, we won't know until we can get a closer look at him," Monroe said.

"And if it's what we think it is, Jimmy," Rowley added, "you'll be grinning from ear to ear."

"And what if it isn't?" Nicholson countered.

"Then we just close him up and nobody's the wiser."

A slow artful grin spread across Nicholson's face. "I knew it! You guys are on to something." He nodded vigorously. "Got to be, only it's so iffy you don't come here with a properly sworn out search warrant. You come with a smooth line in bullshit to con your old friend Jimmy Nick, the honest civil servant. Nudge old Jimmy along and he'll do the dirty work. Am I right, or am I right."

"You don't need a warrant, Jimmy," Rowley reminded him. "You people have got more power than Jesus Christ. We just want a look, that's all."

Nicholson wagged a finger. "OK, OK, just thinking out loud, fellows, I mean, who cares it's my pension going down the pan. I'll open him up on one condition only. Whatever it is you've got up your sleeve, I'm in on it, is that a deal?"

Rowley looked at Monroe. The DEA agent nodded. "OK, Jimmy," Rowley said. "That's understood. It's a deal."

Nicholson said, "It had better be," as he took a pair of tin snips from a tool tray and began to remove the seals from the zinc lining of Daniels's coffin. When he had them free, he peeled back the top. Gary Daniels lay under a white cotton shroud, his body drained of blood and pumped with formaldehyde which had transformed his waxen cheeks into a ruddy pink complexion. Embalmed, Daniels looked healthier in death than he had in life. Only his face was visible above the shroud, eyes slightly bulbous, expression tranquil, lips parted in an enigmatic smile.

Nicholson finished his work and stood back. "There he is," he said. "Isn't he a beauty?"

Rowley reached over and gingerly eased back the white gown until he revealed Daniels stretched out on the PVC liner like a pink porpoise. The body had been sliced open from throat to groin and laterally across the ribcage, the incisions neatly sewn with nylon thread, and although the Yard DS was accustomed to pathology procedure, up close, the sight never failed to jolt him.

He turned to Wolfe. "You sure he wasn't PMd?"

Wolfe shook his head. "There was no need," he confirmed. "It was natural causes."

Rowley looked back at the body. "Well, somebody sure as hell opened him up and made it look like a post-mortem job."

Monroe took a pair of surgical scissors from the tool tray and began to snip the stitches. Nicholson stood back, arms folded, puffing on the cigar clamped between his teeth. He was frowning but he offered no protest.

Rowley joined Monroe and steeled himself as he helped the DEA agent open up the body and remove a section of the ribcage. He caught a glimpse of plastic and recalled that it was usual after an autopsy for the organs which had been removed to be placed in plastic bags and packed back into the cadaver with wood chippings and green cavity filler to bulk out the abdomen and thorax. But if there had been no autopsy . . .

Despite himself, Rowley flinched as the DEA agent used all his strength to open up the rock-hard corpse. Despite his intuition which had suggested the possibility, his eyes popped at the sight of Daniels's pink embalmed body packed tight with kilo-sized plastic bags. Without hesitation Monroe stabbed the point of his scissors into the nearest bag up under the throat. White powder trickled out. Bending over the body, Monroe licked a forefinger, touched the powder and tasted it with the tip of his tongue. He looked up triumphantly at Rowley. "You were spot on, slick!" he exclaimed making no attempt to conceal his excitement. "Pure cocaine. They shipped the product after all!"

"Yeah." Rowley sighed, leaning back against the adjacent marble slab. "They shipped it all right, in a snow man."

20

"What d'you say, Monroe?" Jimmy Nicholson invited the American to confirm his own calculations.

"Twenty million pounds sterling," the DEA agent replied. "What I always said it would be." He chewed his moustache thoughtfully. "The pump-primer. Step on it once, you double your money. Step on it twice and you're on the roller-coaster. Mix in the talc, get it down to street strength, cook up with baking soda, you're into crack, rock, any of the designer stuff you care to name. Angel dust white-out, freebase cocaine. Three, two, one, zero, blast-off!"

They were in Nicholson's office at Heathrow Customs SIB, fidgety, hyped up as they anticipated the prospects. On the desk-top lay a single one-kilo bag of the product, the one Monroe had punctured and later resealed. The rest, removed, weighed and counted, had been replaced inside the corpse of Gary Daniels, the fat man carefully restitched and resealed in his coffin. The work had been as grisly as it had been painstaking.

Across the office Rowley was on the phone to the NEL duty squad. Detective-Superintendent Andy Barnes had left the Yard but was quickly reached on his bleeper at the Beefeater steakhouse in Park Lane, half way through a sirloin with French fries and a green salad. It was his wedding anniversary. Now Barnes was on the other end of the phone as Rowley described the situation, trying to stay calm, keep the excitement out of his voice.

"Bingo! Sounds like you hit the jackpot!" Barnes became euphoric, his dinner and his long-suffering wife already forgotten. "Listen, Tony, we've got to think about this. We've got to set this up with no loopholes. Nail 'em bang to rights. What time have we got to play with? What time's that hearse due in?"

"Any time now," Rowley said into the phone. "We won't have time for anything fancy, guv'nor. We'll have to go with what we've got."

"OK, OK, you stick with it!" Barnes was thinking rapidly, considering their options. "Meanwhile, I'll get some NEL back-up, whistle up all the troops I can lay my hands on. Hot damn, Tony! You pick your time, don't you? First off we're going to need a tail on that hearse, one that sticks but doesn't show out. The one thing we've got to do is follow through all the way, pull 'em in the act, no messing about. After that last fiasco we can't afford to cock this up. Listen," he went on, "I've got to make some calls, get something lashed together pronto. Look, you're going to have to hold that end down yourself, only whatever you do, don't scare 'em off, you got that, Tony? I'm going to be mobile any minute, you can reach me in the car, switch to channel nine, I'll get MP to clear it for NEL priority."

Rowley chose his words with care. "Guv'nor, one thing. Monroe and Wolfe are with me. They'll be all right, but Jimmy Nicholson's in on this too, you know Jimmy Nick, the Customs guy? Do we have a demarcation problem with him?"

"Tony," Barnes replied, "Jimmy Nick's OK, we can work with him. Take him along, OK? But no one else. Let's keep this in the family."

"Right, guv," Rowley said thankfully, bit his lip and then plunged on. "Guv'nor, we may not need to tail that hearse."

There was an astonished silence and then Barnes said, "What! Why not?"

"I think I know where the fat man's going."

"Where?"

Rowley gave Barnes a location, repeated the address.

"How in the name of Christ do you make that connection?" Barnes demanded in a puzzled voice.

"Guv'nor, believe me it'd take too long to explain."

"OK." Barnes didn't pursue it. "I'm up and running, just keep me posted. Oh and listen, keep your head down, don't do anything that'd blow it. Tell the others I'm taking charge and I don't stand any nonsense." Barnes chuckled. "Yeah, you certainly pick your time, Tony. You know what night this is? Hallowe'en."

Rowley put the phone down. He felt angry with himself for blurting out his theory. What if he hadn't guessed right? What if his imagination had played tricks with his recollection when he had salvaged that fragment from his memory . . . angel wings. But there was no time to double check, be absolutely sure. The only course of action was to let it run.

Still uncertain of himself, Rowley returned to the others and filled them in on the hastily conceived plans. "You know, Tony," Nicholson said, "by the book I ought to call my boss. I know you guys did all the legwork, but this is still Customs jurisdiction."

"Since when did you ever do anything by the book, Jimmy?" Rowley said.

"Come on," Nicholson said. "A favour's one thing, twenty mill in cocaine is something else."

"Barnes said he'd square it," Rowley said.

"Yeah, well." Nicholson relented. "I suppose I do owe him a couple, so I'll go along, but no dealing off the bottom of the pack, OK?"

Rowley said, "There won't be time for any nonsense. You're in, Jimmy, and besides . . ."

The shrilling of the internal phone on Nicholson's desk interrupted him and the Customs investigator picked it up, listened for a moment, a frown of concentration creasing his brow. He issued a few instructions and then said, "You're right we won't have any time. The hearse just pulled in. Couple of minutes and they'll be picking him up." He got up. "You want to watch this happen?"

As they left the office Monroe slipped the kilo bag of cocaine into his raincoat pocket for safe keeping. They hurried down to the loading area, where Nicholson took them into the shift supervisor's cluttered office from which they could watch the proceedings on closed circuit television.

A stretched Granada hearse, gleaming black with curtained rear windows, backed into the bay. A pair of heavy-set men in dark suits got out and Nicholson said to Rowley, "Recognize anybody?"

The Yard DS took a close look at the men and shook his head.

Nicholson manipulated the camera and went in close on the driver's window, where a third man remained behind the wheel of the hearse. A glimpse of profile in the shadow was enough for Rowley to identify Harry Vance, a known villain who inhabited the gangland subculture of the London underworld. But again he shook his head at Nicholson's questioning glance, although he was beginning to feel more confident.

The coffin was wheeled out on the metal trolley and manhandled into the back of the hearse.

"We'd better start doing something, slick," Monroe urged. "That snow man's hitting the trail."

Rowley knew the DEA agent was right. He had to trust his own judgement. "Well," he said, "we can forget the back-up. There's no way they can get here now. We're on our own."

"So let's move it!" Monroe said.

"Who needs back-up when you've got us?" Wolfe said, showing his teeth in a grin. "You only get one chance." He remembered his experience at Munich airport. "You have to make up your mind, then you have to do it, right or wrong."

Rowley was already moving, his mind made up. "Come on," he told them. "We'll take my car and the hell with it." He shot Nicholson a glance. "You coming with us, Jimmy?"

"Damned right I am," the Customs man replied. "Right now I'm committing the cardinal sin of letting that snow man through my fingers, so I'm certainly not about to let you jokers out of my sight."

Fifteen minutes later, jousting with heavy traffic on the motorway heading back into London, Rowley finally lost the hearse in the weaving mosaic of tail lights up ahead. As soon as they had left the airport, Monroe beside him, Wolfe and Nicholson crammed into the back seat of the Capri, Rowley had raised the Yard on VHF, identified himself as a November Echo Lima unit and had requested a PNC check on the target's registration number. The computer had told him that the hearse was registered at a rental firm, Canterbury Cars, with branches around London and the Home Counties. Another useless piece of information.

Rowley requested a channel nine priority, car to car, and as the crackle of static cleared, Detective-Superintendent Andy Barnes came up on the set, his speech badly distorted.

"Guv'nor," Rowley said, "we've got no chance for a tail. He'd make us in no time flat in this traffic. What's the score with you?"

"One team," Barnes replied. "Not enough, but we'll just have to do the best we can. Rewrite the manual."

Rowley said, "Shall we all go for the target?"

"Absolutely," Barnes said emphatically. "We've got to get lucky sometime." He gave Rowley a rendezvous point and closed down.

They drove on, discussing their predicament. There was no way they could throw a full-blown surveillance net around the target, for that would have required a minimum of sixty detectives and twenty unmarked cars. That kind of operation, pivotal peripheral surveillance as it was called, required manpower and time to establish. They had neither.

When he finally pulled into a Rotherhithe side street and allowed the Capri to drift to a stop at the kerb, Rowley's self-doubts were returning as crunch time approached. They got out of the car and walked around the corner into Black Wharf Street, the tang of the nearby Thames in their nostrils. Barnes was waiting for them, his light camel topcoat swinging open as he reached into the boot of a squad Cavalier and handed out short-barrelled pump-action Remington shotguns, nodded a greeting to Nicholson and told Monroe and Wolfe, "As far as I'm concerned, you two are special constables just for the night. We'll skip the swearing in."

They checked their weapons as Barnes quickly ran through the details of the plan of action. He showed them a hand-held Motorola surveillance walkie-talkie and said, "We're all set. The blue team were on the location when the hearse arrived, they've got themselves a good vantage-point on the roof opposite with a starlight scope. The minute anything starts to happen I'll get two clicks over the radio here. Red team are around the corner ready to follow us in and secure the scene."

Rowley understood. It was standard Metropolitan Police practice.

Barnes explained, "There's another three crews on their way and I've called for the local rapid response team to stand by just in case we need extra back-up. One shout and we'll be up to our ears in woodentops."

He gave Rowley a shrewd glance. "You were spot on with your surmise as to the target, Tony. When we've got the time you'll have to tell me about that. Nice work anyway." He looked from one to the other and then said, "OK, let's go!"

Misty yellow light haloed the lamps as they moved down the street, which had stood still since Victorian times. They crossed into Lady Walk and approached the town mansion which had been converted into the Sacred Heart Funeral Parlour. The Motorola gave two urgent clicks and Rowley felt a nerve in his neck jump as Barnes broke into a jog, calling out softly, "That's it. Follow my lead."

Swiftly they moved down the street, holding the shotguns against their bodies, each man absorbed in concentration. They ducked down an alley at the side of the building where the Granada hearse was parked outside double doors which led directly into the chapel of rest. A figure emerged from the shadows, wielding a sledgehammer, and without hesitation Barnes nodded to the man.

In the alley Rowley raised the Remington to waist level, taking a grip on the forestock, knowing that the spread of shot could demolish anything within fifty feet, and there were five fat red shells in the magazine under his hand. The others followed suit as the heavy hammer-head came swinging down, shattering the lock and bursting open the door.

Barnes led them inside. Rowley and Nicholson at one elbow, Monroe and Wolfe on the other flank. In the soft light from the cherub wall lights the chapel looked exactly as Rowley remembered it, ornate gothic.

Four men were gathered around the fat man's coffin, which stood on wooden sawhorses. The casket was gaping open, the zinc lining stripped back. They had unceremoniously ripped open the corpse and were in the process of removing the consignment of cocaine.

Four men, stunned expressions of disbelief on their faces. Three of them heavy-set, built like boxers; they were the minders, dwarfing the fourth man, a slight figure, hook-nosed, Latin-featured with bright bird-like eyes. The *capo di tutti capi*.

Before they could recover or react, Barnes levelled his shotgun, tuck-ing the stock into his hip with his right elbow and gripping the pump action with his left hand. "Trick or treat, gents," he announced, savour-ing the moment. "It's your funeral."

21

News of the snow man bust spread like wildfire on the Met grapevine. Pretty soon the street outside the Sacred Heart was alive with winking blue lights. It seemed as if every glory-hunter in the force was there, half the NEL hierarchy, cock-a-hoop at the reversal of their fortunes, the M Division Commander with a bevy of local brass eager to bask in the aura of success. Deputy Assistant Commissioner Raymond Moss, the drugs supremo, made a grand entrance, sweeping in, his boyish blond hair casually mussed. Everyone was clapping Andy Barnes on the back, feeling involved, and even the scene-of-crime team preserving the evidence seemed overawed by the spectacular nature of the haul.

A prison van with barred windows collected the handcuffed prisoners now identified as Francis Spinelli, no previous convictions but sus-pected of links with organized crime; John Reyfus, CRO, wounding and armed robbery; Derek Holdaway, CRO, possession of controlled drugs with intent to supply, and Ronald Doyle, CRO, conspiracy to supply controlled drugs.

Barnes deputed half a dozen of his own detectives to accompany the prisoners, instructing them, "Get 'em down to the local factory and book 'em in bed and breakfast. We'll be there shortly."

Flanked by escort cars, the prison van set off for the nearby M Division station in Lower Road, Rotherhithe, with a triumphant blare of two-tone horns. In the euphoria of the moment no one had any doubt that the subsequent inquiries would smash a major drugs ring.

Andy Barnes broke away from the crowd of admirers for a moment and told Rowley to rendezvous at the Lower Road station in one hour, instructed him to keep Monroe and Wolfe with him but leave Nicholson out for the time being. He said he would personally take care of Customs.

Jaundiced by the pantomime of rank-juggling which was being enacted over the open coffin and its grisly contents, Rowley acquiesced. With a similar expression of disenchantment on his face, Monroe gripped Rowley's elbow and urged him, "Let's get out of here, slick." They took Wolfe with them, and outside in the chill night air, each of them in their own way began to feel the onset of deflation now that the excitement was over and the operation had been taken out of their hands.

They walked to where the Capri was parked, hunched in their raincoats, ignoring the groups of curious onlookers gathering on the street corners, not even bothering to conceal the shotguns they still carried. When they reached the car Rowley unlocked the driver's door, reached inside and placed his shotgun on the back seat. Wolfe followed his example and then climbed into the rear of the Capri. Monroe went around to the passenger's side and got in when Rowley lifted the catch. He rested his shotgun across his knees.

During the short drive to the police station the American remained silent, staring out of the window at the passing streets. The station yard was already jammed, so Rowley found a space at the kerb and cut the engine. After the adrenalin drive of the bust it seemed as if everything was happening in slow motion.

Rowley was removing the keys from the ignition when Monroe told him quietly, "I'm going to need the wheels, slick. Unfinished business, got to close that fat man's account. It's dues time."

Rowley leaned back in his seat, just sitting there listening to himself breathe. Then he said, "How did I know you were going to say something like that?"

"You don't have to do a thing," Monroe said. "You're out of it. Just lend me the car and don't ask any questions. Just get out and walk away."

Rowley said, "You know I can't do that, Jack."

Monroe shrugged. "Then I'll just call a cab."

"Around here, this time of night, not a chance," Rowley said, unable to see the DEA agent's expression in the darkness of the car.

"Then I'll walk if I have to," Monroe persisted.

"With the shooter?" Rowley indicated the shotgun resting across Monroe's lap. "All you'll do is get yourself nicked. First uniform claps eyes on you. This is London, not the South Bronx, Jack."

Monroe turned towards him. "Have you got a better suggestion, slick?"

Rowley sighed as he restarted the engine. "What the hell, I'll drive you. After all, I'm still officially the minder, I'm still supposed to look after you. You need a wheel man, you've got one."

Wolfe leaned forward from the back seat. "You'll want a lookout, too," he suggested, "just to be on the safe side."

"Yeah." Rowley laughed. "Three-handed makes sense. You're among friends, Jack."

Monroe said, "You two are nuts, you know that? This is my beef, nobody else's. All you're apt to get tagging along with me is a barrel of trouble."

"Requiem for a fat man," Rowley said. "We'll just sing the chorus, eh, Wolfe?"

The German chuckled. "Whistle the tune and I'll pick it up."

They drove to Battersea, parked well down from the crumbling façade of the Gladstone Hotel. It had begun to drizzle. The three detectives got out of the car and stood in a huddle on the pavement. Monroe slipped his pump action Remington under his coat, inserting his right hand through the lining so that he could conceal the weapon against his body.

Rowley said, "Listen, Jack, one thing. Nothing stupid, OK? Blow it now and we're all finished. You know we can't touch the guy officially."

A crooked smile formed on Monroe's face. "I'll be in and out of there in no time flat."

Rowley said, "We'll wait for you here, in the motor. But if anything goes wrong, we're coming in."

"Give me half an hour," Monroe said. "If I'm not back by then, do what you have to do."

The DEA agent began to walk down the pavement towards the illuminated lobby of the Gladstone. Rowley and Wolfe got back into the Capri, cleared the mist of drizzle from the windscreen with a flick of the wiper and then settled down to wait.

As he approached the hotel, Monroe could see that the routine was as before, the foyer was deserted, the reception desk left in the custody of the night porter, who was fortuitously away on some errand. The DEA agent pushed open the glass door and went inside. Several of the ceiling lights had already been extinguished, adding to the gloomy rundown atmosphere of the place. Without pausing, Monroe crossed to the stairs, went on up and began to negotiate the warren of corridors until he came to the passageway which led down to the room he was looking for.

In the dimly lit corridor, his footfalls muffled by the tatty runner, the nightmare from Monroe's past caught up with him again and transported him back to the jungles of Vietnam, the triple canopy shading the sluggish brown water of the Song Tra Bong. He was back in the deserted VC village with his LURP guide, inside the hooch, crouching beside the pile of body bags, watching in mesmerized fascination as the stream of angel dust trickled from the bowie knife puncture. Monroe twisted around, narrowing his eyes at the silhouette of the green man lounging in the doorway, realization full on his face. This wasn't Charlie's coke run, there had to be Americans in this. American soldiers! The green man had the light behind him, his face hidden. Jesus but it was stifling in there, the still air so thick that Monroe could hardly breathe. Sweat poured down his ribs, his lips moved, tasted the salt of his own sweat. "Hey, you know who's behind this?" Sweat stung his eyes, blurred his vision. "Hey!" He didn't see the grenade, just heard the metallic snick as the spoon flew. "Hey!" Monroe was getting up, the exclamation still only half formed when the green man said, "So long, snooper," and the blast flung him into the air. Grenade shards sliced into his chest in a whirl of shock and pain and he was hurled backwards into a void of blackness and oblivion.

Jack Monroe, U.S. Marine Corps SIB, swimming back to conscious-

ness, clinging to the threads of life, drenched in his own blood in a
jungle hooch in Vietnam, South-East Asia, left for dead; crawling by
will-power alone to the hidden radio, calling for the dust-off which
saved his life.

Jack Monroe, Federal agent, United States Department of Justice
Drug Enforcement Administration, moving carefully down a dimly lit
passageway of the Gladstone Hotel, Battersea, London, reaching the
door he had previously reconnoitred, slipping a strip of celluloid between the jamb and the door and expertly releasing the cheap lock, the
old wounds aching as he caught the sound of sudden movement inside
the room.

Monroe brought the pump-action shotgun out from under his coat,
levelled the barrel and pushed the door inwards, moving swiftly into
the room, adopting a shooter's crouch. One quick sweep with his eyes
took in two orange vinyl easy chairs, a green candlewick spread thrown
over the bed, a cheap table on which stood a portable computer hooked
to the phone, screen winking green symbols. His eyes fastened on the
man coming towards him, white cotton polo neck, blue slacks, white
loafers. Gold Rolex and chunky gold bracelet on scrawny wrists, a wiry
man in early middle age, sinewy, once athletic, but now out of condition. A walnut face dried up and wrinkled by the climate of the tropics,
contorted in astonishment, rheumy eyes swimming in black pools
widening in shock.

Monroe held the shotgun on him, kicking the door closed with his
foot, locked his gaze into those red-rimmed eyes, watched his reflection
drown in their murky waters. Recognition was instantaneous. The man
stopped, frozen in his tracks, spread his hands, palms outwards in some
mute appeal. Monroe released his grip on the ribbed forestock of the
shotgun, reached into his pocket and took out the kilo of superfine
Colombian cocaine he had filched from the fat man's corpse. He threw
the bag on to the table beside the bed with such force that the seams
split open. Angel dust gushed out.

Monroe took a step forward, jabbing the barrel of the shotgun into
the wrinkled berry-brown face. The man cringed back. "On your
knees!" he rasped out the command. The man sank down, twisted his
head upwards, a pleading look in his eyes. A little froth bubbled from
the corner of his mouth. Standing over him like an executioner,

Monroe pressed the cold muzzle into the man's forehead, forcing his face down into the white powder. "Eat it!" he instructed in a voice like a death rattle. "Eat it, or I'll blow your head off!"

22

Detective-Sergeant Tony Rowley drove Jack Monroe out to Heathrow the following morning to catch his plane. When the DEA agent had returned to the waiting Capri after his visit to the Gladstone, neither Rowley nor Wolfe had posed any questions. They had simply returned to the Rotherhithe police station and had spent the night with Detective-Superintendent Andy Barnes setting the follow-up inquiries in motion. It had been a triumphant night for the Metropolitan Police and everyone was riding on a high. Before dawn they snatched a few hours' sleep in the adjacent section house, then showered and shaved. Monroe announced that he was obeying his instructions from Washington and was leaving. "Always quit while you're ahead," he told Rowley. "Besides, I've got a feeling I've outstayed my welcome. Time to get back Stateside, get back in the saddle while the trail's still warm."

Barnes pumped Monroe's hand and offered to put in a call to his bureau chief and describe in glowing terms his role in the snow man bust. It was the least he could do. With unusual diffidence Monroe accepted the fraternal gesture. "Much obliged," he thanked Barnes. "I can use some credit in that direction."

And so the detectives hung around, vaguely awkward as Monroe called TWA and made his reservation, booking Washington via New York. Rainer Wolfe grasped his hand as he was leaving the station. "No hard feelings over our little preemptive strike, I hope. We were all just visiting firemen on that one."

Monroe chewed the ends of his moustache. "Forget it, Wolfe. You only get one roll of the dice in the big game. If the numbers come up, you play 'em." He shrugged. "In your shoes I guess I'd have done the same."

On the pavement outside the police station Monroe threw his airline bags into the back of the parked Capri. Rowley got in and started the engine. The DEA agent took one last look at the bleak rain-streaked street, turned up the collar of his coat and got into the car.

"Maybe I'll swing a trip down to Miami," he told Rowley optimistically. "Drink some wine, soak up some sun, give The Enterprise another squeeze. Ah, what the hell, maybe I'll just make it a vacation."

"Sounds good," Rowley said, pulling away with a swish of tyres.

"Nothing like Florida sunshine," Monroe said. "You want to try it sometime, give me a ring. Some foxy ladies down there, help you forget your blues."

Now at the TWA check-in, elbowing through the crush, Rowley felt a warm affection for the American despite their brief acquaintance. When he thought about it, he realized that the DEA agent had helped him to regain his self-respect. The boarding light began to flash and Monroe, touched by a similar pang of emotion, squeezed Rowley's shoulder and told him, "Keep the faith, slick, there's precious few of us left."

"And getting fewer," Rowley gave the stock reply. The drooping moustache spread in a grin, then Monroe turned, walked down the boarding channel without looking back and was gone.

On Rowley's return to the Yard, Detective-Superintendent Andy Barnes called the DS into his office. "Got some good news for you, Tony," Barnes announced, tipping back in his chair. "You're on my firm if you want it. I squared it with the guv'nor, he was pretty impressed with the way you handled yourself."

Rowley made the right responses, wondering when he would have to tell Barnes about the connection he had made, Spinelli's trade mark, the angel wings carved inside the fat man's coffin. Angel wings to carry him to heaven. But that would lead to his illicit contract with the capo, clinched in blood. Whichever way he looked at it, that was bound to come. Spinelli would certainly play on it in his defence, a bent detective on his firm. Some sharp defence lawyer would cut him to ribbons in the witness-box. Bleakly Rowley wondered whether Barnes, the straight-arrow drugs chief, would be so delighted with him when he learned the truth.

Across the desk Barnes was toying with his pipe, mystified by Rowley's introspective silence. He had expected the DS to jump at the offer. "You got something on your mind, Tony? If so, let's have it."

Rowley chewed his lip. He was on the point of blurting it all out when a NEL detective poked his head around the door and broke the awkward silence. "Funny job just came in from across the river, guv'nor," he told Barnes, consulting scribbled notes on a message pad. "Division got a shout to a flea-pit over in Battersea, Gladstone Hotel. Some guy OD'd on coke, ingested. Must've been a real flake, they say he tipped out a kilo on the table and gobbled it up. Rocket ride to heaven and his bulb blew out."

The detective looked at his notes. "This is the weird bit. OD turned out to be a Yank, Vietnam veteran no less. Must've blown his mind, because he sure as hell wanted the world to know it. You know what he did, guv? He put his old Marine Corps dog-tags under his tongue like they did with killed-in-actions. Handed us a positive ID on a plate." The detective looked at Barnes questioningly. "Just thought you ought to know, guv'nor. We want any of this one?"

Barnes grimaced. "Ate a kilo of coke!" He looked at Rowley, shaking his head in disbelief. "Makes you wonder what goes through their minds out there, Tony. Crazy people, what a way to go."

The detective was still standing expectantly in the doorway, waiting for a decision. Barnes frowned and picked up his pipe. "What was the name on those dog-tags?" he asked.

Rowley felt a tightening in his stomach as the man glanced at his scribble. He knew what he was going to say.

The detective said, "Ryker."

Roger Busby began writing crime novels twenty years ago when he was a crime reporter in Birmingham, England. His appointment as Public Relations Officer for one of England's leading police forces has taken him even deeper into the action. Working alongside homicide detectives on major cases completed his education in the streetwise world of law enforcement. For *Snow Man* he won the *Police Review*'s Award for the title with the most authentic police background published in 1987. This is his Crime Club debut. He lives with his wife in a village on the edge of Dartmoor, England.